Death Scheme!

"I can't hang the jury," said the lawyer. "No jury-man picked from this town would ever dare to vote 'not guilty' against you, Hugh Alton. He'd be lynched by his brother jurors at the end of the case! I understand what I'm talking about."

The rancher turned greener-gray than before. "Very good," he said. "I understand what you mean. Every juror picked will long ago have made up his mind that I'm guilty!"

"He will."

"Then the rope's around my neck, or else I die in prison. My family's disgraced. Wisner, I'm paying to have brains! What are you going to do?"

"I'm going to kill Joe Good. . . ."

Books by Max Brand

Published by POCKET BOOKS

Max Brand

SHOTGUN LAW

PUBLISHED BY POCKET BOOKS NEW YORK

SHOTGUN LAW

1

At the top of the Cronin Pass, Joe Good paused to look back into one world and forward into another. Behind him, he could see the bold, treeless hills that made the cattle range around Fort Willow; and before him, on the rainier side of the mountains, there was smoother, richer country, checkered by silver or golden fields of growing crops and dark squares of fallow plowed land, although this pattern was subdued by the mist of distance.

He paused at this high point for other reasons than to look sadly back upon a wasted past before entering a new future.

For, as he steered his way forward, sighting between the ears of his burro and over the hump of the pack that burdened it, he had been amusing himself by playing tricks with his black snake. It was not an ordinary black snake, thick and heavy at the butt and tapering to a thin, cutting lash. The cutting lash was there, but behind it the whole body of the black snake was of one dimension, not a great deal wider than a thick pencil. It was covered with the finest rawhide, so carefully treated that it was more supple than the skin of a snake, more supple, even, than the rawhide which the Mexicans know how to treat so that in their lariats it becomes like liquid iron, so to speak.

Either in his pocket or in his hand, this black snake was ever near to Joe Good. It was in part of his own invention. He had discovered that bulkier whips are likely to lead to inaccuracy; and Joe Good loved accuracy as much as he loved laziness. So he had developed this black snake after his own idea and given it weight with flexibility by loading it with leaden shot, not only on the handle, but down nearly to the very tip of the lash. The shot diminished in quantity and in size, but it was there, never-theless.

Only at the butt, the handle flared out a little to make a suitable grip for the palm and fingers. As he walked along, Joe Good had amused himself by performing little tricks with the whip. Sometimes, to be sure, he used it to encourage the burro, but this was very seldom. That burro was said to have the toughest hide of any burro on the range, but somehow it always responded to the magic touch of Joe Good.

For he knew how to take out a chunk of skin and flesh with a snap of the lash; and he knew, also, how to draw a gash in the thickest mule hide. More than this, he was aware of other arts and, once an animal realized what the master could do with that tormenting whip, it needed only a touch to make it put forth its full efforts to whatever task lay before it.

Sometimes, too, he exercised his skill by performing a feat often talked of, but very rarely seen; that is to say, now and then the black snake would uncoil from his hand and throw out its thin point like a snake's tongue, flicking away a fly without more than brushing the hair of the animal. It was a trick that pleased Joe Good. He would have liked to do it before an audience, but he was a fellow who never had an audience.

There were many other things he could make the black snake do, besides serving as a whip, however. Sometimes it poured fluidly from hand to hand, up one arm and over his shoulders, descending sinuously into the opposite hand.

Sometimes it even reared up like a living snake and for an instant seemed to be supporting its eight feet of length on its thin tail, while the handle rose and steadied for a moment above, like the head of a snake.

Sometimes he threw it high, high in the air, until it diminished to a mere pencil stroke, and caught it again by the handle as it shot downward.

Now and again, as he passed under a tree, he flicked the lash upward, dexterously allowed it to twist around a branch, and then cut the branch in two with a slashing pull. Again, with exquisite care, he nipped off leaves, cutting directly through their stems as with a knife touch.

But now and then, and this pleased him more than all else, to judge by the smile he wore, he took the almost liquid coil of the black snake in the palm of his hand and then threw it like a ball at a sapling, or a tree trunk, and watched the ball dissolve and the arms of the black snake whirl suddenly around and around the trunk of the tree.

Suppose that a man were struck in the breast by that weight, even if he were not knocked down by it, his arms would be suddenly lashed to his sides!

That was why he smiled when he performed the trick, always unerringly. It was not so easy at it looked. The head and the tail of the whip had first to be disposed of in a certain way; otherwise, the lash simply rebounded from the trunk and fell limply against the ground.

He was making the black snake coil in his hand and then spring up, snakelike, again and again, when, at the crest of the pass, he saw the new country before him and turned to give a final glance at the big hills behind him.

And then it was, also, that he saw the eagle.

From a high crag of Cronin Mountain, on his right, it launched suddenly forth and began to circle rapidly, cupping the air under its powerful wings, as it struggled upward.

He forgot the rest of the scenery in order to watch, for he recognized the maneuvers of an eagle taking its pitch, in order to swoop down on its prey.

Presently he saw the answer. A fish hawk slid out into view above the tops of the trees, with a fish gripped in its talons, a big, silver flash of a fish held firmly by the back, with its head pointing forward, so that it would cut the air in the best fashion and cause the least wind resistance.

Joe Good, admiring, pulled up his coat sleeve a little and, with a single twirl, wrapped the lithe line of the black snake around his arm. When he pulled down the sleeve again, the handle of the whip was concealed under the cuff, just above his wrist. This he did automatically, as the result of having practiced the really difficult trick a thousand times before.

His eyes, all the while, watched the flight of the hawk, which was beating its wings rapidly, to sustain the weight which it carried. Somewhere a nest filled with long-necked ugly-headed youngsters was waiting for that same food. Well, there would be enough to go all around, unless—

But the eagle was thinking of nestlings, too. It knew the taste of fresh fish perfectly well, and preferred it to anything in the world, even the hottest and juiciest of lamb cuts. It lacked the art of procuring the tidbit from the water, but it knew how to take tribute from more cunning workers.

Now, from its high tower in the air, it turned and dipped over. Down it came in the most magnificent style, opening its wings once to give a swift beat and increase the rate of its fall, then closing them again as it became a metal bolt out of the higher heaven.

Just above the hawk those wings shot outward—young Joe Good distinctly heard the sound. With talons and beak, the king of the air threatened, but the hawk, clumsily dodging, loaded down as it was, continued on its way more rapidly than before.

The eagle had feinted and failed; but now it rebounded on stiffened wings almost to the height of its former stand. Again it turned over and, even to the eye of the boy, there was savage business in its gesture through the air.

The hawk knew perfectly well that the game was ended.

It persisted until the tyrant was just overhead, then it dropped the prize, and the monarch shot down, caught the burden in one claw, and skimmed away toward the nest.

The harsh, enraged scream of the hawk now floated down to the ears of Joe Good, but the hawk itself, released from the weight that had anchored it, now shot away to take its watch again over the waters of the hidden lake or stream.

Grand was the eagle's flight, but nothing compared to the way the long, narrow wings of the hawk knifed through the air.

Joe Good, watching it, shook his head, and soliloquized: "It's always the same. Even the hawks, they've got the eagles over 'em. Same way with me; no matter where I go, I'll land in trouble. Everybody's got trouble. There's no use running away from it. Not even if you could walk on air, because a new brand would find you out, wherever you landed and started again."

He was so impressed by this thought that he whistled.

The burro instantly understood the welcome signal and, coming to a halt, began to tear eagerly at the long grass that fringed the trail.

Joe Good sat on a rock and looked sadly forward to the new land, sadly back upon the old.

As he reflected, he took from his pocket a small news clipping, and his eye glanced over the following notice:

Vincent Good was buried today in the cemetery, by Doctor Oliver Wain and the Episcopal Church. Attending the funeral was his son, Joseph Good.

Vincent Good met his death under tragic circumstances last Wednesday. During a saloon brawl he drew a gun and shot and seriously hurt Harry Alton.

He was pursued by an impromptu posse composed of the father and brother of Harry Alton; also, Tucker, Dean, Samuel and Christopher Alton joined the pursuit. They overtook the fugitive in Chalmer's Creek Canyon, where he resisted arrest, and was fatally wounded by a volley poured in by the posse.

The Episcopal congregation paid the expenses of the funeral.

The eye of Joe Good dwelt, strange to say, chiefly upon that last line. It was true. The congregation had paid, although grudgingly, the cost of the burial. For he, Joe Good, had not a penny.

"You got the wrong name," said an irate member of that congregation. "You ought to be called not Joe Good, but 'No Good'! You ain't worth a darn for anything."

That was what had decided Joe Good to leave the town of Fort Willow. But now, as he sat on the rock, he considered, and shook his head in doubt. There was labor and trouble in every part of the world, even in the blue heavens where the swift hawks and the eagles fly. Perhaps it would be better for him to return to the home community.

2

When he thought of the home farm, his heart sank, however. It was not a thing that commended itself to his thoughts. The only good thing to say about it was that it lay close to town, but the hundred acres were blow sand, cactus, and mesquite, with bristlings here and there of other thorns and worthless weeds. Sometimes, when the spring was very wet, they could pasture a few cows, and when the great cattle drives came through the country, they often made a little money in renting pasture rights to the herdsmen.

On the whole, however, it was worthless ground. No plowshares would ever turn its surface. Even for grazing land, it amounted to almost nothing. Once, to be sure, the Good property had extended twenty times as far and as wide, but his father had sold off bits here and there, and finally the last morsel, and the most worthless one, was that brier patch that lay close to the town of Fort Willow.

As he considered these things, however, there was another element in his memory that made him determine to go back.

He had not even said good-by to the house. For the bed, the bedding, the stove, the few pans and dishes, were almost worthless. As for the ground, people would not have wanted it even for a gift. Taxes would eat the whole thing up in a year or two.

No, it was not the value of the place that called his thoughts back to Fort Willow, but it was the recollection that the man who had said his name should be No Good, was, like those fellows who had killed his father, an Alton.

That thought was barbed, stuck in his heart, and would not come out for any pulling.

So, like one who stands at the verge of a promised land, he considered the fair new country beyond the pass, and then grimly looked back over his shoulder toward the Fort Willow Hill.

A dog came down the trail, a dog moving at a steady trot, as traveling coyotes do. There was something of coyote in this beast, except that it was smaller, and the black and white spots on it gave proof of a domestic mixture that was in the blood.

It saw the man, halted, and began to make a wide detour.

"He's been kicked out of somewhere, too," said the boy. And he whistled.

At the whistle, that sign of human notice, the dog put its tail between its legs and scurried forward.

Joe Good laughed. It amused him, when he saw that any living creature was afraid of him, even a dog. He knew his own worthlessness too well. When other people talked with him, it was usually on that subject.

"Hello, Professor," said he.

The dog stopped, raised its head, and then paused a moment longer with one forefoot raised, ready to be gone with instant expedition.

"Don't be a fool, Professor," said the boy. "Come over here and talk to me. I never hurt any one. I can't."

As he said it, he laughed. In fact, it had been that way all of his life. People never fought with him, because he was not worth a fight. As a boy, he had always been rather small. Even when he finally grew up, in one rapid year, to his full height, he could not stretch himself past five feet nine inches. It was not much. And the men of Fort Willow were generally six-footers. Every one looked down on Joe Good. Every one always had.

The dog turned squarely around, canted its head over one shoulder, and regarded him thoughtfully.

"It's all right, brother," said Joe Good. "I can't catch you and, even if I could, I wouldn't bite."

The dog sat down.

"I haven't got a gun," said Joe Good, "but if you start laughing at me I might do something that would surprise you."

The dog let its red tongue loll farther out and laughed more deeply, more silently than before.

Joe Good gave a slight shake to his arm, and the limber length of the black snake slid down into the palm of his hand. He knew every outline of the whip as another might know every page of a textbook. Textbooks had never troubled the mind of Joe Good very seriously.

"Professor, are you coming here?" asked Joe Good.

The dog lifted its head a little, then with deliberate insolence, turned it and looked behind him. That moment, Joe Good took for his shot. His right hand rose and shot out faster than thought, fast as the beat of the hawk's wings, as it fled through the sky.

The dog saw the missile coming, and it sprang up to flee, but it was just a fraction of a second too late. The darting ball grazed it on one shoulder, and at once the ample coils of the black snake flowed over it, almost like a black liquid. Around and around body and legs, the whipping lash circled, twisting itself tightly about the limbs. The dog, with a howl of mortal terror, struggled to flee and fell headlong in his tracks.

Before it could pick itself up, before it could shake loose the unwinding coils of the loaded rawhide, Joe Good had it by the scruff of the neck.

It flattened its body on the ground, closed its eyes and waited for punishment.

He said: "That's all right. I'm the same way, myself. I've been kicked around. Don't worry about me, brother. I've been kicked as hard and as far as you've ever been kicked. Don't curl your lips. I don't think that you'll bite. There's my hand. You little beast! You've got your teeth on it, but not in it. You won't bite—not me! Steady down, now. Here we are, and ready to walk along."

He passed a noose of the supple whip around the neck of the Professor—its wise little face had put the name in the mind of Joe Good—and led it back to the trail. The Professor held back, struggled, found that the hard coil strangled it, and came on freely enough.

"Here we are," said the boy, sitting down on the rock from which he had just risen. "And where do we go from here?"

The Professor sat up, cocked its ears, and looked at this new master.

"You're not big enough to fight, and you don't know

anything, I suppose," said Joe Good. "So you're about like me. Tell me where we go from here?"

The Professor suddenly reared, placed its forepaws on the knee of Good, and licked his hand.

"You know me, eh?" said Joe Good. "If you know me, you can go free. You scamp!"

He loosed the coil that held the dog by the neck.

The Professor turned into a blurred streak of speed, ran in a circle, and came back to Good again. By that time, the boy had turned the head of the patient burro and was herding it down the trail again. He laughed a little as he saw the dog come back.

"Other people have families and things to run. I have a burro and a dog," said he.

And he laughed again, as they went down the trail.

For the Professor, it was plain, had adopted him, at least for the moment, and, running up the trail in the lead, it stopped at every suspicious scent, and looked back with an attitude half of warning and half of pleasure, toward the burro and the man.

They steadily slogged on down the trail until it was noon. Joe Good was hungry, but he had often been hungry before. So he tightened his belt and went on, when the Professor jumped a jack rabbit out of a pile of rocks. Joe Good laughed heartily to see the tail of the little dog bobbing with effort as it legged it after that winged rabbit. Even a greyhound would have been put to shame; and how could the Professor have a chance?

But the dog did not run far. Presently he paused, cocked his head and, running off to the side, lay down in the long grass.

Two minutes later it appeared again, bounding forward, and out of the grass before it rose a jack rabbit and went away with flying leaps up the hill.

Joe Good began to notice now.

Swiftly the rabbit ran, but the dog, pursuing only a short distance, seemed to take notice of the curve of the jack's flight, for no rabbit can do other than run in circles, large or small. And when the curve was noted, the Professor ran off to the side, lay down, waited, and rested. It pursued only long enough to make the frightened jack flee furiously for its life, after which the dog went to a strategic point and kept watch.

Sure enough, before long, it had started the jack again,

and sent it wildly away. Six times that game was played, and the last time of all, the rabbit, exhausted by its own glorious running, died in the teeth of the dog.

The Professor brought it back, the long legs trailing on the ground, and laid it before the feet of the new master. Joe Good was touched.

He was moved by the canny intelligence that the mongrel had showed. He was moved, even more, by the odd sign of affection which the beast exhibited toward him. But, best of all, was the rabbit's flesh itself. He toasted it over a small fire and ate. The Professor had the bones and oddments, and they both drank at the same stream.

Joe Good was in a thoughtful humor and he said aloud to the crisp mountain air: "Brains will do everything—brains and teeth!"

"But what teeth have I?" he added to himself, and he sighed.

They marched on, Joe Good and the burro, the Professor scouting well ahead, until they came down to the house which was posted highest up the side of the pass. There a huge beast that seemed half mastiff, and half wolf, came rushing out at the Professor. Joe Good gave the dog up for lost.

For it had not the strength to defend itself; it had not the speed to keep away from those long legs. And he himself had no gun to defend it.

The Professor bolted under a barbed-wire fence, whirled, and as the crossbred hound sailed over the fence, the Professor ducked back under the lower wire, sat down, and lolled its red tongue in laughter at the foe.

Joe Good stopped the burro to graze, and himself to laugh loudly and long.

"Here's brains again," said he, "and brains will always win."

3

For a moment or two, the game was repeated, the big hound vaulting over the fence, or rushing vainly toward the barbs, while the Professor deftly ducked back and forth under the lowest strand.

Then the little dog introduced a new idea; it ran to the side of a big, conical rock and waited there, while the hound, in a fury of joy, bolted in pursuit.

It was a new game. Joe Good was so close that he could have interfered, now, but he was too interested to move.

The hound first chased the little dog around and around the great rock but, though it was twice as fast of foot, it could not turn comfortably in such a small circle. It ran so wide that the Professor finally doubled back between the teeth of the larger dog and the rock; then it sat down and lolled its tongue and laughed.

The hound, grown wild with rage, leaped the very top of the rock to get at its enemy; the Professor waited until the danger was fairly hanging in the air over him; then he began to slide around the huge stone again.

"Brains!" whispered the boy, rapt with admiration. "Brains always win!"

The Professor was not content, for as the great dog, frothing with fury, raced after it, the Professor gained so much that suddenly it was on the haunches of the hunter and twice slashed it across the thighs, wolfishly.

A howl of rage and pain answered. The hound bolted away and then stood, dancing about. The enemy was so small, so elusive! If only the honest strength of downright jaw power could be applied to the problem!

He rushed the rock, feinted at one side, feinted at the other, and then again vaulted clear over it.

As he landed, the Professor waited to nip once again at the defenseless hind quarters, then fled around the stone, with the hound terrible in pursuit!

But the Professor's small size and canny footing made him gain as before, and presently, slash, slash, he was drawing blood again.

The hound, with a wild howl, tucked its tail between its legs and fled for the house. It had adventured much for the sake of science, but this was sheer necromancy and home was the best place in this cruel and mysterious world. The Professor, licking his thin lips, came back to his master, and fawned upon him, as much as to say: "See what a danger I have disposed of in your behalf!"

Joe Good did not laugh; he was too deeply buried in thought, for again it occurred to him: "Brains will do everything!"

Not only in the world of dogs, but in the world of men, also!

As he went down the trail toward the hills of Fort Willow, he spent much time talking to the Professor and caressing him, for it seemed to him that there were certain object lessons that he had learned on the way, that must be retained in the mind. If only he could apply them!

Then came a beat of horse's hoofs behind him and behold! The crossbred hound, again, with no barbed-wire fence, no great conical rocks in sight, of which the little dog could take advantage. But the hound had its lesson well in mind; it held aloof. Savagely, it snarled and barked, but always at a distance. That was not the danger, but the big mountaineer, who reined up his absurdly little mustang and stepped, not jumped, to the ground.

He was middle-aged, huge, black-bearded, with a beard that covered most of the face and showed only the glint of the eyes and a red streak of mouth. He was in a towering rage, with the reins of the horse over one hand and the rifle over the other.

"You and your vicious dog, what kind of tricks you been up to?" said he.

Young Joe Good began to adopt an apologetic air, but suddenly he remembered that he was no longer in the town of Fort Willow. For all this burly fellow knew, he might be the most dangerous gunman in the entire West.

Then again, he said to himself, brains will do every-

thing. Was he as stupid as this gross creature, all beard
and brawn?

So he straightened himself up to the full stature of his
inches—alas, how pitifully few they seemed!—and said:
"You keep a fighting dog, and you shouldn't mind if it
gets into trouble, partner."

"I'll partner you!" said the mountaineer. "I'll make you
a red partner, is what I'll make out of you. Because I'm
gunna teach you something, is what I'm gunna do!"

And he came straight at young Joe Good, with vast
strides.

He was, to Joe Good, as the hound was to the dog,
longer of leg and fleeter, vaster of bulk, far more powerful of leg. And what could he do? He was not a fighting
man.

"You stand where you are!" said Joe Good.

The other hesitated half an instant.

"Words," said Joe Good to himself. "Even bare
words—they're enough to stop even a brute like this."

And he marveled.

He had always felt that every one saw through him, but
this man did not see through him—quite!

The big fellow strode on.

"You gotta have a lesson. You and your dog. I'm gunna
shoot that dog, after I get through with you. But you're
too mean for shooting. You ain't worth a cartridge."

Joe Good shook his right arm a little, and the heavy,
supple coil of the black snake came down into his hand.

"I'm asking you again—will you stand there?" said he.

"I'll see you dead first!" said the big man.

"Then take it!" said Joe Good.

For a flash of blood-red lightning had crossed his brain
and, as it cleared away, he saw that he had hurled the
coiled ball of the black snake.

The mountaineer, with an oath, jerked the rifle to the
ready. Had the loaded whip, in a knot, struck the breast
of the big man? At any rate, he reeled and staggered; the
rifle hurled a bullet aimlessly into the blue of the skies.
Then the supple arms of the whip coiled about the body,
about the arms of the big man.

He stood there with his hands lashed to his sides, the
rifle fallen to the earth.

Young Joe Good stepped forward, picked up the gun
and leveled it.

"You'd better back up a little," said he.

As he watched, he saw the most curious thing that ever had come under his observation. For the big man seemed to melt away, as the coils of the black snake disentangled themselves from his arms and his body.

He stepped back, muttering.

And then he held up his big soiled hands before his face, as though to shut out the thought of death.

"I ought to drive a slug through the middle of you," said Joe Good. "You're not worth a damn. You're no good. That little dog licked your dog, and made it howl. I've licked you. You understand? I could lick you again, any day of the week!"

The hot fury of the tyrant surged through him.

"Don't shoot!" moaned the man of the mountain.

"I ought to, and I think I shall," said Joe Good. "You came down here to murder the pup! I ought to do the same for you. You were going to manhandle me and then murder the pup. I think I'll let you have it."

The big man moaned. "I didn't know who you were. I didn't know you was one of these here gunmen. I just thought you were ordinary like me. Don't shoot, partner!"

"You back up!" said the boy slowly, tasting his words and the power behind them. "Throw off your ammunition belt and your revolver, and then back up out of here."

He was implicitly, foolishly, he felt, obeyed. The good Colt and the belt of cartridges, half for the rifle and half for the revolver, lay on the ground, and the big fellow, mounting his mustang, started off, his head turned over his shoulder, and his mouth gaping through the black beard.

Joe Good motioned with the butt of the rifle toward his shoulder; the other bowed over the pommel of his saddle and spurred away for life.

"Brains do everything," said Joe Good to himself. "Brains, and a little bluffing."

He began to laugh. The Professor came and fawned about his knees. "Down, boy," said Joe Good. "You've taught me everything I know, and now you begin to think that I've taught you. Brains and bluffing, they're all that count in this funny little old world!"

He was still laughing as he picked up the gun belt, and

then, hitching up his coat sleeve, gave the black snake the proper whirl to twist it around and around his arm.

A sort of childish wonder overcame Joe Good. For he saw that dreams could come true, and that the black snake on which he had wasted so many idle hours that even his idle father had reproved him—even this toy could make the difference between life and death, between victory and a brutal manhandling, at the least. So he was amazed, and held his amazement close to his heart.

On the day before, his father had been buried without honor, without a mourner following his body, except his son, buried by public subscription. And on the day following, he, Joe Good, had stepped into a strange empire of his own, based on the power of a whip and a small dog.

A dog for a teacher and a whip for a weapon.

And yet who could tell how far the limits of that empire might extend, before the finish?

He only knew that he felt in himself the beginning of limitless strength, limitless resources. The world would have to wait, to see what he could do.

He remembered the story of the man who had been thrown off a stage for failure to pay his ticket, a man who was rushing toward a newly discovered gold field. And where he fell, stunned, in a creek bottom, his kit of tools flung out beside him, there he had risen and cracked a great pebble with his hammer, and had seen the gleam— of priceless gold shine out invitingly at him.

So, perhaps, he, Joe Good, had stumbled upon his fortune.

4

He left Fort Willow with the burro and the black snake. He came back with a dog scampering ahead, a rifle over his shoulder, a revolver strapped about his hips. He would have been a strange lad if he had not been pleased and, in fact, in all the twenty years of the life of Joe Good, nothing had happened that meant so much to him.

He took a shortcut over the hills and came to the house of his father, his own house now, and as he looked at it he wondered that he could have been tempted so easily to give it up.

To be sure, it was only a little ramshackle house with four small rooms, but it had its good points that were sure to appeal to the eye of a really indolent man like Joe, or his dead father. If the house itself were not important, at least it possessed an excellent deep veranda across both the front and the back of it. The grass was worn away under the two big oaks and the vast fig tree that leaned above the roof of the cottage.

It was worn away by the moving of chair legs, for this was the favorite reading place of Vincent Good; and here from morning to night he would sit, lost in the pages, or taking notes for the great work which he was one day to write. For years and years he had been stacking up these notes on the manners and customs of the ancient Indians, but he never had been able to write more than the title of the first chapter.

The only crop which the tag-end of the old ranch grew in quantities was leisure. No one could go hungry when fish thronged in the creek that trickled just behind the house and when the rabbits came knocking at the kitchen

door, so to speak. Then there were the seasons when the
ducks flew, when the melon patch supplied an abundance
of fruit, when the berries ripened on the banks of the
creek, and when the half acre of corn that Joe tended was
ripe enough for roasting. As Vincent Good had often
said: "All the old place needs is a coat of some paint."

Joe Good, leaning on the front picket fence, nodded
his head and decided that he was right. The old place
needed paint, and it should have some.

He turned out the burro in the scant pasture—at this
season of the year nothing but a burro could have lived
on the pickings to be found in the big field—carried the
pack into the house, and then strolled downtown to the
hardware store.

The proprietor greeted him with a frown; every one
greeted Joe Good, in Fort Willow, with either a sneer or a
frown, or sometimes it was both.

"I want this turned into white paint," said Joe Good,
and laid the revolver on the counter.

The storekeeper lifted the gun, examined it. It was
brand new and it was loaded. "Where did you get this?"
he asked sharply.

"Fellow tried to murder me this morning," said Joe
Good, with some truth in his words. "I had to take his
guns away."

"You took his guns away? How did you take 'em
away?" said the doubter.

Joe Good shook his right arm; the heavy pile of the
black snake slid down into his hand, and he showed it.

"With this," said he, and smiled.

He had an insinuating, rather twisted smile. That and
his dark-blue eyes were his only good features in a thin
face that had colorless eyebrows and sun-faded hair
above.

The storekeeper looked at the whip and scowled. He
did not understand, but meanwhile he was losing time,
and the gun really had a value. He gave Joe Good half its
worth in white paint, and the boy carried it back to the
house.

It was middle afternoon now, but he fell to work at
once with a great zeal, and at the end of the day a horseman, going slowly past the Good place, was astonished to
see a clean white face on the old shack, a pure white that
shone out like a light through the overhanging shadows.

He looked closer, and saw that young Joe Good was there at work, now finishing off the veranda.

The rider uttered a profane exclamation.

"Here, you!" he exclaimed.

Joe Good turned, paintbrush in hand; the little dog beside him turned also. And the boy saw, sitting a horse at the gate, none other than Hugh Alton, the father of the lad whom Vincent Good had wounded in the saloon and the leader of the posse that had killed the fugitive on Wednesday.

All the Altons were magnificent, but Hugh Alton was the most magnificent of them all. He was nearly fifty, but he looked ten years younger. He kept the thin waist and the muscular shoulders of a Western rider; and in his face was that noble beauty which all of the Altons had inherited from him. He was a very successful rancher, but every one who knew him wondered why he was not the governor of the State or a United States Senator. He had the brains necessary for such a post; more than that, he had the bearing.

The heart of Joe Good fluttered as he saw the great man; it fluttered still faster as he remembered that Hugh Alton had led the posse that killed his father. Then the boy went slowly toward the gate.

Alton rested one hand on his hip and looked down with much disapproval on the lad. "I thought that you'd pulled out of here, Joe?" said he.

"I did," said the boy. "But I pulled back again."

"Why?" said Alton. "Think you can make anything out of that sand heap of yours?"

"It's home for me," answered Joe Good.

Mr. Alton brushed his mustache away from his upper lip, a characteristic gesture. He did it with the tip of a gloved finger.

Then he said: "I'm glad that you've come back, Joe. As a matter of fact, I came around here late this morning, hoping to find you in."

"What made you come?" asked the boy.

"Because I've decided that I'll take the place off your hands, that's why."

"Have you?" said Joe Good.

He turned and looked all about him.

"I don't know what you'd do with it," said he. "You don't need the house; and the barn has a broken back, and the hundred acres hardly puts out five tons of volunteer hay in a year."

"I know those things," said Alton. "Nevertheless, the land has a value, for me."

"Have you struck gold in the creek?" asked Joe Good, with his twisted smile.

"Nonsense!" said Alton. "Stuff and nonsense. Nevertheless, the land has a value for me. It would bring my property down to the road, and that's an advantage. I don't want to be shut off from the main highway, as I am!"

He pointed toward the rolling ground which marked his own boundaries.

"You can understand that, Joe," he said rather confidingly.

Joe Good looked in the indicated direction, and he remembered that all of that land, almost as far as his eyes could reach, had one day belonged to his father. The Altons had it now, and they were making it produce a steady stream of gold.

"I can understand your wanting it," said Joe.

He turned back to the other man.

Suddenly it seemed to him that the attitude of Hugh Alton had in it a certain degree of patronizing sympathy and kindness. Hugh Alton, the boy remembered, had brains, and brains will do everything in this world. But why should Alton be using brains on him, poverty-stricken Joe Good, or on the patch of desert which Joe owned?

Well, the hawk had a use for the fish in the pool, and the eagle had a use for the hawk in the air. So from great to small, the stronger prey upon the weaker.

"I'll offer you a price, Joe," said the rancher. "The house and the barn are worthless, as you've already said. I'd simply be at the expense of tearing down the fire traps. The ground itself, as you've also said, isn't worth a penny. But I'll pay you something. Partly because I can use the acreage as a border to my own land, and partly because I can't help feeling sorry for you just now, my lad. You know, of course, that there was no malice in the unfortunate affair of Wednesday. It was simply apprehending a fugitive. Whisky was the whole trouble. Infernal, brain-rotting whisky! Your poor father could never stand the stuff, you know!"

Joe Good stared.

It struck him as very odd that Mr. Alton should be explaining these matters with such care. Very odd indeed. He had taken it for granted that his father had flown into one of his accustomed passions, and in those humors he was capable of the greatest violence. Vincent Good had stood a thousand times in the danger of the law because of his frightful temper; last Wednesday had been the final stroke. That was all.

But now Alton was explaining this proposition.

The great man went on: "I'll make you a price on the land. I'll give you—what do you say?—well, five dollars an acre. That's five hundred dollars, Joe. As a matter of fact," he added, glancing at his watch, "we've time to drop downtown right now and fix the thing up."

He gathered his reins, as though about to start at once.

It seemed to Joe Good that he heard a faint, far-off booming in the air, as when the stooping eagle had suddenly spread out its great wings above the hawk.

Five hundred dollars was really a great deal more than the shack was worth, of course, together with the ground that surrounded it.

But Joe Good found himself shaking his head.

"I don't think that I'm interested."

"What?" cried Alton. "Not interested? Stuff and nonsense, Joe. You're not such a fool as to refuse five hundred dollars, I hope!"

Joe Good smiled without mirth.

"I'll keep the place, I think."

"Young man," said the rancher, "you don't think that I'm bargaining, do you? You don't think that I'm really beating you down with a small offer that I will raise?"

"No, but you see how it is," said Joe Good. "I've just put a whole coat of paint over the front of the house. You wouldn't want me to throw away all that good paint and the time it took to put it on, would you?"

Mr. Alton stared. Then he exploded: "Half-wit!" and drove his horse furiously up the road.

5

The boy looked long and earnestly after the retreating form of the rancher. "The eagle missed me that time," said he, "but he'll be stooping at me again before long, I have an idea."

The Professor whined, sitting on the ground before his new master and watching the face of the man with affectionate interest. Joe Good then made up his mind.

He snapped his fingers at the dog and walked outside the front gate. There he paused a moment to admire his brush work, which had given the house a face so astonishingly bright and new and clean. No one would have thought of calling it a shack, now. It seemed rather a delightful cottage, a lovely retreat, tucked away under the cool shadows of the trees, a perfect place for the summer. And the boy smiled with pleasure.

He himself, once he was out of rags, might he not seem fairly presentable?

Then he went downtown, following his former thought. Hugh Alton had seemed to think that there was something that required a little explaining. If that were the case, it was not from an Alton that Joe Good wanted the explanation.

He went into Mort Pemberton's saloon, where the brawl between young Alton and his father had taken place. Mort himself was behind the bar, looking vaster than ever in his white coat. He leaned on his fat elbows against the inner edge of the bar and perused a newspaper. There was no one else in the bar; most people were having their supper at this hour.

"Hello, Joe," he said, with a side glance and no more. "What are you after? A beer?"

Joe Good had fifty cents, it was all he had in the world. Now he slid it onto the bar, saying: "I'll have a touch of whisky. Have one with me."

Pemberton looked at the money with some surprise. Then he nodded, produced with one hand a bottle of whisky; with the other, two glasses wedged firmly between his fat fingers. He put down the glasses, uncorked the bottle, and spun it into place in front of his patron. Joe Good poured himself one finger.

"That ain't a drink. That's only a taste," said the bartender, helping himself heartily.

"A taste for you is a drink for me," said Joe Good. "I haven't got a steel lining to my brain, the way some of you people have."

"Yeah," said Pemberton, holding up the glass and regarding it with a squint that was only half for the contents, and half for his own thoughts, "yeah, there's some that can hold it and there's some that can't. Your old man, Joe—I'm sorry about him, too—but your old man was one that couldn't hold his liquor none too good."

"No, I don't suppose that he could. He was quick-tempered," said the boy. "I don't think that quick-tempered people ever can stand alcohol well."

"Are you quick-tempered, kid?" asked Mort, with a rather disdainful smile.

"No," said Joe modestly. "But you don't need a whole ocean to sink a small ship."

The bartender grinned.

"Well, here's how," said he, and put down the drink.

Joe Good did the same, and coughed and winked the tears out of his eyes. "Mighty hot, but mighty good," he gasped.

The bartender smacked his thick lips and grinned again.

"Have another one on me, Joe," said he.

"No, thanks. One's enough."

"I'll have another one myself, then," said Mort Pemberton. "Where'd you get the dog, Joe?"

"I picked him up. He's just a stray. But he has brains," said Joe.

"You oughta have a lot of brains yourself, Joe," said the other, with the comfortable friendliness of the whisky taking hold upon him. "Take the books you've read, you oughta have a lot of brains from reading them. You oughta go and do something for yourself, one of these days, maybe."

"Thanks," said Joe Good. "Some day, maybe. We're a lazy lot, though, my family."

Pemberton lowered his voice to gentleness. He leaned his chin on his fat hand.

"Kind of lonely out there, ain't it, kid?" he said.

Joe Good straightened a little and looked the other man in the eye.

After a moment, his voice came, and he said: "He was a father and a mother and a brother to me."

Pemberton frowned with pain. He looked suddenly away from the boy's face and down toward the floor.

"I know," he said. "It's terrible! I wouldn't've expected your old man to shoot anybody. He never gave any signs that way, before."

"He had a temper," said the boy. "But there's one thing that surprises me."

"That he pulled a gun?"

"No, but that he was actually able to hit anything after he pulled it. It must have been an accident."

"Oh, I don't know about it being an accident," frowned Pemberton, speaking as one who has given all the ground he can. "I guess his pulling the gun was no accident or shooting at Harry Alton."

"I don't suppose that it was," said the boy calmly. "I was calling the hit an accident, that's all. But no one knows exactly how it happened, I suppose. They were alone in here, weren't they? You'd gone into the back room?"

"Yeah, I'd gone into the back room, but they weren't alone. Wally Chase was in here with them. Wally seen everything. Wally was the one that give your old man a run out of the place."

"I didn't know that Wally was in here," said Joe Good.

He looked up at the mirror and seemed to see there a picture of the veteran gunman, lean, hard as iron in soul and body. He was barely twenty-five, but his hair was silvered; he had been through enough, men said, to whiten the hair of a whole army.

"Yeah, Wally was here, all right," said Mort Pemberton. "He came in with Harry Alton, in fact, and they was having some words. Your old man was standing there in that corner, drinking a little, and being mighty quiet. He hadn't showed no signs at all."

"What were Wally and Harry having words about?" said the boy.

"Something about money. I dunno what. Harry'd given Wally some money. Maybe it was poker. Wally seemed to think that he ought to have more coin. Harry got hot, and cursed him."

"That's a strange thing to do," said the boy. "To curse Wally Chase right to his face, I mean."

"Well, Wally ain't fool enough to take a shot at an Alton, I guess," said Pemberton.

"How did my father get mixed into the trouble?" asked the boy.

"I guess," said Mort Pemberton, "that he was just standing there in the corner loading up poison against the Altons. You know—they've bought up all his ranch, bit by bit, until they come to the last bit, that they didn't want. Must've sort of worked on your father, to see Harry Alton standing there in fine new clothes, with a gold watch in his pocket and a diamond in his necktie. He was kind of swelled up that night, Harry was. He was gunna go out with his girl, I guess. And when I went out of the room, I suppose he just boiled over. There couldn't've been many words. I just heard the shot and your old man shouted at the same time."

"What did he shout?"

"I dunno that I remember. Just kind of yelled out."

"As if he were angry?"

"I suppose so. I heard the shout and the gun go off, and Harry groaning and the sound of him falling. As I tore back into the room, there was Wally Chase giving your father the run out of the place. Your father looked kind of surprised and staggered. Wally was yelling to get your old man, and shouting out that he'd dropped Harry Alton. Your father ran out to the street and jumped the first horse he came to, and Wally went out and gave the alarm. It just happened that there was a lot of the Altons in town, and they started on your father's trail."

"It's a strange thing," said the boy, "that Wally didn't ride in the man hunt. He likes that sort of thing well enough, and he's usually on the other end of the thing."

"Yeah, that's true. But Wally acted real decent, that night," said Mort Pemberton. "He came back inside the saloon and picked up Harry. He said how sorry he was and took care of him like a brother. We had the kid bedded down on the table in the cardroom, back there, till Hugh Alton come back from the chase. He and Wally and Harry confabbed a while, and then the buckboard came and carted Harry home. He wasn't hurt very bad. Just a clean cut through the top of the thigh."

"Ain't gunna have another, Joe?" he asked briskly.

"No, I'll be rambling," said Joe.

He went out into the street, with the dog behind him.

There were hawks in the sky. One of them had struck down his father. And he, No Good, might now have to play the part of an eagle and hunt the hunters.

The thing became clearer and clearer as he stood there outside the saloon, watching the crimson of the sunset blur and streak the west with blood.

Then he walked down the street, feeling the puff and squirting of the dust beneath his feet.

He wanted to find Wally Chase, and he knew well enough where the man would probably be. If Wally was not on some nefarious mission outside of the town, he was to be found at Mort Pemberton's saloon, or on the veranda of the hotel, slumped back against the wall and thinking his own dark thoughts in lonely silence.

When Joe Good came to the hotel, he spotted his man at once. There was Wally, as usual, at the end of the line of the indolent, and, again as usual, with no chair pulled up close to his.

The boy went down the veranda. No one took the trouble to speak to him. No one guessed that anger was softening the fall of his feet. And if that had been guessed, who would have cared for the thoughts and the passions of No Good?

So he went down to the end of the veranda and stood in front of the gaunt, doubled-up form of the gunman.

"Hello, Wally!" he said.

Wally Chase gradually lifted his head from his broodings, but he said nothing. He wasted no words on people like Joe Good.

6

Joe leaned against the near-by veranda railing and shook the black snake into his hand. He began to make it pour from hand to hand, and the hard, supple coils made a soft, clicking sound as they struck on one another and then flowed loosely into the nearest empty space.

He made the long, shaky thing glide up his arm, over his shoulder, and around his neck, slithering down inside his coat and so into his hand again. He had played with the whip for so many years that his hands performed instinctively with it.

The Professor sat down against his toes.

Said Joe Good: "I wanted to ask you something, Wally."

Wally Chase said nothing. He pulled out the makings, and began to construct a cigarette.

"I wanted to ask you," said Joe, "about Wednesday night."

"Got a match?" said Wally.

"No."

"Go fetch me one, then."

Joe Good went and borrowed a match. A faint chuckle of scornful amusement arose from those who had overheard the command of the gunman and watched its execution.

Joe lighted the match and held it for the cigarette of the other man. Wally lighted his smoke and then leaned back, puffing, without a word of thanks.

Some interest, of a mild sort, was taken by the line of

observers in young Good, as he stood there before the gunman. The contrast between the man of terror and the obscure youth was sufficiently great to keep heads turned in that direction.

How could they tell that under his careless surface, Joe Good was as tense as a violin string, ready for the bow?

But he was telling himself that now he must play the eagle, indeed, if he were to hunt down such a hawk as this.

"About Wednesday evening," he said.

Wally Chase took no heed of the words.

"I was wondering," said the boy, "if you'd tell me just what happened there in the barroom, Wednesday night? You and Harry Alton are the only men who know."

"You lie," said Wally Chase. "Your old man knows, too."

"What?" gasped Joe Good, unable to believe that words so brutal could really have been spoken.

"Your old man knows about it. Go to the infernal regions and ask him," said Wally calmly. "And stand out of my way. I don't wanta be bothered with you!"

"I won't bother you long," said the boy.

"No," said Wally Chase. "You said one thing that's right. You won't bother me long. Stand out of my way, will you?"

His voice rose a little. All other conversation along the veranda ceased. No one was amazed to hear the snarling tone which announced that the poison was mastering the brain of the great gun fighter; but all were utterly stupefied to see that young Good did not flee at once, for his life.

If he were presuming upon his insignificance, he was very wrong. Wally Chase, like the beasts of the field, killed when the humor came upon him; he killed men as a cat kills mice.

"I'll stand out of your way after you've answered a couple of questions," said the boy.

He was measuring the distances, accustoming his eyes perfectly to the dull light of the dusk.

"You'll what?" said the voice of Wally, soft, so soft that the straining ears of the others on the veranda could hardly make out what had been said.

"I'll stand out of your way when you've answered a few questions," said the boy.

Wally said nothing. He merely began to lean forward a little in his chair, and his feet moved gradually back under him. His body, at the same time, swayed slightly to the left.

There was a muttered exclamation not far away.

The suspense was beginning to tell; every nerve was strained to the breaking point, as Joe Good said, as gently as ever: "I want to know why you shot Harry Alton and then threw the blame on my father?"

"You want to—" began the voice of Wally Chase.

Then the gun flashed, exploded, and fell with a rattling bang on the floor of the veranda.

People arose with groans. They waited for the slender body of Joe Good to topple forward on his face, quite dead from a bullet either through the heart or the brain.

But, instead, Joe Good remained standing easily where he was.

"I asked you a question," said he.

For answer, Chase cursed him, and reached for his fallen gun with the left hand, not the right.

Something hissed and sang in the air. Wally Chase did not pick up the gun, but straightened with a jerk and an oath.

With incredulously staring eyes, the observers at last understood. Wally Chase was not about to kill Joe Good. Instead, he had just received a slash from the black snake of the boy—and still he was not in the killing vein, it appeared.

"You've broken my wrist!" said Wally, and added with a vile oath: "I'm gunna eat your heart. You've broken my wrist."

"I asked you a question," said the boy. "Why did you shoot Harry Alton and then lay the blame—"

The right wrist of the gunman might be broken, but he still had another resource. With his left hand, he drew a hunting knife that was so ground, so drawn to a tapering line of light, that it was quite clear the owner never intended to use that delicate edge on the hide of a deer. With that knife, he lunged straight at the slender body of Joe Good.

That is to say, he started to lunge, but a coil of the

loaded black snake struck him across the face and sent
him staggering to the side. And as he stood there, reeling, the accurate lash of the whip flicked out and curled
around the left wrist of the gunman.

When it was jerked back, it burned through skin and
flesh almost to the bone. Fire cannot burn like rawhide,
as every Westerner knows. And the lash of the thin whip
was almost like a knife. Wally Chase yelled with the pain
and the knife dropped to the veranda floor.

Wild oaths rushed from the lips of Chase.

Young Joe Good picked up the knife. He held it in his
left hand, while in his right the black snake rose and
fell, stood up snakelike and dropped away again, for all
the world like a column of black water springing out of
the fountain of his hand.

Wally Chase stopped cursing. With his blood-dripping
left hand, he cursed the broken bones of his right wrist,
and he watched with fascination the evil play of the
black snake.

No one else so much as breathed. For they knew Joe
Good. They knew that he was No Good, as well. And
yet there he stood, and there stood the iron man, the
slayer, Chase.

The eye could survey this scene, but the brain could
not really comprehend it.

In Joe Good there was a strange feeling of calm and
assurance.

A small eagle he might be, but an eagle, nevertheless.
And now he had a great hawk in his talons and the
lesser creature would have to bow to his will in all things.

Said he: "I've asked you the question several times.
Are you going to answer me?"

"You've spoiled my gun hand!" screamed the other.
And this was followed with more oaths.

"Will you talk?" said Joe Good.

"I'll see you dead, first," said the gunman.

The last words were cut sharp, for the lightning-swift
lash of the whip went out, like a snake's tongue, and
licked straight across his face.

Rage more than pain made him howl, and he turned
to flee from that supple sword of fire.

The black snake slid out again through the dusky air,
curled about an ankle, and Wally Chase was jerked flat

on his face. He got up slowly. No one had offered to assist him. Perhaps there never had been a more feared and detested creature in the town of Fort Willow. And now the men stood about in a wide circle, breathing hard. Not a one of them but wished he had in his grip a whip like that which now lay compactly coiled in the hand of Joe Good.

"Will you talk now?" said Joe Good, "or do you want me to take off some more of your hide?"

"What do you want to know? I'm gunna have your heart for this, you yellow sneak," said the gunman. "I'm gunna eat it, is what I'm gunna do."

He stopped and jerked himself more erect. The lash of the black snake had snapped loudly, under his very chin. Wally Chase shuddered and was still.

"You shot Harry Alton, didn't you?" said the boy.

The answer was faintly enough muttered, but it boomed more than the explosion of a cannon in the ears of the crowd.

"Yes, I shot him," said Wally Chase.

Four small words, but they had gigantic implications.

And young Joe Good was drawing them out.

"Why did you shoot him?"

"He got fresh. He was trying to beat me down in a— a business deal."

"What was the business deal?"

"I've said enough."

"What was the business deal?" said Joe Good. "What was the business deal, or I'll cut you in two!"

"It was about your old man," said the gunman.

"What about him?"

"I ain't gunna say no more. Go ask Alton what the deal was about. Curse you!"

Said young Joe Good: "Harry Alton hired you to kill my father. Is that it?"

"Yes—no! You lie! I won't speak again!" shouted the gunman.

Then, in mortal fear of the stroke of pain from which he could not flee, he cowered. A strange sight to see the tyrant shrink!

But no blow answered him.

Joe Good was saying: "I imagine this makes the affair clear. The Altons wanted my father out of the way. They tried to hire this thing. There was an argument about the price. The deal was confused, but eventually they got what they wanted. Now, then, was my father shot by a posse, or murdered by a gang of Altons?"

7

The next morning, Sheriff Dick Purvis found a small mongrel sitting on its haunches near the house of Good, watching while its master, with care and some skill, applied a coat to the south side of the old house. The front and the north side were already of the purest and snowiest white.

The sheriff took off his hat, shook the dust from it, and gave a shake also, to the bandanna that surrounded his throat, for there had been no stir of wind as he jogged out from the town, and now a little cloud of white drifted slowly away from him. Joe Good, seated on a plank that was supported by two ladders, looked down from his work, and waved his hand.

"Hello, Mr. Purvis," said he cheerfully.

"Morning, Joe," said the sheriff, making a smoke and looking curiously up at the worker. "That house worth the paint you're puttin' in it?"

"It's worth its paint to me," said the boy.

He began to stroke the brush across the wood, putting on a thick slab of the paint, and then working it well in with supple strokes that brought out the paint from the very depths of the brush.

This was not rudeness on his part, for he continued to talk as he worked, saying: "The old place is brightening up a little, Mr. Purvis."

"I came out to talk about something more'n paint," said the sheriff.

"Go right ahead, will you?" said the boy. "You don't mind me painting while I listen, do you? I want to finish this side of the house before noon."

Said Purvis grimly, puffing out a thick cloud of cigarette smoke: "I dunno but what I'll have to take you back to jail with me, kid!"

"Dear me!" said Joe Good, his voice filled with great horror. "I'm sorry to hear that."

"You're sorry to hear it, are you?" said Purvis. "You may be a whole sight sorrier than you are now when you get behind the bars, young feller!"

He was rather a young man himself, to be holding such an important post in the county. He had been elected out of respect to his distinguished father, who had held the office before him for many years, and who had died in the execution of his duty. Then young Dick Purvis was chosen for the place, and stepping into his father's shoes he had done fairly well.

He was big, strong, fearless, and honest. He would attack anything up to wild tigers. And he could not be corrupted by the use of money. However, there were other points in which his character was not quite ideal. He was a little too rough, a little too pleased with his own importance, and sometimes he lacked the cleverness which every officer of the law ought to possess.

Joe did not look down as he listened to this outburst. He merely said: "But I'm not going to jail, I hope. What could be the charge against me?"

"Theft!" bellowed the sheriff, almost maddened by the indifference with which the lad received him. "Theft, and breaking the peace, and assault with attempt to kill! Isn't that enough of a charge for you?"

Joe continued the painting, laying on the white with great precision and humming a little, very softly.

He now said: "You know, Sheriff, I don't know whether you're with the fish, the hawk, or the eagles."

"What in the world are you talking about?" demanded the sheriff.

"Not quite with the fish," said the boy thoughtfully, "and it is equally certain, not quite an eagle. A hawk, let's say. One of the shortwinged kind, that robs the hedges of the little singing birds and catches the field mice."

"Why, what are you raving about?" asked the sheriff. "Are you out of your head? I tell you what you're charged with, and you talk about fish and field mice."

"About the charges," said the boy. "The theft, for instance. That had to do with the revolver, eh?"

"Exactly that! And what you got to say in answer?"

"I don't say a thing until I'm charged," said Joe Good. "As for the gossiping of an old gray-headed fool like our friend of the hardware store—"

Tomlinson was one of the most respected of the merchants of Fort Willow. But he was a cruel man in the collection of bills, and most sharp had he always been, most sharp and curt in his treatment of the worthless Goods.

Now, with precision, with a wonderful relish that passed from the roots of his tongue to the roots of his soul, Joe Good applied these opprobrious terms to the well-known dealer.

The sheriff himself was amazed. It was a fact that young Good was not expected to advance such ideas with an air of calm decision and of calm knowing.

"What Tomlinson suspects does not matter," concluded the boy, lifting his brush and squinting to examine the smoothness of the white layer he had just put on. "And as for the fellow who may once have had the gun, he will bring no charges against me. Does that cover the point, Sheriff?"

He turned and favored the sheriff with his humorous, twisted smile.

"Point be blowed," said Sheriff Dick Purvis. "It don't cover nothing. The gun wasn't yours if you didn't buy it, and—and—"

He paused, staring at the blank which confronted him. He hardly knew what to say. His words seemed to have conducted him down a blind alley.

"Breakin' the peace," he went on angrily, "and assault—"

"Assault on whom?" asked the boy, dipping in the brush and flicking off, against the inside of the paint bucket, the superfluous fluid.

"Will you stop that painting and talk to me?" demanded young Purvis.

"I can hear every word you say," said Joe Good. "Unless you want me to study your face, Sheriff, as you speak!"

The words were innocent enough; the sheriff could not tell why he felt that there was a not too covert insult hidden in them. "Assault on—you know well enough what I mean! Assault on, well, on that same Wally Chase!"

Somehow, the words half died in his throat as he spoke them. Assault on Wally Chase?

It was a thing to make the county laugh.

"Is Chase in jail?" asked the boy.

"Him in jail? Why should he be?"

"He pulled a gun on me. There were twenty men present who saw him draw a gun on me. Let things like that happen in your town, Sheriff?"

Young Purvis ground his teeth together audibly and dangerously.

And Joe went on with the same smoothness: "Also, he attempted my life with a knife."

He pulled a long, glimmering blade from somewhere in his clothes, and held it up to view, turning and smiling again at Purvis.

"This is the knife," he said. "You could shave with that blade, Purvis. He attacked me and tried to kill me. I barely managed to defend myself with a whip."

"His gun hand is broke," said the sheriff. "It'll never be the same. You went and ruined him for life, practically."

"He'll have to give up murder and take another line of honest work, perhaps," said Joe Good. "Like house painting, eh?"

The sheriff swore loudly and long. His rage grew, because he found less and less that he could actually put his teeth in and call it a crime.

His three charges, which he had come trotting out to lay against the boy, and frighten him into submission and a proper attitude toward life, had dissipated.

And then he heard the voice which he had begun to detest, speaking once more, and this time it was saying: "Besides, you won't allow Chase to go free, will you, after he confessed, in public, that he shot down young Alton?"

The sheriff gaped.

And Joe went on: "Besides, I'd like to know what you've done about the Alton murderers. Anything?"

Young Joe Good was himself incredulous, as he heard these words flowing from his own lips. He rose and stood upon the plank that supported the paint bucket, also.

"What about it?" he repeated, controlling the almost

hysterical joy of danger that was taking him by the throat. "Have you done a single thing about the Altons?"

"Are you butting in and trying to tell me what to do with my job?" asked Dick Purvis.

He roared, as he found a slight semblance of an excuse for fury: "I'm gunna put you in your place, you young loafer! You're the town joke. I'm gunna teach you manners, too!"

Said the boy: "The Altons pretended that they thought that their boy had been shot by my father. But everybody knows that my father couldn't hit the side of a barn. He never hit a mark in his life, even with a rifle. Everybody knew that. But the Altons wanted him out of the way."

"You fool," shouted Dick Purvis, "why would the Altons want to kill your lazy tramp of a no-good father?"

An hysterical impulse came over Joe Good, like that which a man feels when he is perched on a dizzy height. He gave way to the impulse and climbed down the ladder to the ground. There he stood close to the sheriff and looked calmly up into his eyes.

It was wonderfully easy to do, and the effect of that calm confronting was extraordinary, for the sheriff blinked and actually withdrew a half step.

Then Joe spoke: "Maybe the Altons sent you out here to bully me. But you can't bully me, Purvis. You're not even a hawk, I see. You're just a buzzard, a carrion-eater. You go back and organize your posse and arrest the Altons. They murdered my father. That's proved now. They hounded him and ran him down. And if you don't arrest them, I'll have you arrested, Mr. Sheriff, for failure to do your duty. I'll ride back into town with you now, and swear out a warrant for the whole gang of them. We know their names!"

8

The sheriff wanted to blast the young interloper, but he remembered that he was hired by the county to enforce the law, not to break it. He could think of nothing else to do, except to condemn the boy quite fiercely to his face, and tell him to do as he pleased; he, the sheriff, was riding back now.

And back he rode.

Joe Good followed on foot, and went to the office of the judge. The judge was a brother of the hardware merchant. Already he seemed to have heard of the story of the revolver, for he was not wearing a pleasant expression when Joe Good appeared before him.

"Young man," he said, "I was afraid that you'd be here before me before long. You've been raising a scandal in this town. What have you to say for yourself?"

"I've come to swear out a warrant," said Joe Good, "for the arrest of Harry Alton, for conspiracy which led to the death of my father. I've also come to swear out a warrant for the arrest of Hugh Alton, Jess Alton, Tucker Alton, Dean Alton, Chris Alton, and Sam Alton, as the actual agents who committed the crime and murdered Vincent Good. Will you issue the warrant?"

The judge stood up from his chair. He was hearing the most respectable names in the county, and certainly the richest ones, all grouped together under one scandalous charge.

"What dumfounded nonsense is this?" he asked.

"You know what it is. You speak English," said the boy.

He stepped a little closer, and his dark bright eyes glinted as he looked into the eyes of the judge. He was

43

discovering, with amazement and a sort of wicked joy, that there is a power in the eye against which few men can stand. He himself, all his life, had been quickly subdued by a level and savage eye. Now he had learned, since the light pressure of the coiled black snake around his arm filled him with more assurance than the touch of any heroic and friendly hand, that in his own glance there was the same power.

So, as he stepped closer and stared at the judge, who was staggered by the last remark, he went on: "I want the warrant. I'll raise up Satan himself if I don't get it. My father was murdered. There was no charge against him. He was murdered by a gang. You know the names of the gang. Everybody knows 'em. I want the warrant."

"You can't have it," said the judge. "In obedience to a general hue and cry, because it was thought, however erroneously, that young Harry Alton had been shot down and perhaps killed by your father, certain men at once pursued the fugitive, whose flight seemed to prove his crime, and they performed what they considered was their duty."

"It wasn't a general hue and cry. It was a hue and cry of the Altons," said the boy. "Not a soul by any other name rode with them."

"Are you going to tell me what the law is, and what the law isn't?" exclaimed the judge. "Leave this room! Some of the most respected members of the community, men of tried and proved integrity, have been insulted by an idle loafer. Leave the room!"

"Don't go wrong at the start, Judge Tomlinson," said the boy. "Are you going to quash the case against the Altons?"

"There's no case to quash," said the judge, more loudly and angrily than ever. "Jameson! Jameson!"

A burly fellow broke into the room.

"Throw this young fool into the street!" commanded the judge.

Jameson said: "I'll throw him out on his head!"

He came with hands prepared and savage eyes; not for nothing had he enforced order in courtrooms and guarded prisoners for many years.

But he was stopped by a very strange sight. Joe Good was laughing.

"You're only a fish in the pool, Jameson," said Joe Good. "Don't come a step nearer, if you want to keep a whole hide!"

And under his eye and before that laughter, Jameson stood frozen to the spot. Joe Good actually turned his back on him; but still Jameson did not stir. He was busily remembering what he had heard of the scene on the veranda of the hotel the evening before. And Wally Chase, that terrible man, had been the victim on that occasion. He was not a Wally Chase. He was only a Jameson.

Joe Good, as he faced the purple judge, went on: "If you drop out all the other Altons, what about the case against Harry Alton?"

"Case against a man who was shot down?" thundered the judge. "Are you a blithering idiot? What case is there against him?"

"He only had a surface wound on the leg," said the boy. "But he let the gunman who shot him, he let Wally Chase run out of the room and raise the hue and cry, that you speak of, against my father. Was that conspiracy with intent to kill, or what was it?"

"A boy shot down on a barroom floor—you expect him to have the presence of mind—" began the judge, and ended with another roar: "Jameson, take him out of the room!"

Joe Good did not even turn to warn Jameson away. And Jameson licked his thin lips, but dared not stir. The heart was willing, but the flesh was now too weak.

Said Joe Good: "He may have been confused at the time. But days passed before my father was buried in shame, as a man who had attempted to commit murder. If Harry Alton was not a conspirator and conniving at the crime of murder, he would have spoken at once to clear the name of my father. He let the days go by. No one would have known, from Harry Alton, that my father was innocent."

"And who knows now?" asked the judge, his rage swelling, as he saw that a clear legal case was being built up. "As for a poor boy who was shot down—"

"Shot down for doing crooked business with a murderer. What was that business? No one knows. Why should Harry Alton have money dealings with a hired murderer?"

"You can't touch Harry Alton," said the judge, "unless there is actual testimony, and be careful how you call citizens of this county hired murderers!"

"No," said the boy, "I see that I can only call you a hired fool! That's all!"

He turned on his heel and left the room, while the judge, on the verge of apoplexy, sank speechless down into a chair.

In the street, young Joe Good stood for a moment, letting the fierce, honest heat of the sun burn against his face.

His soul was wonderfully calm and composed. Just across from him was the veranda of the hotel, with a dozen loiterers on it. Some of them were pointing him out to one another, and some were standing up, as though to see him better. A grim, cold pleasure went through the heart of the boy, like a poisonous wine. It was long, long years since people had stood up to see a Good, father or son.

Another figure, to his left, attracted him. It was the notorious miser of the county, old Zeke Stevens, a man hated by thousands for his pinching ways, his great wealth, his high rates of interest, his narrow soul, his cruel foreclosures. He had ruined many a promising life by his savage greed. He would always make a loan, when banks refused, and from his victims he never failed to wring more than a sufficient return. People said that he loaned money not so much to increase his hoards, as to give pain to others.

Wifeless, childless, friendless, he was a millionaire. Some said that he was a multimillionaire. Yet, as he stood there on the sidewalk under the open window that gave air to the chambers of Judge Tomlinson, he was dressed like a beggar. His coat had been black, but now it was chiefly green. It was pinned with a safety pin across his hollow breast, and over the hump of his crooked back it was guarded by a huge patch. The cuffs of his trousers were a soiled and tattered fringe. His hat was a dismal rag of ancient felt.

He had two pleasures in life, money and whisky. Though he indulged himself in the first, the second, if it had reddened his lean, grinning face, never had obscured his wits, at least, never during his business hours, which, it was said, consumed twenty-four hours out of twenty-four.

Now he remained standing beneath the window of the judge, with his head canted a bit to one side, and his habitual wolfish grin widened to a smile of actual pleasure. He was as one who has just heard heavenly music and still stands harkening for more.

Most amazing of all, he now turned his undiminished smile upon No Good, and then began to beckon to him with a forefinger.

Joe approached him with wonder.

"There's Mort Pemberton's saloon across the way. Come and have a drink!" said Zeke Stevens.

The very breath was knocked from the body of Joe Good. For it was famous through the county that the old man never bought a drink, except for himself.

Joe made the point clear.

"You mean that you want to buy me a drink?" said he.

The miser twisted his face.

"I gotta buy you a drink," he said, and shook his head, rather bitterly. "I'll buy you one whisky! Come along."

The marvel of the thing carried Joe Good along with it, and he went in a daze across the street and held open the swinging door while Zeke Stevens, with the half-dragging and half-running gait which was forced on him by his very bowed posture, went before him into the saloon.

No one was there at that mid-morning hour. There was only Pemberton himself, who waved to them in surprise.

"Bring in a couple of whiskies," said the miser and led the way into the back room.

There he took a chair. The whiskies arrived, and old Zeke began to turn his glass with loving fingers, after he had paid. But he did not look at the liquor. He continued to eye the boy with that vast incomprehensible smile.

"Joe," he said, "I like you. I pretty near love you. I'm gunna drink your health. Here's to you!"

"Here's how," said the boy, more utterly amazed than before.

He raised his drink and downed the stinging, fuming stuff. A crash startled him. Old Zeke had dashed his glass upon the floor.

Now he said, while the ears of the boy tingled with incredulity: "When I drink the health of a man like you, I always smash the glass, like I would in honor of a king!"

The startled saloon keeper appeared at the door.

"Charge me with a broken glass," said the miser. "And bring me in another—and a fresh bottle. The whole bottle, d'ye hear?"

9

Many marvels had been seen in the short and stirring history of Fort Willow, from early Mexican and Indian wars, through a gold rush, and the wild days of the cattle drives. There was still excitement enough in its dusty streets, from time to time, but nothing had ever occurred to rank, as a marvel, with the spectacle of Zeke Stevens ordering an entire bottle of whisky and paying for it.

Mort Pemberton was actually pale with excitement; his eyes were large as he carried in the bottle. He looked earnestly at the money he received in exchange, as though doubting its real value. Then he withdrew, backward, so that he could be sure of seeing everything as long as possible.

"Close the door!" said Zeke.

Mort Pemberton slammed it with a muttered oath. He would have given his very teeth to hear the conversation to which this miracle was the prelude.

Zeke Stevens filled the glasses. The boy left his untouched, but the old man, staring down into his own glass, turned it about, again and again, with zealous fingers, admiring the film of oil that collected along the sides of the glass.

Strange words came from his lips.

"Skunks and starved coyotes and mangy dogs and molting hens that smell of the sage," said he. "That's what they are. Tomlinson, he's one. The Altons, they're some

49

more. But they've got a front to 'em. A fine front. They dress fine and they talk big, and they been to school, all of 'em. But they ain't real. They ain't real men. They ain't the kind that I seen out here. They ain't got the men, and they ain't got the women.

"I seen men out here that burned themselves up like candles. No, they didn't last long. But they made a light, is what they made. They made a light that even me could see by. They used to make me wanta be different. They came and they went. They went fast. Rich miner today, dead drunk tomorrow. Cattle king this year, cleaning spittoons the next; cattle king again, the next; dead in a gun fight, the next. Them was men. They burned themselves up, and they made a light that even I could see by.

"And today, when I stood there under the window of the judge, and heard you lay out the Altons, I begun to see by the old light ag'in. It made me wish to be different. It made me wanta shine. And when you laid out old Tomlinson himself, the fat faker, I says to myself: 'Zeke, you can't never shine yourself, but maybe you could help somebody else to shine.' When I say that, I mean you."

He lifted his head. He looked into the eyes of the boy, and Joe Good saw terrible, hungry inquiry, doubt, criticism, and, finally, relief and belief. For he answered that stare with another, equally profound, into the dark soul of the moneylender. He could not have done it the day before. But now this was a sort of gunfire to which he was accustomed.

The old man grinned again and nodded.

"They used to have eyes like that," he said. "They looked straight through and through you. They had a ring about 'em. These others, they move like men, and they talk like men, and they look like men. But they ain't. Only bell metal makes the bell and today, over there under the window of the judge, I heard the old ring!"

He nodded his head.

Then he went on.

"Your father was a gent with substance to him. He knew something. But he didn't have no action in him. He just had sitting. But your mother was different. You never knew your mother, Joe, did you?"

Joe Good lifted his head.

He said nothing, but the miser merely smiled.

"You don't need to get mean," he said. "What I got to say about her would sound good even in a saloon. She was small and she was clean. You take thoroughbreds and raise 'em in a cactus country, and they grow small. Maybe only fourteen-three. But they're all iron, all fire, and no smoke. No wastage. They run a hundred mile a day for a month. Their legs is steel, and their hearts, they fill out their ribs. She was like that. She was small, and she wasn't the most beautiful in the world, but she would've made any fool the king of the world, if she'd had the time. She made your father a big man in two years. And when she died, he sort of faded out. And you, you got her in you. I never seen it in you till this morning. But you're her son."

He finished his second glass.

"I gotta mind to get drunk," he said. "I'm happy, is what I am!"

Then he shook his head.

"Talk is all right, but we gotta be practical. Answer me some questions."

"All right," said the boy. "I'll try to."

"Are you good with a gun?"

"No."

"Ah, that's too bad. The old-timers, they was artists with guns. Pretty pictures they could paint for you with six-guns. Pictures all in red, all in red."

He laughed gaspingly. "Now, son," he said, "if you ain't good with a gun, what about a knife?"

"No."

"Not a knife, either? But a real workman, he don't mind about tools. What's your tool?"

"A black snake," said the boy.

Blankly at first, then with a grimly dawning light of joy, the moneylender stared at him.

"A whip!" he said. "That's the best of all. That's what they need, more'n horses or dogs!"

He repeated several times, relishing the taste of the word: "A whip! A whip!"

And he broke off to laugh in his horrible, strangled fashion, once more.

"More questions!" he snapped.

"Go on," said the boy, still feeling that he was fumbling through a miraculous labyrinth.

"Got any friends?"

Without needing time for thought, Joe Good answered: "Not one."

"Any girl on the brain?"

"No."

"Any profession or work you wanta do?"

"Nothing."

"It's perfect," said Zeke Stevens. "And now, who d'you hate?"

"Nobody," said the boy.

Blank dismay fell upon the old man.

"Nobody?" he echoed.

"Of course, the Altons murdered my father," said Joe Good. "I think they ought to be removed. But I don't hate 'em."

"You're right," said Zeke suddenly. "A good surgeon, he don't hate a cancer, but he cuts it out! What about Judge Tomlinson?"

"He thinks there is nothing in the county except the Altons. He ought to be removed, I feel."

"Good. And Dick Purvis?"

"The Altons made him sheriff. He can't think against them. He ought to be removed."

"And you're going to do it?"

The boy did not hesitate.

"I'll remove them," he said calmly.

Zeke ran the red tip of his tongue over his lips. His eyes were the eyes of a fox.

"Then you gotta do it in style," said he.

"I don't follow that," said the boy.

"Don't you? Well, then think again. A killing by a ragged tramp, that's murder. A killing by a fine man in fine clothes, with servants in the house—that's a gentleman's honor vindicated. Look in the newspapers, and you'll find all kind of words to call it!"

The boy nodded.

"I think I know what you mean," said he.

"If you're gunna be thorough, you'll get the whole lot."

"Just a minute," said Joe Good. "I'm not interested in killing. That's short and easy. Besides, it gets the killer hanged, sooner or later. I don't intend to be hanged."

"Eh?"

"I take no chances," said the boy.

"By the jumping thunder of the powers above," said the old man, "how you gunna down 'em, then?"

"Well, there are worse things than dying," said the boy.

"Such as what?"

"The Altons are the top of the heap, now. Suppose that they're put at the bottom. That would be a lot worse! They'd feel that more than dying, one by one."

Said the miser: "The Altons have everything. They have mines, ranches, newspapers, town real estate. They have everything. What have you got to down 'em with?"

"Brains," said Joe Good, with a twisted smile.

The other drew in a long breath and said: "You have 'em too! I see that you have 'em, and I believe what I see. You got brains! But brains, or not, they'll throw a man in rags like yours into jail. Believe me?"

Joe Good hesitated for a long time.

"I think they would," he said at last, slowly. "The whole town knows that the Altons did crooked work about my father. But the whole town does nothing. Why? Because I'm a beggar, my house is a shack, and I'm a tramp."

Old Zeke Stevens drew out a wallet and held it firmly grasped in both his hands. He stared at it. His lips twitched and trembled.

"Here's a gentleman," he said. "I've got it in my hands. A whole gentleman, from the light in his proud eyes to the shine on his boots. Look! I'm—gunna—give you—this!"

He passed the wallet across the table.

"How much is in it?" said the boy.

The moneylender writhed.

"Don't ask me how much there's in it," he said. "I'd pretty near as soon throw away a leg as throw that money away. But it ain't throwed away. It'll dress you. Nothing but the finest. It'll give you hosses, nothing but the best. It'll put a coupla servants in your house to take care of you. And it'll make a mystery out of you, because nobody will know where you got it.

"And when this here is spent, I've got more for you. More, and more, to pull 'em down, the Altons and the rest. More money to burn under their chins and toast their beards. Every now and then, I'll sneak in, and sit in your fine sitting room, and soil your grand rug with my dirty boots, and listen to what you've done, and what you're going to do, to pull 'em still further down!"

10

Joe Good did not do his shopping in Fort Willow. Instead, he took the stage to the railroad line, and boarded a train that put him down, not many hours later, in a town with paved streets and street lamps that burned all night, in certain sections. And there he outfitted himself, first with a big trunk, and then with clothes and boots and hats and all else that he needed in order to outfit himself according to his mental picture of a gentleman's exterior. That picture was based on bits of his father's conversation, some remnants of former splendor that lingered about the house, but chiefly on the boy's own observation of the world. So he dressed himself very quietly, but very well indeed.

He still needed a horse and a servant. And there was plenty of money left.

So he went down to the town jail and saw the head jailer. This was a man with a face of stone and very few words.

"There are a lot of prisoners filling your yard, Mr. Leigh," said the boy. "You've got some more in the cells. And I need the brightest man that's held in your strongest cell. Some one whose term is about up. If you turn him over to me, I'll keep him straight the rest of his days."

"Will you?" said Mr. Leigh, with no expression on his face of stone.

"I make new men of them," said young Joe Good. "I teach 'em to respect higher principles."

A faint smile came upon the face of Leigh, and he said: "This afternoon we're going to turn loose one named Budge Morrissey. We picked him up on a vagrancy charge. We know that he's a safecracker, yegg, second-story artist, smuggler, gunman, pickpocket, and other things, but we haven't managed to get evidence together during the three months. So we have to turn him loose. Perhaps, you'd like to see him?"

"I'd love to see him," said the boy.

Mr. Leigh pressed a bell, gave instructions. Presently four guards entered, pushing before them a black man who filled the doorway. He was three or four inches over six feet, and from his massive shoulders, lines of strength and speed swept down to long-fingered hands and slender feet. His jaw was hinged high up on his head; his forehead was a vast, shining slope. He wore a huge, golden smile, and set in the lobe of one ear was a diamond of good size that flashed like a speck of fire as he turned his head.

"Take the irons off his hands," said Mr. Leigh.

It was done, and the guards were ordered from the room. They went willingly, but in surprise. Then said Leigh: "Budge, this is midmorning, and I didn't intend to turn you loose until this evening. But here comes a gentleman named Mr. Joseph Good. I don't know him, but he says that he turns bad men into good ones. He intends to take you home with him. I won't prevent him. And I won't prevent you from stepping through that window onto the street—if you can get through this Mr. Joseph Good. I'll leave you alone to talk things over, if you want to take your chances with him, Budge."

"Mr. Leigh," said the black man, bowing a little, "that would be fine."

The jailer left the room, and again the faint smile stirred the corners of his mouth. He was not a kind man, this Mr. Leigh. He was in this business because he liked it and, as the door closed after him, Budge Morrissey said: "I suppose that you have a gun, Mr. White Man, and you think that you can stick up Budge Morrissey. But a lot more than air moves through this jail. White Man, shove up your fool hands."

And suddenly his right hand was inside his coat and coming forth again with a sheen of blue-steel revolver in it.

Joe Good did not stir. He had given his right arm a stealthy shake the moment before, and now from his hand leaped out a shadowy streak and the lash of the black snake curled around Morrissey's wrist. The burning, binding cut of it, as it was jerked backward, opened the fingers of the black man as if with a magic touch, and the revolver thudded on the matting of the floor.

"That's smart," said Morrissey. "But it's not smart enough, brother."

And he came at Joe Good with a knife in his hand. For all his bulk, he came with catlike speed, his left arm raised to protect his face and head. But that guard was not enough. The more heavily loaded butt end of the whip shot up and over, and whacked on the base of Budge Morrissey's skull.

His rush was not ended, but it merely carried him blindly past the white man, and left him standing, tottering, in front of the window that looked upon the street.

Joe Good followed, picked the knife from the nerveless fingers of the black, laid it, together with the fallen revolver, upon the desk of the jailer, and then turned to Budge Morrissey and steered him back into a chair.

He sat down in a slump; it was a whole minute before intelligence began to gleam like two diamonds in his eyes again.

Then Joe Good pointed to the weapons that lay on the polished mahogany.

"We can start all over again, whenever you say," he suggested.

Budge Morrissey laid a hand on the back of his skull. The smile widened and flared like a golden flame on his face.

"Mr. Joseph," said he, "I never bet on the last horse when the winner is under the wire. Who dropped out of the ceiling and hit me on the head with a hammer, Mr. Joseph?"

Joe Good smiled in turn, his twisted, humorous, appealing smile. Somehow there was much sympathy in it.

He said: "Budge, you've been a bad man. You've earned your living with guns and knives and nitroglycerin."

"Yes, sir," said Budge Morrissey.

"You've never worked for anyone in your life."

"No, sir," said Budge.

"But today you commence," said Joe Good.

"Yes, sir," said Budge Morrissey.

"As long as you're a good man," said Joe Good, "I'll pay you well, give you easy work, and treat you like a human being. If you're bad, or if you lie or steal, I won't discharge you, but I'll flog the skin off your black body."

The smile of Budge Morrissey went out. His eyes opened.

"Yes, sir," said he.

"Can you cook?"

"My wife can cook, Mr. Joseph."

"Where is she?"

"In this town, sir."

"Go get her and bring her to the railroad station by three-thirty."

A gleam of joy and relief spread over Morrissey's face. "Yes, sir," he gasped, and rose hastily to his feet.

"Don't forget this knife and gun," said Joe Good.

"No, sir," murmured Morrissey.

And his brow puckered with a faint doubt and hesitation of a new sort, as he gathered up his weapons which had been so mysteriously taken from him.

He went on more slowly to the door.

Said Joe Good: "Wait a moment. You can't come to work for me in dirty, greasy, torn clothes like those. Here's a hundred dollars. Get something of a sober color, but decent. See that your wife has a neat dress, too. Now don't forget. At three-thirty."

Budge Morrissey had opened the door. Now he stood transformed into a statue, with the sheaf of unexpected money grasped in his mighty hand.

His eyes looked out at Joe Good as a child looks upon a seer, a magician, whose magic is real.

"Yes, Mr. Joseph," said Budge Morrissey huskily. "I'll be ready with my wife at three-thirty, sir!"

He made a step back. He bowed to Joe Good. And then he went down the hall with the money still clasped in his hand, and the look of a sleepwalker in his face.

Mr. Leigh saw him go and came back into his office, stealthily, looking fixedly at his visitor.

Joe Good went to the door and nodded farewell.

"You had exactly what I wanted," said he.

"Mr. Bell-the-Cat," said the jailer, "you'll always find everything that you want in this world, I have an idea. What diabolical business you want to use that black for I don't know. But I see that you begin with hypnosis!"

Joe Good merely smiled and went forth.

When he walked onto the platform of the station that

afternoon, he saw a great black man in a dark-gray suit rise up like a tower, and a slender little mulatto woman rose beside him. With stalking strides, Budge Morrissey conducted his wife forward.

"Mr. Joseph, sir," said he, "this is my wife, Betsy, and if she don't cook better for you than anybody ever cooked before, I'll beat her, sir, from yellow to black."

Betsy looked at her man with affection and pride; she looked on Joe Good with staring awe; then she smiled with content.

Said Joe Good: "Budge and Betsy, I've been looking for both of you for a good many years. Now I've found you and there's only one thing that you need to remember: in my house no voice or hand is ever raised except my own.

"Budge, here is five hundred dollars more. Buy yourselves tickets to the station of Willow; then go on the stage to Fort Willow. Find the house of Joseph Good—it's my house; now it's your house, too. It's a small cottage. Finish painting it white. Buy food and such dishes as we'll need. Then get a map of the county and chart down in your own mind every house, every road, and every hill, creek, and mountain. I'll be there in three days."

He extended the money; a slight quiver passed through the body of the big man as he reached for it, but the thin yellow fingers of Betsy arrived first.

"I'll keep the money, Mr. Joseph," said she. "Because I've got a bigger purse."

Joe Good, without further words, waved to them, smiled on them, and was gone.

11

He had sent them three days ahead for a special purpose; the town of Fort Willow had to be prepared for a strange alteration in his way of life. Also, the town of Fort Willow must begin to waken, and rub its eyes, and hum with gossip as it never had hummed before.

Then, on the third day, when the westering sun had lost its strength, Joe Good came out of the mountains, and jogged down the main street of the town. No one recognized him at first. It was not alone the clothes he wore, but it was the horse he rode, a slim-bodied chestnut mare with four black stockings and a sooty muzzle. She was not more than fifteen hands high, but at a glance it was plain that she was one of those animals that Zeke Stevens had described so eloquently—a desert-raised thoroughbred, made of hammered iron and muscled with lightning flashes.

The town of Fort Willow opened its mouth and gaped in silence.

A pair of lordly grays came prancing up the street from the opposite direction, bearing in their saddles magnificent Hugh Alton, and in a sidesaddle on the second horse a red-haired girl with pleasant eyes and a good-natured smile. As they drew nearer, the great Alton spoke to her, pointed with the handle of his quirt. And her face was sober as she went by Joe Good.

He raised his hat and bowed; there was no response from either of them.

Then, as he came to the verge of the town, with the wide fields extending under his eyes, a rattle of wheels rolled up behind him, and old Zeke Stevens reined in his sweating, broken-down nag.

The eyes of Zeke burned redder than his face.

"You been spending like water—my good money like water," said he. And he writhed in his place. "But you're turnin' the trick," he continued. "Them Negroes—them Negroes—they got the whole town started to callin' you Mr. Joseph. I wanta see you and talk. But nobody must spot me with you. So long. Work slow, and work sure. Blow up the foundations, and the house will tumble down!"

And he put the whip on the back of the horse, and went off in a dust cloud, the nag raising a humping, broken-kneed canter.

Young Joe Good reached his father's house and called. Suddenly, in answer, an immense form in an immense white jacket appeared outside the front door and ran down the path to the gate.

Budge Morrissey held the bridle and the stirrup of his master.

"Good evening, Mr. Joseph," said he. "Good evening, sir. I'll put up your horse and be right in. Betsy will have your bath ready in one minute, sir. It makes a pleasant day for us to have you home, sir!"

He took the mare toward the barn; and young Joe Good went slowly to the house and walked still more slowly about it. It was completely coated over with the white paint, now, and looked in this light like glistening marble. The grounds were in good condition. The very fences had been repaired. The leaves were raked beneath the trees. The front yard was dug up and leveled off, and over the soft soil several sprinklers were whirring, cooling the air with their spray and soothing the mind with their murmur. Gaily, rapidly, the well-oiled gears of the windmill clicked and purred, and to the boy these sounds seemed as a promise that life had returned to the place, and that a new heart was pulsing strongly here.

He went in the front door, and Betsy, in spotless white, came to meet him. She took his hat and, while he listened to the deep-voiced pounding of the water as it ran into the tin bathtub, she conducted him to his room.

He paused a moment, amazed, for all was altered in it. It had been a dingy place of shadows. Now it was painted white and cream, a bright rug shone on the floor; there was a deep easy-chair, covered with chintz; outside the sill, appeared a window box filled with blooming plants. Their fragrance spread gently through the room. Now Betsy was lighting a shaded lamp. Now she was asking what clothes she should lay out for him—his trunk had preceded him. Now she was withdrawing with a faint whisper of skirts, and the door closed without a click.

Joe Good closed his eyes and felt fear as one in a dream. He opened them and the clean, shining truth poured in upon his mind. He had started up a ladder, and he swore that he would never turn down again.

He dined that night as he never had dined before, with Budge Morrissey standing behind his chair, and the great hands offering new dishes, noiselessly removing the finished courses.

Afterward, he sat on the front veranda and smoked and sipped such coffee as would have gladdened the heart of an Arab chief.

"Budge," he said, not loudly.

He felt, rather than heard, the step of the giant on the floor beside him.

"Budge," he said, "there's a house not far away belonging to Mr. Hugh Alton."

"Yes, sir," said Budge. "I know where it is. I heard in the town about the Altons and their murder, sir."

"I think they have a house guest, a girl. Go over there tonight, and don't come back until you know the girl's name. Also, find out where young Harry Alton sleeps, and whether he's alone, or his brother with him."

Budge left. In an hour he was back, the dark of the night dissolving and letting his shadowy form appear only when it was almost beside his employer.

"Where did you learn to stalk like that, Budge?" asked Joseph Good.

"In South Africa, sir," said the other. "The lady is Miss Katherine Garnet. Mr. Harry Alton sleeps in the bedroom in the second story in the southeast corner of the house. He sleeps alone. His wound is much better. He can walk a little, now. The servants believe that Miss Kate Garnet is to become engaged to Mr. Harry Alton. Mr. Hugh Alton has sent for the sheriff and received him in his house. They were still talking together when I arrived. I learned from them that it is felt you must have committed a crime to appear suddenly with so much money; the sheriff will look into the business."

"How did you overhear what they were saying?"

"The room they were in had a window," said Budge, "and the veranda roof under the window made a comfortable place for me to sit. I happened to be sitting there enjoying the cool of the evening after my hot climb to the roof. And while I was sitting there, I happened to hear what they were saying."

The boy smiled.

Then he said: "I'm not surprised that you've done all this so quickly, Budge. I imagine that you'll do much cleverer things still, before we're through with one another."

It was a moment before Budge answered:

"I've been around a good many parts of the world, Mr. Joseph. But nobody ever gave me money, trust, and a licking all at one time. It's a black day for Budge Morrissey when he's fool enough to leave his first boss, Mr. Joseph. If I left you, Betsy would leave me."

"Thank you, Budge," said Joe Good. "That's all for tonight."

He sat on through the cool of the evening and watched new stars gradually pricking through the mist of the eastern horizon, then rising clearly into the upper sky.

It seemed to Joe Good that he was a new being, that he was rising into strange, lofty, and dangerous regions, far above his old wont. But joy was in him like wine.

He numbered his enemies, such as all the Altons, seven men, strong, rich, and clever; and the sheriff himself, and the judge, to say nothing of that poisonous criminal, the famous Wally Chase. His gun hand was broken, but his evil brain remained to contrive mischief, even if his hands could not execute it.

Against this opposition, already he could present allies of his own, a strange group of them.

There was the miser, Zeke Stevens, who had both brains and hard cash.

There was huge Morrissey, strong, fearless, and silent as a panther in the night.

Finally, there was Betsy, with thought ever smoldering in her eyes.

With three such partners, his back was guarded; and he began to feel that he could take care of all the dangers that rushed at him, face to face. So he began to brood upon his first great problem.

And the Professor lay at his feet and brooded upon the face of his master, silent also.

12

That night Joe Good slept as never before. The next day he sat, as his father had often done before him, reading and taking notes under the shade of the great fig tree. But the book he read was little more than meaningless print to him, and the notes which he jotted down were his own thoughts, as they drifted into his mind.

At noon, and again in the evening, he burned those notes. So, after supper, he sat once more on the front veranda, but this time with a table beside him and a shaded lamp burning upon it.

There was more reading, more note taking but, strive as he would, he could only reach this conclusion: That with the material he had in hand, there was no possibility of drawing proper deductions. Plainly, Hugh Alton and the rest of that tribe wished to see both Vincent Good and Joseph Good dead, or run out of the county. They could not have such a savage determination because of personal malice. For decades the Good family had been far too poor and too weak to effect anything against a tribe as powerful and as increasing in power as the Altons. No, there was some other motive than personal hatred.

What other motive could there be?

It appeared that there was none other possible than the motive which so often had entered in the lives of all the Altons—their individual and tribal love of gain.

Suppose that one reduced the matter to this conclusion: the Altons desired to push the Good family out of the way, either by killing them, or by threatening them in such a manner that they were frightened away from the town.

But what could the Altons gain by this? A chance to pick up the land cheaply at a public auction, when, for a few dollars of merchandise owing, some tradesman forced a sale of the place.

That was clear enough. But what was the land worth?

Hardly a penny, unless there was gold on it. And Vincent Good had once prospected the place for minerals from head to heel.

No, there was nothing hidden under the soil, and yet it seemed that in some mysterious manner, the acres had a great value in the eyes of Hugh Alton.

More notes were scribbled on pieces of paper and gave indication of his thoughts, but he found that he was surrounded by a wall too high to be surmounted.

The Professor touched his knee with a paw. He looked down and saw that the little mongrel was sharp-eyed with some excitement. It was panting a little and wagging an eager tail. Now it backed away from the master, and scooted into the darkness toward one of the big oaks, where there was a dense tangle of shrubbery. Halfway to the place, it halted and looked back over its shoulder, as though asking to be followed.

When it saw the master immobile, he turned and scampered back to him, and again touched his knee with an eager paw.

"Budge!" called Joe Good.

The great black glided out onto the porch, and in a lowered voice, Joe Good said: "There's something over there in the shrubbery under the oak tree. Go out from the back door, and don't make a sound. Circle around behind that shrubbery and see what you'll find. You'd better have a gun with you; but don't shoot unless you have to."

"Yes, Mr. Joseph," said Budge, and the great golden smile spread upon his face again.

Though he could be a perfect valet, in a pinch, it was plain that other lines of work were more to his liking. He disappeared into the house, and Joe Good continued to read there by the lamp on the front porch. He quieted the Professor with one word, but that silently sagacious little beast sat down close to his master and continued to stare toward the oak tree. Certainly he was not fool enough to be so excited about a stray wild cat, a skunk, or a coyote?

A quarter of an hour went by in this manner, until Joseph Good began to feel prickles of cold forming along his spine; then followed a sudden outbreak of voices and a crashing among the brush.

Out came the vast head and shoulders of the giant, carrying before him, by the elbows, a slenderer, writhing body.

"I'll break your back over my knee, mister," said Budge, "if you kick me in the shins again!"

The captive suddenly ceased struggling, and on the veranda, before his master, Budge Morrissey put down the slender, evil form of Wally Chase. His right hand was covered by a bandage that was wrapped stiffly around what seemed to be splints. A drop or two of blood trickled from his left.

"Did you hurt him, Budge?" asked Joseph Good.

"He tried to knife me," said Morrissey. "And cut his own hand when I took the knife away."

"I would've ripped the insides out of you," said Wally Chase savagely, "if I'd had two hands to use."

"You wouldn't've ripped the insides out of me, white man," said Budge, unmoved. "I had you covered five minutes before I jumped you. He was laying out there on the edge of the bushes," said Morrissey to his employer. "And he was watching you on the porch."

"I could have shot you through the head," said the gunman.

"Here's his guns," said Budge.

And he laid in the lap of his employer, two Colts. "Careful of them—careful of them!" exclaimed Chase apprehensively. "They're on hair triggers, both of 'em! I could've shot you dead, Good, and you know it! I couldn't miss at that distance."

"You could, though," answered the other, "and you knew it. You're no good with your left hand. I saw that the other day, when you tried to use a knife in it."

Said Wally Chase, actually more consumed with curiosity than with fear: "What made the black come out there to hunt like a cat in the dark?"

"The dog told me that you were there, Wally," said Joseph Good, a little inexactly. "So I sent Budge around to cut off your retreat."

"The dog?" snarled the other. "I got a start when he come nosing around, but after he went back onto the veranda, I didn't think that there'd be any trouble. You're lyin' to me, Good. The dog couldn't've give you a warning."

"He did. You must have seen me call out Budge. And I sent him around to pick you up, which he did."

He smiled on Wally Chase, and the man scowled savagely back.

"Now what?" asked Wally grimly. "I come here and take a look, that's all. There ain't any harm in that!"

"You lie out in the bushes and have a pair of guns with you; and you try to knife the man who routs you out. The blood on your hand now, Wally, will send you to prison. Judges and juries won't be too friendly to you, Chase. It'll be a long term."

The gunman held down his head, as he glared at the other from under his hanging brows.

"You gunna slam me in the jail?" he asked. "All right. Take and slam me there. I gotta stand it."

"You'd like it, in fact," said Joe Good. "You think you have friends who would take you out again. But that isn't my motive. Budge, tie his wrists together and his ankles, too."

It was done. The omniscient Morrissey instantly took from his pocket some lengths of stout, waxed twine and, with this, he had secured the wrists of the gunman behind his back, before Chase muttered: "What's the idea of all this, Good? The black's murdering my wrist that you burned open the other night."

"I'm going to hang you up by the hands to that oak tree you were hiding under," said Joseph Good, "and then I'm going to flog some information out of you. Shall we gag him, Budge?"

"If you gag him, Mr. Joseph," said Budge, with his most amiable smile, "you won't have to make me flog him so hard. When they feel themselves choking, they quit right away. There are plenty of men who'll stand flogging till they faint, but they won't stand throttling, in my experience."

He took out a large white handkerchief and began to wad it significantly together. "Wait just a minute," said Wally Chase. "Good, you're a low hound. Whatcha want?"

"In the first place, I want to know who sent you tonight?"

"I sent myself."

"Gag him, Budge," said the boy. "He's asking for a flogging, and he'll have to get what he asks for."

The hand of Budge Morrissey was raised.

"Hold on," said Wally Chase. "What if Hugh Alton sent me? Well, what of that? You been talking around town about him so big and high that he's gotta right to look after you. Don't make no phony play, will you, Joe?"

"He sent you to do what?" asked the boy.

"He sent me to barge in and listen in on things over here," said Wally Chase. "That's all I came for. I couldn't figure that the dog and the black—mostly, I couldn't figure on your blasted luck, but one of these days that luck's gunna change. We're gunna get you, and we're gunna get you good."

"That's all right," said Joseph Good cheerfully. "Now, about the arrangement that you were making with young Harry Alton, that other day in the saloon, the money that he was to pay you, I mean. What was the money to be paid for?"

"That? That money?" said Wally Chase. "It was just some coin that he'd lost to me at poker. I staked him and he lost it. It was seven hundred and fifty. He said that he was busted, and that he didn't dare to ask his old man for any more than five hundred. He said that he'd pay the other two hundred and fifty later on, and I—"

"Gag him, Morrissey," said Good. "He's really got to have it—"

"Wait! You!" said Wally Chase with a snarl. "I wish that I'd shot the rotten heart right out of your body the other night. Whatcha want me to say about my deal with the kid?"

"Just tell me the truth. I know so much that I'll be able to spot the lie. Listen to me, Wally, you need a flogging, and I'd be glad to flog you, you dog. If you lie again, you won't have another chance to speak till your back is dripping blood."

The face of the gunman worked.

Then he said, with bitter slowness, the words blending with curses: "It was like this. I was broke. Alton knew it. Harry come to me and says that he's got a stake for me."

"How much?"

"Five hundred bucks."

"For what?"

"For running your old man out of the county."

"To run my father out?"

"Yeah. The idea was that, once your old man was out of the way, you'd drift pretty soon and drift pretty far."

"Why did they want to run us out?"

"I dunno. I got the job, not the idea. I didn't care about the idea."

"Was Hugh Alton behind his boy? I suppose he was."

"I dunno anything about that, either. Harry come and told me that he wanted me to give you and your old man the bum's rush. That's all I know; that's enough for me to know."

"And you do the job for five hundred?"

"I said that I'd do the job for five hundred down and two hundred and fifty after you're both on the way. He promised me the five hundred one day, and the next day he takes back his promise. He says that the job's too easy and that, if I don't want the five hundred after the work's finished, he'll get somebody else to do it. Well, I got sore, because I was counting on that coin. I needed it. I tried to make him show down. He wouldn't, so I dropped him. I kind of wish that I'd tore his insides out with that shot, instead of playing him for an easy get-away. I'd still have my gun hand left to me, if I'd done that."

"How do you happen to be playing with the Altons now?"

"How else and where else am I to play, if I want to eat three squares? I got the drop on them if I wanta tell how Harry offered to bribe me. So they have to play me along. I get living expenses, and that's about all I do get, out of the cheap gang!"

"Set his hands free," said young Joseph Good. "And the next time you see him on my ground, day or night, shoot him down. Wally, walk down the path to the gate, and good-by!"

13

Joe turned to Morrissey. "Stay here with me a moment, Budge," he said, after Wally Chase had gone to the gate, had swung about to curse the house and its inhabitants, and then gone on. "Stay here, while we talk things over a little. There may be some hard work ahead for both of us before the evening's over."

A smile spread upon the face of Budge Morrissey.

"I hope I know the ground we're going to work in, Mr. Joseph," said he.

"What ground do you think?" asked his employer.

"Alton ground, sir," said the big man.

"Call Betsy," said Joe Good.

Budge disappeared, and came back a moment later with the little woman walking before him. She stood straight, small, and intent of eye, before her employer.

"Betsy," said he, "I have some work on hand this evening. I'm going to enter the Alton house, which is burglary. And the house is filled with armed men, which may mean a gun play or so. I want to take Budge along with me, but not without your permission."

Joe Good looked at the big man and saw the brow of Budge was contracted with painful doubt.

But Betsy answered calmly: "There's all sorts of bad ways to good ends, Mr. Joseph. He's been a burglar and a gunman before, for his own worthless hide. Why shouldn't he be one once more for your sake, sir?"

"You want two guns, a jimmy, and silent shoes," said the master to Budge Morrissey.

"I've got the guns, the shoes, and a little kit with more than a jimmy in it," said Morrissey.

"I'll be ready in five minutes, Budge," said Joe Good.

"I'll be waiting for you, sir."

In five minutes, in fact, they were walking across country, and not a word did the white man speak until he came in view of the house of Alton, sitting back on the brow of a hill and thrusting its big roof high above the tops of the surrounding trees.

Then Budge Morrissey heard Joe Good say: "I'm not quite sure. They may be eagles, but I think that they're only hawks. I think that we'll outfly them, and outfight them, and take away the fish."

Of this strange speech, Budge Morrissey understood not a word.

But he answered: "We'll take what you want, Mr. Joseph!" And he followed on, until they were closer to the house. Then, holding up his hand by way of apology and to ask leave, he silently glided in front of Joseph Good and began to make the way.

Joe could instantly see why Budge had taken precedence. He himself had gone ahead with a good deal of caution, but with something of what he would have called unavoidable noise. But when Budge stepped, there appeared to be eyes in his feet that found out every fallen twig, every dead leaf, every loose stone. Joseph Good had simply to put down his own feet where he had seen Budge step. So, noiseless as cloud shadows, they drew under the trees and close up to the house of the Altons.

They came in time to see an odd spectacle.

In the first place, a hanging lamp from the ceiling of the front veranda lighted it up and showed three women and no fewer than seven men.

Crouched behind some shrubbery, Joseph Good named them to Budge.

"Beginning on the right," he said, "write every name down in your memory, and file away every face. For that's the cream of the entire Alton crowd. There's Sam and Bud Alton at the right side, talking together. That big man with the mustache is Hugh Alton, the chief of the gang. Next to him is his brother, Tucker Alton, the father of Chris and Sam, and Dean Alton, who's sitting by the big, broad-shouldered girl. That's Alice Alton, the daughter of Hugh.

"Jess Alton is sitting beside his mother, the gray-headed woman with the necklace, and that fellow with one leg propped up in a chair and a pair of crutches beside him is Harry Alton. The girl beside him, you know. She's Kate Garnet, and you found out about her. She doesn't belong in that sort of a den! Have you got them all in mind? You know what Harry is, and the other six men are the fellows who murdered Vincent Good."

"It was a bad day for them, even if they don't know it yet," said Budge. "And I've written 'em all down. I've drawn their pictures. I'd know them in spite of false whiskers. I'd know 'em by their ears and noses."

As he ended this whisper, up the driveway came a halting figure that moved into the light cast from the ceiling lamp of the veranda.

It was Wally Chase, looking taller, meaner, more bent than ever. He dragged off his hat at the foot of the steps, and then the loud voice of Hugh Alton was heard, exclaiming: "There's a poor fellow I have to see."

Hugh Alton himself came hastily down the steps, and drew Wally Chase by the arm back under the shadows, back close under the shrubs which also sheltered Joseph Good and his companion.

"You fool," said Alton through his teeth. "Have you no more sense than to come here and show your face before all these people, at this time of the night?"

"Don't call me a fool," said Wally Chase, with an equal energy. "You can't talk down to me, not with what I know about you."

"If you take the blackmail line with me, my fine fellow," said the great Alton, "I'll soon show you what my friendship means in this part of the world and what my enmity means, too."

"Your friendship and your enmity can go to, for all I care," said Wally Chase, snarling. "I've been through another hot dose tonight, and all on account of you."

"What d'you mean by that?"

"You had to pick me out to go scouting around the Good place. There wasn't nobody else. You had to pick on a cripple. If I hadn't been a cripple, I would've had a chance to lie quiet in the dark, and put a bullet that would've done for him!"

"What have you done," said Hugh Alton. "If you tell me that he's had his hands on you again—"

"He's had his hands on me, all right," said the thug.

"You have the brains of a weakfish and the strength of a house fly," said Hugh Alton. "All you can do is to turn up where you're not wanted, and at the wrong time. He's had talk out of you. He's made you talk, and now you've come whining back to me! That's what you've done."

"Alton," said the gunman, softly and fiercely, "when I hear you talk like that, I've got a mind to go back and really talk to him."

"There's no point in losing our tempers," said Alton, his manner changing perceptibly. "We've been through too much together, in one way or another. You've shot down my boy—and still you see that I treat you as a friend. Let that be the proof."

"I shot him because he was a double-crossing hound!" exclaimed the yegg. "And if I hadn't thought of you at the last minute, I would've sent that slug straight through the middle of him."

"I know that you were tried. Harry is young and foolish," said the chief of the clan. "But matters have come to a bad state now. There's too much talk in the town. Who could have imagined that the boy had so much in him! Who could have dreamed that the little lazy worthless idler was a man-tamer! More than that, he's beginning to fill the eye of the people. There's talk around the town. There's a great deal of talk, Wally!"

"There's talk," said Wally Chase, "and all of it is about the kid. He's done to me what nobody else in the world ever done, by tricks and sleight of hand, but not in what I call a fair fight."

"A black snake against a gun and a knife?" said Alton. "But go on. What are they saying in town? What do you hear?"

"They can't talk at all, except about Joe Good. Him and his new money, the two blacks and the thoroughbred mare. I seen her, and she ain't no fake. I seen the blacks, too, and they ain't no fake. But the people in Fort Willow are beginning to ask, not what sort of a bank did young Good crack to get all of that money, but what sort of a bad deal did you put over on him when you killed Vincent Good. They're talking about what you called a posse, and they're calling it a murder gang, just the way the kid called it. I tell you what, Alton," he said, shaking a forefinger in the very face of the rancher, "you've covered up a lot of things in your day. But you ain't covering this up, very well. There's trouble in the air. Maybe the most important folks still think that you're all powerful. Maybe the judge and the sheriff still think that you can't do any harm, but the saloons are full of buzzing. When the punchers talk about you, they frown, and they talk down, deep and low. For every ten friends that you had when you killed Vincent Good, you ain't got more than one left."

"But the ones who remain," said the rancher, "have the county and all of its affairs in their hands. As for the opinions of the rabble, I'm above being influenced by them. That covers the ground. But what did Joseph Good wring out of you, if anything?"

"Nothing that he didn't know before," lied the gunman.

"How did he get hold of you anyway?"

"His servant is a regular lurcher. He's a silent, runnin' hound. And he come slidin' at me while I was lyin' out in the brush, watching the veranda and edging close enough to pretty near make out what was being said there. He grabbed me. He's a gorilla, and I only got one hand, or I would've laid him dead, the black varmint. They took me in and held a gun to my head. They'd as soon've killed me as taken a breath. And they had me dead to rights; I was caught on their grounds."

"Blast you and your rights," said Alton. "I know that they made you squeal, but now tell me what you said. I don't care. I can cover it up. But I must know exactly what they got out of you."

"He knew it already," said the gunman. "I dunno how, but he knew that I was to get five hundred for running his father and him out of the county. He knows that Harry offered me the money. He doesn't know that you're behind the deal. He's got no idea of that! He don't have any idea, either, why that sand patch of his is worth a mint of money, right now! They would've tore me in pieces if I hadn't talked, and now you know what he knows."

Alton took a deep breath, and then, with the tip of a finger, he brushed back the mustache from his upper lip. Finally he said: "How did young Good take this news?"

"As if he'd known it when he was born."

"He's dangerous!" murmured the rancher. Then, as though by an afterthought, he said: "I know, whatever he thought, that you never would have confirmed any of his suspicions, except that you had to."

"Thanks, chief," said Wally Chase. "That's only fair, but I'm glad to hear you say it."

"There's another thing," said Alton. "I've begun working up the big black. I've started an inquiry, and already I'm getting results. He's a known yegg."

The gunman sighed with satisfaction.

"I knew it wasn't no new hand that took hold of me, tonight," declared Wally Chase. "He had a kind of a professional way about him. He knew a gag from a hand-saw, what I mean."

"I'll get the black first," said Alton, "unless the boy crowds me, and then I'll have to take him. If I can get the giant, I'll spoil young Good's reputation in the town. Crooked servant, crooked master."

"Like me and you, eh?" chuckled Wally Chase sardonically.

"About money," said the rancher coldly. "You need some funds?"

"I ain't a buzzard," said the gunman. "I can't live on my own dead."

"Here's fifty dollars," said the other. "I'll take care of you, Wally, and I'll take good care. Now trot along. And the next time you come, come in the back door of the house!"

He turned and went away toward the lighted veranda, while Wally Chase paused only a moment, to mutter with savage hatred.

Then he slid away into the shadows and down the drive.

14

Shortly after the return of the master of the house, the ladies retired. And big Morrissey was murmuring softly, as if to himself: "This is the kind of a party to be stepping in on. All crooks! All except the little lady with the red hair. This here man always noticed that a girl that's as good as she's pretty, carries a lamp around inside of her. She shines! Look at that veranda now, Mr. Joseph, and see if it ain't kind of dark since she went inside?"

Young Joseph Good thought that the remark was very much to the point, but he gave no answer. He was too interested in the group that had formed, suddenly, on the veranda; Harry standing supported by his crutches, while the others formed in a close knot, speaking with low voices.

"They've all gathered, the whole of the fighting clan," said the boy. "Every one of those men means money, Budge. And every one of them can bring other fighting men into the field. They've come together tonight to talk about me. Hugh Alton is telling them, now, that I've got on their trail through the confession of Wally Chase. And they're laying their heads together. They're planning how to ruin me, one way or another."

"A little lead slug through the head is the cheapest medicine," said Budge Morrissey.

"You see the main point that we have to work for," suggested Joe Good. "Why is my land worth more than a gold mine? What's the mystery?"

"Mr. Hugh Alton knows the reason, sir."

"And we've got to try to get the answer out of him. That's why we'll have to enter that house tonight, Budge."

"We got to enter," agreed Morrissey. "And with all of those stinging wasps inside, it won't be so easy a job, maybe. But businessmen always write letters. And Hugh Alton is a businessman."

"What are you driving at, Budge?"

"Take a real, plain, straightway crook, like me and a lot that I know, we never write no letters, except about the weather. But a businessman like Hugh Alton always has to write letters. It's not the morning, if there's not a lot of letters in the mail. Somewhere in that house is Mr. Alton's study, and in the study there's a desk, and in the desk there are a lot of letters, and in the letters there's the mind of Mr. Hugh Alton. You got to find those letters, Mr. Joseph, and you and I have got to do a little reading tonight."

The boy nodded in the darkness.

He saw the troop of men file into the house. Only Hugh Alton remained for a moment at the head of the steps, chewing at a cigar, lost in the deepest thought, and occasionally lifting his magnificent head to look above the heads of the trees toward the stars.

At length he, also, turned about and, with a brisk step, went through the front door. "He's got some ideas," said Budge. "But maybe he's thinking a mite too late."

A servant came out, stood on a chair, pulled down the porch light with a chain and blew it out.

The lower face of the house was at once shrouded in darkness.

"After all," said the boy, "it appears that we've got to step on the heels of Hugh Alton tonight. Do you know his layout?"

Said the surprising Budge Morrissey: "I know the whole plant. I know the cellar and the attic, and even the smell of the blackberry pies in the pantry on the shelves. I ate one of them pies last night, Mr. Joseph. I hope you don't mind!"

Lights appeared in the windows of the rambling second story which, from the pillars of the veranda façade, retreated on either hand. After a short time, those lights, all saving one, went out.

"That's the room of Mr. Jess Alton," said Budge. "We go this way, Mr. Joseph."

Cautiously, in the footsteps of the big black man, Joseph Good rounded the house, still keeping behind the shrubbery and so came to the side which was to the right of the veranda. There Budge pointed out a series of windows which were already black.

"That's the room of Mrs. Alton," said Budge Morrissey. "And behind those three big windows, you see the little one? That's the bathroom, and next there's three more big windows. And that's the bedroom of Mr. Hugh Alton. Then comes two more windows, with a balcony outside of 'em. That's his study. And that's where we have to go."

"Who's next?"

"No man," said Budge. "In the next room is only Miss Katherine Garnet."

"Good," said the boy.

"Yes, that's good," replied Budge Morrissey. "Because a woman always sleeps sounder than a man. I remember once I was in a hotel bedroom for an hour and a half, a-fooling away at the lock of a little private safe, and the woman that owned the safe, she lay in her bed, and snored and slept, and snored and slept, just as sound! I got a little mad at the way she slept so sound, and at the combination on that safe, and while I used my dark lantern, I swore a little louder than a whisper, but that only lulled her all the deeper."

"Did you get the safe open?" asked the boy.

"Yes, sir! And did I have a trip to New York? Yes, Mr. Joseph, I did, and some of my Harlem friends were pretty surprised when they saw me come prancing out of the West. That was a six-month party before I had to go to work again."

The past sins of Budge Morrissey only amused the boy. "We'd better wait a while," said he. "Let them get deeply asleep."

"No, sir! If you'll excuse me," said Budge Morrissey, "the first sleep is the soundest. You just follow along after me, sir."

And he led the way to a side door that opened just above the ground.

"This door hasn't been used for a long time," said Budge Morrissey. "When I tried it last night, I saw that it hadn't been used for a long time, and it made me sort of sad, Mr. Joseph, to see a lock all clogged up with rust, so I gave it a couple of squirts of oil. It ought to open pretty easy now."

It did open easily.

They stepped into a lower hall. Budge closed the door noiselessly behind them, and the warm air of the interior of the house closed up softly about them, with a faint odor of cookery in it.

A ray of light cut down the center of the floor, and then slashed right and left. It came from a dark lantern in the hand of Budge Morrissey. The heart of the boy stood still, until he understood the source of the light.

But after that preliminary examination, Budge moved ahead, a vast and shapeless shadow.

He opened a door on the left. They entered a big room, whose size could be guessed from the distant gleam of a cigar butt that was dying on the hearth. Here, the thick, choking stench of cigar smoke was heavy in the air.

From this room they passed through another door into a purer atmosphere. They came to steps, up which the single needle ray from the lantern tripped before them.

The whisper of Morrissey was at the ear of Joseph Good.

"Walk close to the wall. Put your toes down first and let your knee sag. Ease yourself every step. If a creak starts, stop short, but not too short. If a board begins to groan under you, let it groan long and soft rather than quick and sharp. Come on!"

At that moment, it seemed to Joseph Good that through the darkness numbers of whispering, mocking forms were trooping down the stairs, with hands ready to clutch at them, with eyes that could look through the night.

Up they went, slowly, slowly, and as they came toward the head of the stairs, a padding footfall came down the hall.

They shrank against the wall. Young Joseph Good made the loaded black snake ready.

But the half-guessed-at form went by the head of the stairs. A little farther down, there was a knock at a door. Then a door opened. The voice of Harry Alton said:

"Here's your book, Kate, if you want to read yourself to sleep."

"I can sleep without reading, I'm so full of fresh air and tired with riding," answered the quiet voice of the girl. "But thanks for the book, Harry."

He said: "Kate, now that you've seen everybody, are you any closer to knowing?"

"Yes," she answered. "Not from seeing them, but from other things."

"And what's the answer?" he asked, excited.

"I'd rather talk to you in the morning, Harry," said she.

"Because you don't want to give me a bad night?"

"I'm sorry," said she.

"You're sorry? It's Uncle Tucker Alton," he said fiercely. "You couldn't stand his big, brawling way of talking. I noticed your face at dinner."

"It's not your uncle, Harry."

"It's myself, then?"

"You know, in such a matter, you and I are the only people who really count."

"And you've made up your mind that I won't do."

"Not that you won't exactly do, but—"

"Listen to me!" he broke in. "It's the rotten talk that's been going about through the town. I know you've heard something. About that beggar, Joe Good, and what happened to his father. Tell me true. Is that partly in your mind?"

There was rather a long pause, for such a point in such a conversation.

Then she said: "Yes, that's very much in my mind."

There was a groan from Harry Alton.

"But he's a tramp; he's a loafer; he's worthless!" said Harry Alton hotly.

And the girl said: "I passed him the other day on the street. And he seemed to me like the horse he was riding—a thoroughbred."

"Kate," gasped the boy, "don't you know that he's been the town joke?"

"Perhaps he used to be," said she. "But from the way you all talk of him, he's certainly not a joke now!"

She added: "I don't want to talk any more now, Harry. I'd rather wait till the morning. You know I only came here—"

"I know that you only came because I begged you to," said he. "But to think that Joe Good—No Good, they've called him—to think that he made you—Kate, we'll talk again in the morning. Good night!"

15

The door closed; the padding, irregular step of Harry Alton went down the hallway, and then his door was slammed. The memory of his muffled curses was still sweet in the ear of young Joseph Good.

"Now!" said Budge, and at last they arose and went stealthily on their way again.

They paused, Budge Morrissey fumbled at the wall, and then his wonderfully controlled whisper came to the ears of the boy: "Locked!"

A hand-warmed, metal thing was promptly placed in the hand of the boy.

"Move the shutter a little. Give me a ray of light," said Budge Morrissey.

Joseph Good, for the first time in his life, handled a dark lantern, and unsheathed a streak of meager light, which he played obediently over the surface of the lock.

A little kit was already unfolded on the hall carpet, and Morrissey, on his knees, fell to work. It was metal against metal, but Good heard never a click.

Presently the door sagged open; a whispering draft came out about them. They stole into a big room with a high ceiling. Budge took the dark lantern and swept the place with the single ray which, it appeared, was all that he used. Like a sword slash, the light clove the darkness and showed the rug on the floor, the deep easy-chairs, two tables, one piled with books, and more books in a set of shelves bracketed out from the wall. But, above all, the main piece of furniture in the room was a roll-top desk of great size, placed between the two windows. The ray of light steadied like a finger upon it.

Handing the lantern to Good, Budge was instantly leaning over the lock.

"These things are always easy," he said. As he spoke, he began to slide back the top of the desk gradually, little by little.

There was no sound. It was raised almost to the top, and then they fell upon the papers.

"We can't spend all night," Budge whispered. "If the papers make some crackling noise when we open 'em up, we've got to chance it."

And chance it they did, while the cold sweat formed on the face of Joseph Good and trickled down to his chin. They tried the desk's pigeonholes. But there was nothing there except the scrawled reports of ranch foremen and small ledgers filled with ranch and other accounts.

"Deeper!" said Budge, and began opening drawers.

There were many drawers, and they were stuffed full of letter files and such matters.

For a whole half hour longer, they worked. Finally Budge looked up and shook his head.

"We're not on the right track," he said. "This Alton, he's a fox. He doesn't go to ground that everybody knows about. There may be some tricks about this desk."

He drew out a drawer, measured it, compared its depth with the depths of the desk, shook his head again.

"We've lost," said the boy, shaking his head. "Let's get out of this at once."

For a flutter of panic was making his heart race.

Budge looked up with his golden smile.

"Young crooks get to jail quick, Mr. Joseph," said he. "And they don't have a full pocketbook to take with 'em. But I'm an old crook, is Budge Morrissey. Don't run till the patrol wagon comes, sir!"

And opening a top drawer, he began to probe about at the top of the desk. Suddenly he straightened, with a startled look.

"Heard something?" gasped the boy.

"No, but I found something!"

He worked a moment over the top of the desk, removed the blotter, and presently raised up what seemed a solidly placed board in the surface of the desk, gripping it with his finger nails. A little compartment stocked with letters and a small notebook was revealed.

They exchanged knowing looks, these two burglars, and faint, joyous smiles.

The ledger fell into the hands of the boy. He opened it. Small notations of cash expended met his eyes. They met nothing else until, glancing further, he saw: "Five more for Dick Purvis's election. He's too honest to be worth that much money!"

It was as though music had sounded in the ears of Joseph Good.

Hastily he turned onto a date which would be forever lodged in his memory, and there he found: "The five hundred and two-fifty bonus to Wally Chase. The rascal was worth his pay, after all!"

Lower down: "Good has left. The last of them gone, and another hundred to Wally. That ought to hold him."

Immediately under: "Fifty to Wally Chase. He knows too much. I wish Joe Good had broken the head of the worthless fool, instead of his hand!"

Later: "Fifty to Wally. This is blackmail, but I have to stand it. Joe Good still away, thank God, perhaps forever."

Then: "Good returns. Fifty more to Wally Chase. He'll have to repay me with blood, one day!"

That was the last entry in the ledger.

The boy looked up to find a broad smile on the face of Budge, a smile so vast that it threw wrinkles into the vast expanse of the forehead.

And there was Budge Morrissey holding out several sheets of letter paper.

"This is the trick!" said he.

Joseph Good dropped the account book into his pocket. Then he took the letters and read: "Dear Alton: I have your letter of the fifteenth. I can't thank you enough. If the railroad runs through, as I think, of course you can clean up. You have bought all the best land through which the line will pass, except the most important bit of all, where the siding will run.

"That will become the center of the town, and what are now waste acres will be sold soon for the price of building lots. This land of which I speak is the hundred acres belonging, I learn, to a certain Vincent Good. Can you buy him out? It will be several days before the news of the railroad's plan to build will be made public. You have that margin to work on. Thank you for your check."

The second letter read: "Dear Alton: Have been working frantically, but nothing can be done with railroad engineers. The place they have chosen is the best for all their purposes. They want, also, the water of the creek that runs through the Good place. That will be invaluable, because it is never dry, winter or summer. I talked to the president today and suggested your plan, but he was immovable. I talked until he said that, no doubt I had a good friend concerned. I laughed it off as well as I could. The station will be just in front of the Good place. There's nothing to be done about it.

"You say that you may be able to get Good off the land with guns or money. Use both if you need to. That hundred acres will be worth all the rest of Fort Willow, the instant the railroad building plans are known. There are to be large yards. Fort Willow will have ten thousand new people in it within a year. Alton, I know that you're a smart man. Now use your brains.

"Thank you for the last check. It was very welcome. I am hoping to buy a new house, and will need ten thousand for that purpose. If you get the Good place, I know you won't miss that much."

At the bottom of both of these letters appeared the signature: "William Proctor."

Joseph Good folded the sheets of note paper and placed them in his pocket.

"It isn't a perfect case," he said, "and it might not even put Alton in jail, but it will smash his name and reputation forever. Budge, I owe you something for myself, and something for—"

The hand of Budge Morrissey flew up in warning. He glided back toward the door that opened on the balcony.

That door suddenly opened, and a figure entered the room, only to be instantly seized by the mighty hands of Morrissey.

There was not a sound, except the whispering of silk, and the boy, striking in with a ray of the dark lantern, fastened it upon—the face of Katherine Garnet.

"Let her go!" ordered the boy, aghast.

"She'll yell," said Morrissey through his teeth.

"Let her yell, then, Budge! Take your hands from her!"

The hands of Morrissey fell away from her. She staggered and slid with a groan into a chair.

16

The boy was on his knees beside her, saying: "Nothing will happen to you. You're perfectly safe! Budge, get out of here! Save yourself. The house will be up in a moment."

"The house ain't heard a thing," said Budge Morrissey, breathing heavily. "Steady, now, and we'll still pull through. Her mouth ought to be shut though!"

She sat up, one hand laid on her bruised throat, the other gathering her dressing gown around her.

She was trembling, but something more than raving fear was in her eyes.

"You're Joseph Good!" she said. "Why are you here? Why have you—I came through the wrong door from the balcony. What—what have you done to Mr. Hugh Alton?"

At that moment, as though inspired, from the next room Mr. Hugh Alton snored loudly.

"I came for this," said the boy, "and I've found it. I came to find proof that my father was murdered, and the motive for it—and I've found it. Will you look at these things!"

His finger marked the places. The names were familiar enough to her; the words themselves would have been enough without such a knowledge. And her face grew a sickly white.

"It was murder," said she.

She stood up.

"What am I to do?"

"Go back to your bed. Say nothing; remember nothing. Can you do that?"

She drew in a breath.

"What will you do before you leave this house?" she asked, her glance bright and steady on him.

The twisted, humorous smile came on the lips of Joseph Good.

"Not what you guess that I might do," he said. "And not what other people in this part of the world might do. My father was murdered, but I'll not be a murderer to balance the account. Will you believe that?"

She paused before she nodded, and then her whisper said: "I'll believe you. This house, I leave it tomorrow. I knew—"

She paused, with a gasp at the things she knew.

"Go back to your room," said he. "Budge, close the desk."

It was done. The board in the top was arranged. The roll top was lowered and clicked softly.

Then they left the room. The flicker of the dark lantern lighted the hallway outside, ending in a glistening point on the knob of her door. Then Joseph Good stood in the darkness beside her.

He said: "My hand was forced. I had to play the cards that were in it. Does it make you think that I'm a common criminal?"

And she answered: "If I could do such a thing for my father's sake, I'd be proud. Good-by!"

Her door opened and closed on her, as he stood mute, silenced by the throng of words that were swelling in his throat.

Big Budge Morrissey took him by the arm.

"We've got to go," said he. "Don't stay for her. A lady never forgets, Mr. Joseph, no more than a gentleman can."

It seemed to Joseph Good that all danger had disappeared. They passed rapidly down through the house and out into the black of the night, striding across the fields toward his own house.

All that he had done seemed less important than another thing, a nameless excitement, sorrow and joy, that lived in him like the breath of his nostrils.

He mounted the mare the next morning at nine, and with a free, cantering gait, he overtook a buckboard that contained the narrow, humped body of Zeke Stevens. Into his hands he passed two letters and a small ledger;

and Zeke Stevens clucked to the horse as he drove on, reading.

He looked up, his long, skinny arm extending the papers back to the boy on horseback. But the red fire was in the eyes of Zeke.

"The foundations are blowed away from under 'em. They're all gunna come down; all gunna come down! Go on, get the newspaper, get the sheriff. The game's yours!"

And he waved to Joseph Good.

"Hawks," said Joseph Good. "They were hawks. And now there's an eagle over their heads!"

In Fort Willow, he let the mare dance through the main street. There was peace in his soul and calm determination. He had done enough. The law would have to reach out now and gather in Mr. Hugh Alton, and perhaps many of his clan.

His way took him straight to the office of Judge Tomlinson, and he saw that dignitary dismount from a carriage that sagged down under the weight he put upon its step in descending.

He waited. He followed the great man to his chambers. At the door, he confronted Jameson.

"The judge is a busy man," said the latter, and started to slam the door.

Joseph Good blocked it with his foot.

"Take the judge this ledger," said he. "I'll wait in the hall."

He waited a long ten minutes. Then the door was jerked open by Judge Taylor Tomlinson in person. He came out into the hall with a drawn face.

"Young man," he said, "Hugh Alton is my best and oldest friend. And I'm not a handwriting expert to pass upon forgery!"

"Hugh Alton is your best and oldest friend," said the boy, "and that means that you know his handwriting as well as you know your own!"

The judge raised a hand and covered his eyes.

"Hugh Alton!" he muttered.

He jerked the hand down.

"What do you want?" he said.

"A warrant," said the boy.

"For what?"

"Murder!" said young Joseph Good. "I showed you only part of the evidence. Here's more."

And he indicated the two letters which he had drawn from his pocket.

Back in the chambers of Taylor Tomlinson, he sat beside the judge and watched the latter read until his head finally fell into the cup of both hands.

Then the judge sat up and shook his head to clear away the dark mists from his eyes.

"I would have chosen him," he said solemnly, "as the most honest man in the world. But if he's what he appears, I tear him out of my heart. God forgive Hugh Alton! I seem to see him before me now, guilty, guilty, guilty!"

He rang a bell. Jameson appeared.

"Jameson," he said, "make out a warrant against Hugh Alton, for the murder of Vincent Good!"

17

Trees did not flourish near the town of Fort Willow; only from the north, on a long, shelving series of hills, a forest-covered promontory extended toward Fort Willow like a dark headland thrust into a bright-colored sea.

On the rim of this standing army of pines sat, on this day, Wally Chase, gunman, thief, cattle rustler, but above all, hired murderer. He had killed in many lands. He had killed for pleasure now and then, purely and simply, but as a rule his gun plays were business strokes.

He had not been seriously engaged for several weeks, and the cause appeared in his right wrist, still large and thickened where the bones had been broken straight across. Whatever else he was doing, his left hand was always tending the injured member, wherein was lodged almost more than the seat of his life—his power to deal death with sudden ease out of his shining guns.

He was sitting on a rock, working at this damaged hand, while his companion sat on a horse not far from him.

It would have seemed absurd for Hugh Alton to be on the same level with the thug. Seated there on a lordly gray gelding, he looked like a general surveying his army, a general in undress field uniform, occasionally lifting the tip of a finger to brush from his upper lip his already perfectly brushed mustache.

Alton had certainly kept his pristine vigor. The roughest lumberjack, if he remained brutally unawed by the bold dimensions of the Alton brow, might well hesitate before tackling the owner of such shoulders and arms.

As he looked from the edge of the woods down upon the great, light-colored hills that surrounded Fort Willow, he thought upon his wide acres, as well as the acres of all the rest of his clan, and his face brightened; he thought of other things, and his eye grew dark.

"There was a time, Wally," said he, "there was a happy time, Chase, when my word was better than any other man's bond, all through this range. I had the trust of every rancher, every business and professional man. I had a position worthy of a king. And now that position is stripped away from me. My authority is gone. Even in Fort Willow itself people look darkly on me. Self-respecting men draw back from me!"

He shook his head and sighed.

"Yeah," said Wally Chase with an odd sort of sympathy, if sympathy it could be called. "Yeah, you had your time for being on top. But the kid socked you. When No-good Joe Good started knocking home runs, the crowd got up and walked out on you. They wouldn't pay to see the Alton team play no more."

Mr. Alton found the comparison unsavory, and remarked:

"Mind you, Chase, no thinking man would ever believe for an instant that young Good can win out in the long run. The regrettable matter of the death of his father is—"

He paused and shook his head.

"Yeah," drawled Wally Chase, "and then the way he found out that you had been dickering with a gent on the railroad that had told you the line was coming through Fort Willow—and just where—when he found that out it was a pretty sick day for you."

"The scoundrel," said Hugh Alton, "entered my house, a burglar. And if there's justice in the land, he—"

"Yeah, there's justice," said Wally Chase. "If there's any real justice, he oughta go to jail for robbery, and you oughta hang for murder, is the way some folks would see it!"

"Hang?" said Hugh Alton in a rage. "Hang? Man, what are you talking of?"

"For murdering old Vincent Good. You know you ran him down. You know, if it hadn't been for that, Joe Good would never have started on your trail!"

"Murder!" cried Hugh Alton. "A sad affair, a mistaken affair, I grant you. But we ran down Good that night because we really thought that he had shot and fatally wounded my boy Harry. You know that perfectly well, Chase!"

"Yeah, I know what I know," said Wally Chase.

The rancher stared haughtily at his companion. "Let it be," he said. "Only trust me when I give you my word that one day shall see the end of Mr. Joseph Good, his two servants, and his horse and his dog. I'm going to blot him out; people will not even know the place where his house was, or the sound of his name!"

A sweeping gesture served to give emphasis to the words of Mr. Alton.

"Yeah," drawled the injured gunman. "If hating was bullets, he'd be loaded full of 'em long before this. But you been hating him for quite a while, and when you started in trying to clear him out of the county and grab his land, he was a beggar and everybody laughed at him; but now he's the favorite bet of the town."

"That town is going to find its favorite bet a dead man, and that before many days," said Alton. "Where is your friend? Where's Martin? He's late!"

"Yeah, but he's worth waiting for. You'll like him when you see him, Mr. Alton. He's a beauty. Just the look of him will be a kind of a pleasure to you."

"His looks are a matter of indifference to me," said Alton. "What I'm really interested in is his efficiency."

"You gotta go by the score in such things," said the other. "You take the fellow with the high batting average, and you expect him to make the hits when he comes to the bat. But every great batter don't get across the plate every game he plays. Only, what I mean to say, Martin ain't ever known to've failed. It ain't known that he's less'n a hundred per cent. One hundred per cent of the gents he's gone for are dead."

"One hundred per cent?" said the rancher, drawing in his breath and pinching his lips.

For, after all, he was a sensitive man, was Hugh Alton, and he was now speaking of murder.

"After all," said Alton, "efficiency is the greatest thing in the world. The very greatest. I certainly hope that this Martin will be worth his money."

"Aw, he'll be worth it," said the other, 'if you can get him to take the job for you. It may cost you some money, but he'll do the trick for you if he takes the job. He's a hundred per center, I was telling you, and I mean what I say. This boy Martin, he's poison. There was the story about the two detectives that give up their work in New York and started on a diamond trail clean across the country that finally brought them into the Martin country. He was the boy that they wanted. He'd done the trick in New York, and it happened that he'd killed a night watchman that was the father of these two dicks.

"So they work for seventeen months until finally they come face to face with Martin in his own mountains. That was all."

"Did he kill them?" asked Hugh Alton.

"Did he kill them?" said the other. "Well, they ain't been seen since, and you can make up your mind for yourself."

"It's a wretched business," said Alton. "This hiring of a gunman is a wretched business. But it must be done. Every day that Joseph Good persists in Fort Willow my name is blackened. Every time that people look in his face they call me a murderer and a villain."

"The things that they call you ain't pretty," said Wally Chase, "and that's a fact. I remember that I was at the Pemberton saloon, not long back, and there was Mort Pemberton himself, that used to bow down when he so much as heard your name, and what he says about you while he was looking at the big picture of Joe Good that hangs on the wall of the saloon—"

"I don't want to hear any more," said Alton. "Saloon chatter on the part of the rabble is of no importance to me!"

"Sure it ain't. You go as you please," said the gunman.

"Only," said Alton acidly, "I wonder that you have the face to show yourself at your old haunts! How do you dare to encounter Joseph Good?"

"Oh, he ain't mean. He don't hold malice," said Wally Chase. "He takes a grand air and pretends that he forgets! Oh, how I'd like to have his heart here under my feet! But he acts grand, like he wouldn't tramp on a man that's down."

"You're down," said Alton with a precise and effective cruelty, "because the boy flogged you before the whole crowd on the veranda of the hotel in Fort Willow; flogged you and broke your gun hand for you at the same time. You were a great figure till that moment, Wally Chase!"

"And you're down," answered Chase savagely, "because he got the proofs that you're a briber and a plotter, and that you plotted the murder of Vincent Good and himself. That's why you're down, and after your trial comes off—you can't keep using your money to put off the day forever—you're gunna be dragged in the mud, Mr. Hugh Alton. You're gunna be nothing but a mess of rags and mud, your reputation, when the evidence comes out against you."

Hugh Alton turned on the other a glance that should have withered all life from his veins.

Then he exclaimed: "He must never live to give witness against me. The same case that throws me in peril of my life involves you, Chase, and never forget it."

"I ain't forgetting," said Wally Chase. "But it ain't the fear of the future that keeps me after him. It's thinking about the past, and the way he's treated me and shamed me. I ain't no more than a low hound when I walk down the streets of Fort Willow now. And you can bet that they side-stepped when I sashayed into that town in the old days. They'll side-step again once I get my gun hand to working in good shape!"

Alton started to speak, but checked himself just as his lip curled, and exclaimed: "Why, who's this?"

He had raised his eyes, and saw stretched out on a great branch of a tree above his head, the form of a man whose brown clothes made him merge easily with the bark of the bough.

Wally Chase sprang to his feet and drew a gun, but as he looked up in turn he exclaimed: "That's Charley Martin! Charley, how long you been there?"

"Ever since you both arrived," said Martin. "I thought that I'd listen in a little to your talking. It might kind of save a lot of explanations later on."

18

He swung down from the branch and hung suspended for an instant, not by both hands, but by one alone, the left, and showed a narrow body, long hands, long feet. Like an ape he hung there and then allowed his weight to slide off the tips of his fingers, dropping to the ground almost soundlessly.

As he straightened, Hugh Alton thought that at any moment of his fall or while he hung from the branch the man had been in the most perfect poise and balance, ready to whip out a weapon with his free hand, ready to strike with it. He seemed more like a gorilla than a man.

Yet he had few of the apish characteristics in appearance. It was rather in his actions.

His jaw, it is true, thrust out a little; but so did the brow above, instead of receding to make the typical ape profile. It was a very high, narrow forehead, widening to a bulge at the very top; and there was an indentation distinctly lined out beneath the protuberance. However, the thing was not so noticeable as to be called an actual deformity. The feature made his entire face seem rather long.

His nose was dish-shaped, and seemed to have been broken again and again; and so, looked at from the side, the whole outline was almost concave, and distinctly suggested concavity. In spite of all this, the face was not really very ugly. But there was a night look about it; it was pale, and the eyes were remarkable for a glassy steadiness.

It was the narrowness of the shoulders that made the neck seem so long, perhaps; but the arms were indeed

long, and one monkey trait was the growth of hair over
the backs of the hands down to the first knuckles. Except
for that feat of hanging so easily by one hand and the
manner of the drop to the ground, Hugh Alton would
never have selected this figure as one of immense strength.

Alton himself had nothing to say. He was speechless
with surprise and with anger, but Wally Chase went on:
"Don't be upset, chief. This is just one of Charley's little
tricks. You can't expect him to be like other folks."

He even added: "You'll get used to him."

Martin, without the use of his hands, sat down cross-
legged upon the ground and put his back to the tree.

"Were you up that tree when we arrived?" asked
Alton suddenly.

"No, but I didn't see very good where I was standing,
so I climbed the tree and lay out on the branch. I was
wondering when you'd see me. But you were thinking too
hard, Mr. Alton."

He took from one pocket a stick of soft pine wood.
From the other he drew out a knife and opened the blade
with a flick of his finger tips. Then he began to draw
from the stick shavings so fine that they were translucent.

He rarely looked up from this occupation, but Alton
knew that the man was aware of every gesture of the
other two.

"You know what the gentleman wants, Charley," said
Wally Chase. "Go on and say what your price is."

"What I wonder," said Martin, "is why you don't file
a claim on the scalp of this gent, seeing that he whipped
you once and broke your hand! Is it still bad?"

Wally Chase drew a revolver, balanced it, and put it
back inside his coat with one gesture.

"I'm only about fifty per cent," he said.

"And that ain't good enough? This here Joe Good,
he's a two-gun devil, is he?"

"He's nothing with a gun," said Wally Chase. "A
black snake is what he carries instead of knives and
guns."

"A what?" asked the other, amazed. Still he did not
look up, but the whittling stopped for an instant.

"A black snake," repeated Wally Chase.

"I don't understand," said the other. "Maybe I'm getting too old to understand that sort of a thing."

"You get within ten feet of him, which is average barroom distance," said Chase, "and he'll make you young enough to understand pretty quick. He'll whip the guns out of your hands, and the knives, too, and slam you into a deep sleep with a slug from the butt end of that whip."

"Will he?" said Martin.

Now indeed he looked up, and his flat, glassy eyes were fastened upon the face of Wally Chase.

"I know you, Charley. You know that I know you and that I seen you work more'n once. But get within ten feet of him and I guess his tricks will paralyze anybody in the world. He's always got that black snake in his hand, it seems to me. And it's always ready to jump like a rattle-snake, and every touch of it is poison, no matter which end."

He held out his hands. The broken wrist was obvious. Around the other was a crimson band.

"He done both of those little jobs," said Chase.

The whittling commenced again; there was no further comment upon the skill of the hunted man.

Martin merely said: "You don't have to stand inside of ten feet of him. Why not stand ten yards away and shoot him to bits, eh?"

"That's a smart trick," said Wally Chase. "But that ain't so easy, either. You can't do no business with him in Fort Willow. Not none at all. Because everybody knows that he don't carry a gun, and the crowd would lynch any gent that happened to step in and slap Mr. Good in the face with a couple of slugs of lead out of a revolver. And when he goes home from town he's still got a crowd waiting on him."

"What sort of a crowd?"

"A big black nine feet tall with a pair of guns on every foot of him all the way from his feet to his head. He can chuck knives with any man, and he's a shooting fool. I've seen him practice. Even you, Charley, would have your hands full."

"You make the task seem impossible," exclaimed the rancher. "As a matter of fact, it's not impossible at all. Nothing is impossible when the agent at work has brains, hands, and courage."

"You can say that, Mr. Alton," answered Wally Chase, "but the fact is, and I know it, and this here job has gotta be done away from Fort Willow. Killing that hound in the town or near it can't be done, I reckon!"

He spoke with decision, and Martin nodded, as though accepting the fact.

"He'll have to be pulled away from Fort Willow, then," he said. "Anything's possible."

"Good," said Alton. "I see that you have the right stuff in you."

Martin dismissed the praise with a shrug of his shoulders.

He said: "Lemme see if I have this case straight from listening in. Vincent Good and his boy are dead broke, living on a few acres of sand. Along come news that the railroad will build through Fort Willow. You get that news. You find out that the sand patch of the Goods' will become valuable ground after the railroad arrives. You want to get the land. I suppose you find it hard to buy. You put Vincent Good out of the way. Young Joe Good then gums the deal and burgles your house, finds out what you've been doing, lays a murder charge agin' you, and you're out on bail, trying to get him killed off before your trial is slated, and before he can appear to witness agin' you. Is that right?"

"That's a very naked statement of the case. The important thing is that Joe Good must be put out of the way forever!" exclaimed Alton.

"It'll cost you big money," said the criminal. "It'll cost you ten grand."

"Ten thousand dollars!" exclaimed Alton. "Nonsense! Ten thousand dollars for the shooting of a bullet? Never!"

"No, it won't cost you ten thousand. The price has gone up," said the calm Mr. Martin. "It'll cost you fifteen thousand for the same job, now."

"Fifteen! Absurd nonsense!" said the rancher. "I'll hear no more about it!"

And he reined his horse away impatiently.

The calm voice of the whittler pursued him, saying: "It'll cost more than fifteen thousand. It'll cost you twenty thousand for your neck, Mr. Alton."

There was one word in the last sentence that struck upon the ears of Alton with a peculiar force. He turned about.

"Take a think, take a think, chief!" said Wally Chase. "You gotta pay for the fancy jobs."

Suddenly Alton said, rather huskily: "How do you want that money paid?"

The whittling stopped, the knife suspended in mid-air.

"About five thousand now will be all right," said Martin.

It seemed difficult for Alton to breathe, he was so oppressed with excitement.

But now he drew forth a pigskin wallet, brown and richly polished by long years of friction against his pocket linings. He drew out a sheaf and counted.

"Here you are," said he, and slapped the almost empty wallet shut.

"Fetch me the money, Wally," said the whittler, resuming his task.

Wally Chase took the money from the quivering hand of Alton, returned with it, and offered it to Martin. The latter made no gesture to receive it, so Chase thrust the doubled wad of it into his outer breast pocket.

"You and me can get along fine," said Martin in the direction of the rancher. "You came heeled like a gentleman should. You may be kind of down on your luck just now, but I'll give you a brand-new reputation, Mr. Alton. I'll polish it all up for you and make it shine like it never shined before. Forget about this here kid, this Joe Good. I don't care what else he is, he ain't got experience enough to deal with me; it takes years to know what I know. So long, Alton!"

Alton did not wait.

Perhaps it seemed to him that a darkness worse than night exuded from the figure of the whittler. At any rate, he now turned the head of his horse in earnest, and with a mere wave of the hand he galloped rapidly down the hill.

Still Martin did not look up, but as he listened to the sound of the retreating hoofbeats, he smiled to himself with a deep and silent satisfaction.

19

The silence and the whittling continued for some time. At length Wally Chase cleared his throat and then loosened the collar of his shirt.

He said: "Well, where do I come in?"

"You see the dough," said the other. "Take what you want."

Chase hesitated, then wet his lips, found no words, came closer, and pulled the wad of bills from the breast pocket of the coat.

Greed fastened on him, on his very heart. He actually thought of pulling a gun and splitting open the skull of this much wanted man with a bullet. Then all of that five thousand would be his! The five thousand, and a trip to the cities of easy spending. But he resisted that savage temptation. His right hand was still a little unsure, and Martin had eyes even in the back of his panther's head.

How much should he take?

He took out two five-hundred-dollar bills and folded them, jamming them deep down in his trouser pocket. Then he thrust the remaining money into the breast pocket of Martin's coat.

"One grand is enough for me," said he, his voice very uneven. "I ain't no hog," he added. "You know that, Charley. This here is only five per cent of what you'll pull down for the job."

Martin ignored the remark entirely.

He said: "You know Fort Willow, eh?"

"Sure. I know the town," said the ex-killer, glad to escape pointed criticism of his greed.

"We'd better go down there now and fish this here Joe Good out of the stream," said Martin.

"Hold on, Charley," said the other. "You dunno what you're talking about! You're dealing with a real man now, boy. You'll have to figure things fine, I tell you. You raise a gun on him in that town and they'll shoot you to bits. Yeah, they'll shoot even a Martin—and I know what you can do."

With the tips of his fingers, Martin flicked the blade of the knife shut and dropped both the wood and the knife out of sight. Then, again without touching his hands to the ground, he rose easily to his feet. He seemed to be constructed of springs which were always ready to react, and whose thrust had to be merely controlled.

"We'll just go down and fish him out of Fort Willow," repeated Martin, "and throw him on a bank and watch him kick and struggle till he dies."

Wally Chase blinked uneasily.

He added, by way of argument: "Strolling around Fort Willow with me, it ain't gunna be your best introduction, Martin. There might be agents down there that would recognize you. And anybody that walks around with me is gunna be carefully examined, you can bet your boots."

"Get your hoss and we'll start now," said the other.

He disappeared with a long stride among the trees, and by the time Chase, still doubtfully shaking his head, had mounted, Martin came riding out of the woods.

He was on a beautiful brown gelding, and Chase carefully looked over its points with the greatest admiration.

"You had that hoss right next to us," said he. "How did you manage to teach that hoss to stay so quiet?"

Martin answered: "How old is this Joe Good?"

"About twenty-one, I guess."

"He has the town by the throat, eh?"

"Yeah. He's got it by the throat. One day he was a bum; the next day he turns out as smart as a whip. It was the quick change, and maybe what he done to me, that got all eyes right on him!"

Martin said no more, and they rode down over the swelling lower hills and into Fort Willow.

"Where would Good be, if he came to town?" asked Martin.

"About half a block from here, down the street. At Mort Pemberton's saloon."

"We'll hitch here, then," said the great Martin, and turning to the side, he immediately dismounted, stepping rather than leaping to the ground.

He was looking elsewhere as his hands, intelligent and seeing on their own account, unknotted the end of the lead rope and fastened it in a running noose around the bar of a hitching rack that extended across the front of the Tomlinson Hardware Store.

"Hey, look!" exclaimed Wally Chase suddenly.

He pointed, and Martin saw a neat roadster going by, drawn by a span of tough little mustangs. In the driver's seat sat the biggest black that Martin had ever seen, the most prodigious pair of shoulders, and the most powerful pair of arms, seemingly. The thick muscles padded the sleeves as though they had been poured full.

In the rear of the roadster was a tarpaulin drawn over a heap of what was probably the day's shopping.

An old man with a red face and a bent back, a man in tattered clothes, who was walking across the street at this point, held up his hand. The giant driver stopped the team and politely lifted his hat to the pedestrian.

"That's your nine-foot black, eh?" said Martin.

"That's the one!" said Wally Chase. "Look at the style of the big lump of black ivory, will you? Look at the shine of him, eh? He's been a thug, and a first-rater, too. I dunno how the kid got hold of him for a servant, but I know that now he eats out of Joe Good's hand. That old goat talking to him is our town miser. One of the richest men around the range, curse his stingy heart. Everybody thoroughly hates him, and he don't like nobody but Joe Good."

Budge Morrissey was saying: "Morning, Mr. Stevens. How do you find yourself this morning, sir?"

"I find the whisky bad and the prices high," snarled Zeke Stevens, rolling his red-stained eyes. "How's you and your job?"

"Me? I'm fine," smiled the big black man. "And my job's fine, too. It's gotta be a fine job when there's a boss like I have at the head of things!"

"What kind of a boss have you got?" demanded Zeke

Stevens. "The laziest critter in the whole county, the most worthless, the most carelessest and tomfoolest white man on the range, I'd say that he is."

"Mr. Stevens, sir," said Morrissey, his smile even broader than before, "I reckon that you got your fingers crossed when you say that! You don't mean what you say, sir."

"If I did," said Stevens, with a sort of savage curiosity, "I suppose that you'd put your buggy whip on my back, eh?"

"No, sir, Mr. Stevens," said the giant. "As sure's my name's Budge Morrissey, this black man don't lay no hands on folks; not unless his boss tells him to do it."

"Maybe you got the scrapings and the savings of some common sense in you," admitted Zeke Stevens. "But I guess you found a boss that keeps you standin' around and up to snuff. He works you, I see!"

"Mr. Stevens, sir," said the big man, "mostly Mr. Joseph never speaks to me except he says 'Please,' and he never tells me what to do or what he wants cooked or anything else. You'd pretty near think that Budge Morrissey owned that house and ran it, to see the way he sits so quiet and does his thinking."

"Don't lie to me, you fool," said Zeke Stevens. "I see you workin' your hands to the bone. I see you diggin' in the garden and patchin' fences, takin' care of the horses and a couple of cows, and everything else that comes along!"

"Because I want to," said Budge Morrissey, smiling more broadly than ever. "And if I was to sit down durin' the day, that wife of mine, that Betsy, she'd go and find something new for me to do."

"Betsy is a grand girl," said Zeke Stevens. "You went and married above yourself, Budge."

"I sure did, Mr. Stevens," said Budge. "But Betsy says my luck getting her wasn't nothing like my luck in getting Mr. Joseph for a boss. And I guess she's right."

"Then get on about your business," said Zeke, as though in anger. "Get along with you. Your time belongs to your boss. Don't you be wasting no more of it."

"Thank you, sir," said Budge.

Lifting his hat, he clucked to the mustangs and drove

on again, the pair thrusting with hardened mouths against the bits, bucking with eagerness to bolt, but easily held, both of them, by one iron hand of the driver.

"Yeah, he's quite a man," suggested Wally Chase. "I guess that Fort Willow ain't wrong in thinking that he's quite some."

Martin looked thoughtfully after the disappearing roadster, but he merely said, as he turned: "We'll have a look at the inside of that saloon, that Pemberton place, now."

"Hold on," said Wally Chase. "He's not there, but that's him. There he comes down the street!"

"That little feller on that little chestnut?" asked Martin.

"Little?" said Wally Chase. "Well, he ain't so big, but nobody else stays looking very big in front of him. He whittles 'em down to his own size. That chestnut is a thoroughbred, and it's the fastest and toughest thing on the range. It's desert-bred and raised, Charley. And don't make no mistake about that kid, Joe Good. You'll find his size all you wanta handle."

At last Martin ventured an opinion: "A good big man is better than a good little man. The folks sort of like that kid in this here town."

"Sure, they like him. Look at them wave and holler to him. Look at the smart way he sits up there in the saddle in them fine togs. And him no better than a bum a while ago. I used to look down on him. I wouldn't hardly speak to him a while ago."

"Is that Pemberton's that he's stopping in front of?"

"That's it."

"He doesn't hitch his mare."

"It'll stand where he puts it."

"Every day except the wrong day!" said the outlaw through his teeth.

After young Joe Good had entered the saloon, the two heard a faint outcry, a hailing in his honor. And instantly half a dozen more men came hurrying across the street to join the drinking.

"He makes business for that saloon," said Martin. "He oughta have free drinks for the business that he brings."

"Hey, look!" said Wally Chase.

There was a whistle from inside the saloon. The mare

at once stepped onto the pavement, put its bright head in at the saloon window, then turned, nosed the swinging doors open, and entered the saloon, letting the doors rub gently against its sides.

20

There was a considerable outbreak of voices from inside the Pemberton saloon; and now a little mongrel dog ran down the street and ducked in under the same pair of swinging doors.

"That's his cur," said Wally.

"He's an animal trainer, too, is he?" said Martin. "He's trained this town, at least, so's it follers at his heels. It's plain that no gun could be pulled on him in Fort Willow. So we'll have to fish him out of the town, like I said before."

"You mind telling me how he's to be fished?" asked Chase, exasperated.

"He's the king of the town, ain't he?" demanded Martin.

"Yeah. I've showed you that he is."

"And his pride is up as far as high C, eh?"

"Yeah. He's proud, all right."

"Then if he was shamed, he would go around the world to wipe out the feller that shamed him, I suppose. Don't ask me any more questions. But just go into that saloon and get close to young Mr. Good and speak to him. I'll take care of the rest."

"I ain't any too welcome in the Pemberton saloon," complained Wally Chase.

"Do what I tell you to do," answered Martin. "Lemme run this show for a while, if you don't mind."

— Chase grunted with disapproval, but there appeared nothing for him to say. Finally he gathered his courage and resolution and marched in through the swinging doors; Martin followed much later.

To Joseph Good the drinking of a glass of beer every day in the saloon of Pemberton was a regular affair. It was never more than one glass, but it was always taken in a large company of his friends and admirers. They had the advantage of seeing their hero, and he had the advantage of finding a number of people pooled together, so many that they could tell almost every item of news or gossip that had circulated through the town.

And that was why Joe Good came to the place. He knew that the Alton clan was savagely ready to reach for him with knives, guns, or poison, even; he knew that every day that brought the trial of Hugh Alton nearer brought Good himself into fierce danger. Therefore he was eager to talk with the people of the town. They also, though dimly and vaguely, understood the danger that was gathering closely around their hero, and every move of every Alton, observed by the people of Fort Willow, was sure to be rehearsed in Mort Pemberton's saloon the next day.

In a way it was likely to drive the Altons to more subtle and underground workings; but in another sense, it was a fine thing for the boy to have this congress of informers.

It was not altogether easy, however. He had to repay and reward them in one way or another. He had to be sure to remember all names and faces. He had to be as aware of all around him as is a politician; his twisted smile had to appear on his face more often.

Besides, there were tricks of his of which they never tired. Most of all, they loved to spin coins down the bar, shooting them along at high speed, while the boy stood off and picked them off with the black snake.

Whatever he did with that famous whip was sure to be greeted with smile, admiration, and applause. He could make it disappear up his sleeve, to lie coiled snugly around his forearm, ready for instant use. He could make it flow over his shoulders, writhing like a snake, or twisting in involved loops. But the most celebrated trick of all was when he made the thing spring up from the palm of his hand until it seemed to stand, for an instant, balanced and supported on its thin lash, while the loaded handle hovered aloft, or seemed to hover, like the head of a viper.

It was a wonderfully and rather gruesomely lifelike imitation. Then the handle head dripped over and dropped back into the slender palm of Joe Good, and the whole loaded length of the thin whip disappeared up his arm, there to wait for use.

When young Good was in the saloon, people kept by mutual consent at arm's length; it enabled more of them to see his next casual, laughing performance, whereas if they had crowded close, his scant five feet eight or nine of height would have been quite lost under the screen of their lofty, massive shoulders. Even for the West, the men of Fort Willow were very big.

On this day, however, there were no whip tricks. The mare took the center of the stage, instead.

"What's the news with you?" asked one of his friends.

"Nothing new with me," said the boy. "But Molly may know something. I forgot to ask her this morning."

"Who's Molly?" asked a newcomer to Fort Willow who happened to be present.

"Molly's the mare," came the muttered answer from another bystander.

"Molly talks to you, Joe, eh?" said another, grinning expectantly.

"She talks to me," nodded Joe Good gravely.

"About the Altons, maybe?"

The boy merely smiled.

"She's a gossip," said he. "Women are apt to be that way."

Bart Collins had started his drinking seriously and early that morning, and now he roared: "Bring her in and talk to her now, will you, Joe?"

The crowd laughed. "Bring her in, Joe," urged Mort Pemberton with the widest of grins. "Let's hear her talk, all of us."

"All right," said Joe Good, and he whistled one note, not overloud.

The mare then crossed the sidewalk; its head appeared at the window, and a shout of welcome and surprise greeted it.

"This way in, Molly," said Joe Good, pointing to the door. And straightway in Molly came, nosing the swinging doors deftly apart and going straight to its master and standing before him with eyes shining.

"I'm not seeing very clearly this morning, Molly," said

the boy. "How many people are in the room here with me?"

Instantly it began to tap, rapidly, lightly, on the floor with its forefoot. Fifteen beats she made. There were fifteen men in the room besides its master.

"Great Scott," muttered some one, "she can count better'n I can!"

"That's nothing," grinned Mort Pemberton. "I guess she spent more time in school than you, Lefty."

"Fifteen you say?" said the master. "All friends?"

The mare's head nodded. A shout of applause answered the gesture.

"I know you're thirsty, old girl," said Joe Good. "Take what you want, anything from whisky to beer. Stack a couple of bottles on the bar, will you, Mort?"

Mort Pemberton, delighted, placed on the bar a bottle of good old whisky and another of frosty cold beer.

"Help yourself, Molly," said Joe Good, pointing.

The mare went to the bottles at once, sniffed the whisky and backed away, shaking its head. A loud cheer went up in the barroom.

"She don't want the kind of poison that you handle, Mort!" they told the laughing barman.

It came again, and this time sniffed the open beer bottle, gathered the throat of it carefully between teeth and lips, and then raised the bottle high. Its contents began to foam and flow. Wild shouts and hand clappings and stampings upon the floor greeted this feat.

"Look at her eyes half closed," said Lefty. "She knows her beer when she tastes it, Mort!"

The mare lowered the bottle safely to the bar again and looked again to its master.

"You might wipe your mouth, Molly," said the master. "Where will people think that you've been raised if you don't show better manners than this? Forget your handkerchief? Well, you can have mine."

He threw it on the bar, and the men crowded to see her press her velvet muzzle on the cloth, and then pick it up and return it to Joe Good. He pretended that he did not see the proffer, and presently she nosed open a side pocket of his coat and left the handkerchief in it.

Like bright-eyed children, those unshaven men looked on breathlessly.

"Well, Molly," said Joe Good, "we might as well talk things over. But I'm tired. Can you find a chair around here for me?"

The chestnut mare went with pricking ears to the line of chairs along the wall, picked one up in its teeth, holding it by the top crosspiece, and brought it back. Joe Good sank into it with a sigh of relief. Gurgles of laughter were instantly subdued as the master continued: "You might as well sit down yourself. Makes me uncomfortable to see you standing. Sit down, Molly and be a little sociable."

And at this its hind quarters sank slowly. It sat on its haunches, straight before Joe Good.

There was no end to the applause at this, and a very absurd and delightful picture Molly made, sitting down as if to talk, and actually talking, it seemed, if speech can be in bright, mischievous eyes.

"The best tricks and the smartest hoss that I ever seen," declared big Lefty. "The whole dog-gone crowd is gunna liquor in her honor. Stand up here to the bar."

"Stand up and thank the gentleman, Molly," said Joe Good. "You might shake hands with him, I think."

She went—it seemed miraculous that she could find the right man—and presented a polished forehoof to Lefty, who seized it and shook it with earnest acknowledgment.

Then, as the crowd lined up at the bar, Molly stood behind the master and rested a velvet, black chin on his shoulder.

"She's whispering in my ear that you're a good fellow, Lefty," said Joe Good, "and she says that beer of yours is the best she's had in a long time, Mort."

"Hello, Joe," said a husky voice close to him.

And there stood Wally Chase, grinning in a twisted way and holding out his hand.

"Hello, Wally," said Joe Good soberly.

"Not shaking hands?" asked Wally. "Can't you forget old grudges and shake hands, Joe?"

"I can't shake hands with you, Wally," said Joe Good coldly.

And then a voice on his other side said with a sudden fierceness: "Who are you—too proud to shake hands with any man? You gutter pup, here's a good lesson in manners for you."

Joe turned, ready, alert for trouble. But that trouble

was already on the wing. Even then the boy was able to dodge, but the blow of Martin's fist that was aimed at Good's jaw landed high up near his temple, instead. It dropped him like a shot!

21

In every part of that room, as the blow was struck, there was a flash of guns; not a single one of the fifteen failed to bring out a revolver, and every man of the lot meant business.

But Lefty said: "No gun play. That was fists!"

Martin sneered down at the fallen body.

"It was time for him to learn something from a growed-up man," said Martin, and strode for the door.

"Wait a minute," said Mort Pemberton. "That was dirty work. He didn't give the kid a chance to put up his hands. Stop, there, stranger!"

But Martin was already through the door and in the street.

"Get him, somebody!" said another. "Come on with me!"

They poured straightway through the door, angry men, with angry faces, but saw Martin already mounting a long-legged horse in front of the hardware store. In response to their challenge to halt, he put the horse at a full gallop and rounded the next corner.

"You see what he's done?" said big Lefty. "He's come and taken a sock at the kid, and that way he's made fools of us all. That's what he's done!"

"He's tried to show up Fort Willow!" agreed another. "And dog-gone me if he ain't done it."

"What'll the kid do about it?"

"I'll tell you what Joe'll do about it," said Lefty. "He'll run that hound down if the trail takes him clear around the world. That's what he'll do."

They went back inside the saloon to find that Joe Good,

rather pale of face, his eyes still glassy, had been helped to his feet.

Then he laid a hand on the bar edge, steadied himself for a moment, and shook his head when a drink was offered.

At last, looking up, he said: "Does anybody know the fellow who did that?"

"I know him," said a middle-aged man in a corner of the room. "I know him too dog-gone well. That's Charley Martin, boys!"

The boiling anger of the crowd turned to cold fear and horror.

"Martin?" exclaimed Mort Pemberton. "It couldn't be him. Martin would never dare show his face inside of any town."

"Martin, he'd dare anything," said the other. "I reckon that he didn't have no excitement and nothing to keep him busy. That's about the way of it. And he come down here to rile Joe Good and lead him off on a paper chase. But don't you go after him, Joe. You'll never catch him, for one thing; you'll only catch a slug of lead between the eyes. That's all."

Joe Good, staring straight before him, was seeing with his mind's eye many things—very many things indeed. For the tales of Martin had drifted up and down the range for fifteen years, now. Perhaps he could not have performed all of the atrocities that were attributed to him, but he was guilty of certain known things that were horrible enough. Murder for its own sake was his talent and his passion.

"Where's Wally Chase gone to?" he asked.

"He's here. No, he seems to have faded out of the picture. Must've slipped away somewhere."

"Wally makes the opening, and the other fellow slugs me," said Joe Good. "They worked a little game up between 'em."

Mort Pemberton nodded.

"It was fixed. It's the last time that sneaking hound of a Chase ever gets inside the door of my place, I can tell you," said Mort.

"Does anybody know where Martin has been hanging out mostly of late?" asked the boy.

"Up in the hole-in-the-wall country north of Cronin Pass," said some one. "That's where he generally hangs out, people say. But nobody knows, except some of his friends, and they keep their mouths shut about him, of course."

"Has that Martin, has he got any friends, really?" asked Lefty.

"People that take care of him, anyway, call them friends or not," answered Mort Pemberton. "They get plenty of money out of him. And then suppose that they try to double-cross him; what happens? The police are likely to slip, and then Martin will pay 'em for double-crossing him. And he always pays in red, everybody knows. He puts his pen in nearest the heart!"

"Thanks," said Joe Good softly, and went from the saloon, the mare following him like a dog.

As for the small mongrel which generally followed at his heels, it was now down the street, lying at the hitching rack in front of the Tomlinson Hardware Store.

The crowd remained inside the saloon, looking darkly upon one another and exchanging murmurs.

A middle-aged man, however, followed the boy to the street and laid a hand on his shoulder, saying: "Don't you do it, son. Don't you go and do it! Who'll gain by you going?"

"I may be able to take care of Martin," said Joe Good, his lips pressing together.

The older man looked into the face of the boy with tired, earnest eyes. "I don't think that you can. About all that you'd get out of it would be a long ride and a bullet through the head. Martin ain't like anybody that you've ever met before."

"Maybe not," said Joe Good. "He'll shoot from behind, they say."

"He's like an Indian," said the other. "A scalp is all that he wants, and the best way to get a scalp is the way that's the safest for the fellow who finally lifts the hair. Other people like to play fair and win fair and square, but Martin don't care about no reputation, partly because he ain't got none, and partly because he's a nacheral murderer."

Joe Good considered the other with care.

"I think you're a stranger to me," he said.

"Yeah. I'm new to town. You never seen me before today, Good."

"Will you tell me who you are, and how you happen to know so much about Martin?"

"I don't mind telling you; but I'm not telling every-body. I'm Sid Sawtell. And I'm first cousin to Martin. I've known him all my life. I know what I'm talking about when I tell you that no man can ever handle him! Not up there in his own country, anyway."

"No man?"

Sid Sawtell shook his head.

"I know that you're clever, Good," said he. "And I know that you're brave, too. It takes a man to stand with a black snake against a Colt and a bowie knife. And you did that. But that's a parlor trick compared with what you'll need to be able to do when you get to Martin's country."

"Thank you a lot," answered the boy. "But I've got to go. You know how it is. He came down to start a game, and he's tagged me first. I want to tag him back."

The other nodded.

"I knew that I couldn't do nothing with you," he said. "But I had to try. And I'll tell you another thing that might turn out useful for you before the finish."

"What's that?"

"Every house that you go into up there you'll have to be careful of. Because you can't tell who might be under the thumb of that hound of a Martin. He's got beggars, and he's got folks that seem respectable on his list. You ain't safe till you know you're safe. And you wouldn't be safe in the country until you shot Martin and felt his heart and found it still. He's been left for dead before. But he's still got some of his nine lives left to him."

"Thanks again," said young Joe Good. "Between you and me, I think that I'm on a hopeless trail. But I've got to stick at it. Good-by."

He shook hands with the other, mounted on Molly, and cantered straight down the street to the place where the Professor was lying in the dust. Up jumped the lithe little dog and trotted around the corner, looking back at its master.

"What d'you mean by that, Professor?" called Joe Good. "This way, son! Straight down the street."

But the Professor sat down and barked defiantly.

Joe Good considered. But he well knew from of old the uncanny wits of the Professor; after all, the dog had seen the other man strike him. It was not at all beyond the possibilities that he had struck out on the trail of the enemy.

So he rode Molly down the alley to the place where it ended in a cattle path, and now, clearly printed, he saw the widely spaced tracks made by a horse at full gallop, and, leaning far down from the saddle, he made out the grains of sand still crumbling down the sides of the indentations, a sure proof that the marks had been imprinted only a few moments before.

The Professor was probably right, therefore. And Joe Good rode on.

Presently the little dog had turned to the right and was streaking along at a round pace. Joseph Good, following the new direction, saw that it pointed straight toward the Cronin Pass, and then he was certain that the Professor had been right from the start.

A weird feeling of fate came over him as he looked toward the big mountains that guarded the pass.

Once before, not so very long ago, he had marched through that pass, driving a burro before him, anxious to escape from his past into any new land; now he was riding in the same direction, filled with only one thought, which was to uphold the reputation which he had built for himself in the interim. The old Joe Good was dead, it seemed; that lazy, careless, shiftless fellow; a new man sat in the saddle and guided the good mare forward.

Yet a certain despair came over him as he looked toward the ragged mountains to the north of the pass. It was as rough a wilderness as any hunter of hard game could desire, and he, Joe Good, was to beat the coverts of the forests and hunt through the icy crags above timber line armed only with a black snake!

It made him feel like a fool, but a desperate fool was he; and, setting his lean jaw, he fixed his glance before him and followed the dog.

22

The nose of the Professor was of that hair-trigger variety which reads scents as the human ear reads sounds or the human eye scans words. Neither wolf nor bloodhound could have availed better to follow the trail and lead the master along it.

The Professor was a cheerful worker. He never stopped trotting along except now and again to sniff some new and enchanting odor, or to puzzle for an instant over some forking of the ways; or now and again to lap a bit of water where a mountain rivulet came across the way. And always he was looking back to Joe Good, laughing with red tongue, open mouth, and bright, dancing eyes.

Until mid-afternoon, when they were climbing to the top of the Cronin Pass, Joe Good still nourished a hope that he might be able to overtake the gunman before the latter was immersed in the forests of his native highlands. But by the early afternoon it was plain that the fugitive was far in the lead and could not be overtaken. So the boy resigned himself to a long hunt.

It was a bitter thing to him, to be sure. The trial of Hugh Alton and his clan for the murder of Vincent Good was now posted for a date not many days away, and the case of the prosecution would certainly fall flat unless Joe Good could take the witness stand.

A very happy coincidence for the whole Alton tribe it would be if, when the name of Joe Good was called for the witness stand, he was still laboring through the mountains in search of the man who had struck him in the saloon at Fort Willow. No, if he were still alive, he could certainly leave off the hunt long enough to attend the trial.

But would he be alive?

Only a fool would have undertaken such a quest with a feeling of perfect confidence; and young Joseph Good was not such a fool. He realized that every word that Sid Sawtell had spoken had been laden with truth; and before him stretched an almost impossible wilderness. It would become a question not so much of how he might come to the outlaw, but of how the outlaw might come to him. Nothing could save him except a hand-to-hand fight; if he stood more than ten feet away when the great Martin drew a gun he was a dead man; for that famous man slayer would never miss his mark.

It was not hard for the boy to guess at the influence of the Altons behind this affair. The thing was too pat, too plainly in their favor to be an accident!

Well, this was one more score to mark up against them. Perhaps in the end he would be able to pay them all off at a single stroke!

A mirthless smile twisted his lips as he thought of that possibility.

Now he had to turn to the left and ride north from the pass into the tangle of higher mountains, darkened by forests adrip with recent rains. It was close, careful, and dangerous work every step of the way.

His own eyes could not really serve him very well. In every mile he passed, there were at least half a dozen perfect lurking places for the enemy—and that enemy, he had been warned, was one who killed from ambush by preference.

He had to depend upon the sensitiveness of his advance guard, the little Professor, who was scrambling ahead of him, very weary now, but incessantly weaving from side to side and studying the ground scents, now with lowered head, now reading the stories that streaked through the higher air. He would be exquisitely precise, Joe Good knew from old experience. But still there was always the possibility that the great Martin had doubled far back on his original trail and now lay crouched somewhere beside it down wind.

It was down wind that the boy constantly gave his best attention as he studied the trees that drifted past him, then the tangles of rock, and trees again.

Darkness began to draw down on him as he reached a clearing in a shallow ravine and saw in the open space a little, wretched, knock-kneed shack with a cattle shed beyond it and a moldering haystack beside the shed.

It was not much of a hostelry, but it would have to do for him this evening.

As he came up he saw an old man seated just outside the door peeling potatoes and dropping them with a chime and rattle of tin into the dishpan on the ground beside him.

He was very old, with a sweep of gray beard, and he had on a pair of large spectacles that gave to his face an air of great and abstracted thought.

Behind those glasses he looked up at the boy.

"Evening, stranger," said he. "Put your hoss up in the shed and throw her a feed, and then come in and rest yourself. Supper's gunna be ready in a coupla jiffies."

Joe Good was heartened by this ready hospitality. It matters not the hotel when the host is kindly.

So he put up the mare, as he had been invited to do, and found in the shed four stalls, in one of which a horse was then standing. It was not odd that live stock needed shelter in this region, where snows were deep in the winter and frightful storms might blow up at any time of the year; but it seemed odd to the boy that the horse in the stall of this poverty-ridden shack should be of such quality. It was a long-limbed bay, with a fine, bony head, and plenty of substance and girth to the barrel. He admired the gelding for a moment, then rubbed down Molly, fed her, and returned to the house with the Professor scouting here and there before him, still eager.

His host was inside the shack now, working up a roaring, shuddering fire inside the little iron stove. The smell of coffee, stewing meat and baking bread all reached the nostrils of Joe Good, and he was content.

His host was garrulous to a degree. All the time that he worked over the stove he was talking.

He said: "That a new breed or a chance breed—that dog, stranger?"

"A chance breed, so far as I know," said Joe Good.

"Some of the best is some of the chanciest," declared the cook, while the boy looked around the room at the three bunks that lined the walls, and the moldering clothes that hung from pegs, together with an array of saddles, bridles, bits of broken leather, a thousand huddled fragments. "But the trouble with a half-breed is that it ain't no good in the next litter. They don't carry on true."

"I've heard that before," said Joe Good.

"But," said the philosopher, "I'll tell you this, too. What does a man want with the second generation when he's likely to be dead and gone himself in the first? What I say is, always get what's handy for the time you want it, and then throw it away when it's wore out.

"Patches, they save money, but they cost time, and I'd rather be ragged and full of holes than have to set down and waste myself on the sewing on of patches. Here's Doc coming up the hill, I reckon. Take a look, will you?"

"I don't know Doc when I see him," said the boy.

"He'll have a rod over his shoulder and a string of fish hangin' out of one hand."

From the door, Joe Good looked out and saw a big young man, his face darkened by the dull evening light, and a short growth of beard that covered his skin to the very eyes. The rod was over his shoulder, but there were no fish in his hand.

He reported this.

"No fish?" said the host. "What's the matter with Doc, anyway?"

He called out loudly: "What's the matter, Doc? Ain't you no good any more for nothing?"

"Aw, shut your face, Bill, will you?" said Doc gloomily.

He stamped into the shack, waved a silent hand at the guest, and then leaned his fishing rod in a corner of the room, against the ladder that communicated with the loft above.

"We can get along without the fish, though," said the host. "I seen a big jack rabbit a-skulking along a while back, and I went and got the rifle and took the nose off of that rabbit. He run in a circle for a while, so's I had to set down and laugh my head off. But pretty soon the bleeding begun to settle him, and he lay down in his tracks and died. They die plumb easy; rabbits always do."

"Not them that are out in the desert," said Doc. "Them are real man-rabbits, them are. You gotta shoot the head off of 'em, and even then they'll keep on running long enough to fall down into a hole where you can't fish 'em out."

"Why didn't you get no fish?" asked the old man.

"Because I couldn't find no proper bait."

"Hey! Didn't I tell you where the worms would always—"

"I figgered that I'd try grubs," said the other. "Hunted around under logs and got some, but they wasn't the proper kind. The fish wouldn't bite them none."

"And you wouldn't go and get some of them worms, would you? You had to experiment, you did. You'll starve yourself to death one of these days experimenting," said Bill.

"Aw, shut up," said Doc, with both contempt and disgust. "Who's got this dog. Is this your dog, stranger?"

"Yes," said the boy.

"Don't look like much of a dog," said Doc.

Joe Good was irritated by this criticism more than if it had been leveled at himself.

He said: "You can't judge that dog very easily. I'll tell you why. It has things about it that you don't see."

"What?" snapped Doc.

"Brains," said Joe Good.

The old man laughed heartily.

"That's one on you, Doc," he said. "Brains! You can't see brains, you know. And maybe you wouldn't recognize them very quick even if you could see 'em!"

He laughed again.

Doc looked up at both of the others, then changed his mind about speaking, finished pulling off his boots, thrust his feet and tattered socks into slippers, and walked outside the shack, merely saying: "Rustle along that chuck, will you? And stop shooting off your face!"

"That was a good one on Doc," chuckled Bill contentedly. "He couldn't see brains, and them is what the dog has got!"

He laughed again as he worked over the stove.

23

Young Joe Good saw, as any one could have done with half an eye, that his younger host was by no means pleased. But Joe did not care very greatly. There was a time, not so many months before, when he would have been overawed by the mere thought of the anger of such a formidable fellow. His greasy, dirty shirt clung to muscles that flowed in waves over his broad shoulders. But Joe Good was a changed man since that day when he had watched the eagle fly above the fish hawk; that day which seemed ages ago, in the heart of Cronin Pass.

"Chuck's ready! Chuck's ready!" called Bill, and hammered on the bottom of a pan.

Doc came in.

"Where's Dunker?" he demanded.

"How would I know where Dunker is?" said Bill. "You better ask the dog where Dunker is. The dog has brains. It might know."

"The dog has more brains than you, you old fool!" said Doc.

"Sure, he has more brains than me," said Bill contentedly, still laughing at that. "He's gotta have more brains than me, because he has more brains than you. Ain't the kid said that his dog has got more brains than you?"

Doc turned slowly on the boy.

"He didn't say that," declared Doc. "He ain't such a fool."

"No, I didn't say that," said the boy. "Bill has twisted things around a little."

"You didn't say that your dog has more brains than me," declared Doc. "But you said more'n enough. You were fresh, understand? You were shooting off your face!"

124

"Was I?" said the boy.

The rage of Doc ran up to the boiling point. He strode to where Joe Good sat and towered above him.

Old Bill looked on with an affectionate eye at this growing brawl.

"You be careful now, Doc," said he. "You be careful, because you never know what sort of a sting one of them little fellers is likely to have. Might cut you to bits, that little kid, there!"

"Might he?" said Doc, stifling his rage. "Might he? Why, I'm gunna teach him a lesson in manners, is what I'm gunna teach him. Come on here out of the house, where I got room to teach you, you little runt!"

He took Joe Good by the nape of the neck, dragged him to the door, and flung him staggering out into the open.

"Now, Doc," said Bill, "that ain't any way to treat a guest. That ain't nice, is it?"

The fury of Doc was now feeding itself, however. And nothing could contain it. His big, powerful hands did not seem enough to him. He picked up a stout, iron-shod staff such as the mountaineers used on their winter marches; with that grasped in his hand he rushed on out at the boy.

He had not one of all the people of Fort Willow to tell him what trouble he was running toward. And old Bill, looking contentedly on at the approaching brawl, still laughed with an evil content, as one who cares not what the action is, so long as action there be!

The first thought of Doc seemed to be to thrust with the spearlike point of the staff. But a good, downright blow over the shoulders then appeared to him the better way. So he heaved up the weighty walking stick and let drive at the smaller man.

Joe Good had remained where he was, seeming curious rather than excited. But now, from his right hand, out flew a shadowy streak, and the lean, iron-hard lash end of a black snake wrapped itself around the right wrist of Doc.

Jerked back again, the uncurling lash burned off the skin and some of the flesh, as well.

The staff fell from the hand of Doc. He leaped up into the air like a stricken deer. His howl rang far away and was joined by the nearer, answering echoes.

Still he danced and clutched his injured wrist; he turned to flee into the house and grasp a shotgun that stood significantly by the door, but he had hardly made a step when the lithe lash of the whip curled about one ankle and he was jerked to the ground, his face downward.

The spur that now urged him to his feet was the same darting, curling lash, which almost cut its way through his shirt.

"Get up and dance some more," said Joe Good. "I don't like your lesson in manners, Doc, but I like your dancing."

The burning cut of the lash brought Doc screeching to his feet, insane with pain and fury.

He turned blindly, his hands outstretched.

The gun was one way, but the bare hands were even a better way. He would wring the slender neck of Joe Good; he would smash in the very face of that youth and make him a featureless mask forever!

So he came in, with this blindness of hatred on him, and the gloating laughter of old Bill floated like a streak of lightning through the mad welter of his brain.

But the shadow flew out again from the hand of Joe Good, and the loaded handle of the black snake, darting like the head of a snake, struck home across the jaw of the mountaineer.

It stunned him. It rocked him back on his heels. And as he howled with fear and wonder and the pain of the blow, again the black snake cut him, this time on the legs, fairly biting into the flesh through the thickness of the trousers as it could bite, indeed, through the thickness of hide that armors the back of a mule.

Doc leaped instinctively into the air.

"That's better," said Joe Good. "That's better dancing, Doc. But keep the steps high. I like 'em high, and more of 'em. Dance big and dance fast."

"I'm gunna break you in two and tear you apart," said Doc. "I'm gunna—"

The lash bit the other leg like a gadfly, and he bounded again, interrupting the current of his threats.

Now, carefully covering his head with both arms against the clublike, stunning stroke of the black-snake end, he strove to rush in once more.

He only invited a darting sword stroke that flashed through his guard and cut him across the forehead.

No, to run in on this demon was like running in on a leveled gun. He swerved and lunged again for the house. Again the lash caught him by the heel and downed him with shocking force. Again the whip stroke seared the flesh of his back through the meager protection of his shirt. As he sprang to his feet he saw the maddening picture of old Bill, reeling in the doorway and supporting himself through the sea of his laughter by clutching the door jamb with both hands. Tears of joy streamed down the face of Bill and moistened his beard. He had taken off his spectacles because the water-dimmed glasses now impeded his sight.

Doc wanted to kill Bill even more than he wanted to kill the young fiend who carried the whip. But as he lurched for Bill, getting to his feet, the lash caught him around the neck and jerked him back with a moment's strangle hold.

He turned, literally screaming, no words in his voice, only ghastly passion.

"Dance," said Joe Good, unmoved. "Let me see you dance again, brother. Don't try to run again, or I'll cut you to the bone; but dance, now, you brute!"

The darting lash bit at both legs in turn. Doc bounded high, and he bounded fast. He dared not put down a foot, for the instant it touched the earth the lash seemed ready to sting him like a serpent.

So, frantically he bounded up and up and up. Exhaustion from his frantic effort made his breath come fast, his eyes started in his bearded face, and his brain reeled with the effort. Finally Joe Good said: "The next time you'll know how to treat strangers with respect. The next time you'll be hospitable, Doc, I think. Now you can run away and cool yourself off, my friend."

As Doc turned, the whiplash scored his back again. He fled, staggering, moaning, mumbling, frothing at the mouth. He fled with shame already sinking its poisonous fangs in his heart.

For the scene had been witnessed. The tale would go the rounds of the mountains, told with large embroiderings by old Bill—how Doc started to beat a stranger, a young slip of a boy, and how the boy licked him, stood and made him dance.

Joe Good went back to the door of the house.

He said: "I'd better be going along, Bill. I can't be welcome here after this."

It was a moment before Bill could speak, the sobbings of his joy still strangling his voice.

Then, still staggering, still leaning against the side of the door, he said: "I never seen such a funny thing. That's the funniest thing that ever happened in the mountains. And it'll do Doc good. He got so's he couldn't hardly be lived with. Always cursing everything and everybody. There's too much strength in the hands of Doc, and he can shoot straight, too. It wasn't fair, so many gifts all shoved into the hands of one young feller, like he had 'em. But he can see that there's better things than all he had. He can see that in this here world what rules is brains—and whips!"

He suddenly broke off to laugh again, and then pressed Joe Good to enter.

"You come in here and set yourself down," he invited. "It's gunna be all right. He'll come back after a while."

"He saw you laughing at him," said Joe Good. "He may do you a harm, Bill."

Bill instantly grew sober.

"He may do me a harm?" he said, while a sudden light sprang into his black eyes. "Oh, he may raise the devil here and there, but he'll never do me a harm, my lad. He'll never lift his hand agin' old Bill. He ain't such a fool as that. Not with Dunker around."

Then he added: "We ain't gunna wait. We'll set ourselves down and start to eat. They can eat cold chuck, if they wanta, later on, but it's dog-gone strange that Dunker ain't here."

24

They had hardly sat down when a stumpy, bowlegged man came into the shack, nodded at Bill and said "How d'ye do" to Joe Good. Without taking off his hat, simply pushing it farther back over the matted hair of his head, he sat down at the table and helped himself to the big pot of beans by dipping his tin plate into the pot and bringing it out, heaping and dripping.

The dripping edge he cleaned with a chunk of bread, which he then swallowed, and now, leaning forward, he took a cooking spoon as a tool and began to shovel the beans into his great, hairy mouth.

After that first glance, Joe Good strictly avoided looking at the third man of the shack.

Old Bill, however, regarded him with an affectionate approval.

"That's the way Dunker is," said Bill. "Sets down and grabs the first thing that comes his way. He don't care what it is. Beans, maybe. Just starts in eating, and never asks for no second course. He's an easy man to cook for, Dunker is. Ain't you, Dunker?"

"Huh?" said Dunker vaguely through a mouth filled with beans and now further corked with a wad of bread.

He finished his plate of beans, and paying no heed to the meat or the boiled potatoes, he helped himself to more beans in exactly the same fashion.

As he was devouring these, old Bill smiled upon him more affectionately than ever.

"Always the same, year in and year out, old Dunker is," said he. "Never gets no new fashions. Always sticks to the same old ones. Always happy. Always good-natured. Never complains none. It's never hot for Dunker, and it's never cold. Wears the same clothes all the year through, and he thinks always the same kind of thoughts. Dunker is what I call bedrock, because you always can depend upon him, is what you can do! Always can depend on good old Dunker; can't a man depend on you, Dunker?"

"Huh?" said Dunker, extending his tin cup.

Old Bill filled the cup with steaming hot coffee. Dunker began to drink it. He held the cup in both hands and closed his eyes, and warmed his face in the steam that rose from the liquid, which he took in noisy inhalations.

Bill observed: "That's old Dunker. When he gets to coffee he's done. Never changes his mind and goes back for molasses and pone, say, nor no delicacies like that. But when he gets to coffee, then he's through. Gets to coffee, drinks it, and then he goes and sets and smokes one pipe, and then he goes to bed. Don't you, Dunker?"

"Huh?" said Dunker, lost in the joy of the black coffee.

The coffee gone, he indicated that his meal was ended by turning his cup upside down on his tin plate. Then he went to the door, took a stool just outside, and sat there in the last of the twilight, smoking. It seemed to the boy, from the fumes, that old leather must be filling that pipe.

Said Bill: "That's the way with old Dunker. Always the same. Like a clock. Goes round and round. Any minute of night or day, you can tell where he'll be pointing. Look at that, now!"

Dunker, having finished his pipe, knocked out the ashes, came inside, and went to bed.

This was a simple procedure, for he removed neither coat, shirt, nor trousers; simply kicked off his shoes, and giving a blanket one twist around him, lay down with his face to the wall and pulled his hat a little to one side of his head.

"You can talk right on and right out loud," said old Bill, "because it won't wake up Dunker none. He'll be snoring in a coupla shakes. There he goes, tuning up now."

Dunker began to snore, not loudly, but a long and melancholy sound, something like a roughly played violoncello.

Old Bill listened to the sound with an affectionate smile.

"He's a kind of a rest to have around," declared Bill.

"Always know what he's gunna do. Always know what he's gunna say, which is chiefly nothing. Yeah, he's a relief. There ain't so much use in talking in this here world. Actions is what counts. Actions and whips!" He laughed a little, and added: "And old Dunker, he's full of actions!"

Then he added: "Wonder why the kid don't come in for his supper? Wonder what's holding back Doc?"

Joe Good stared. Then he said: "Perhaps he's waiting for me to get out of the way. I'll be going now."

"Going? Going where?"

"Anywhere—away," said Joe Good. "I'll camp out tonight."

"What should you camp out for," said Bill. "There's gunna be a storm tonight. I can smell a storm in the air, is where I can smell it. You climb up the ladder and you'll find some good clean hay. It ain't much, but it's better than nothing to lie on. Don't you bother none about Doc. He's kind of peeved just now, but he'll go and get over it. We all gotta have our ups and downs. He thought that he was growed up and couldn't learn no more, was what he thought. But now he's found out different, and it'll do him a terrible lot of good: what I mean! Don't you bother about him, but when you're ready, you turn in. You can take that lantern if you want. You go right up and get yourself comfortable. Any kind of a roof is better than trees over your head when it thunderstorms the way it's gunna do tonight."

It was not a very cheerful prospect that seemed to lie before Joseph Good, but he accepted the invitation with thanks. He had grown very thoughtful. Now that he was in the hole-in-the-wall country and had his first sight of its people, his task seemed to him more and more difficult. He decided that he would ask a few questions, for questions would have to be asked if he were ever to achieve his goal.

He said: "You have a man named Martin up here in the mountains a good part of the year, don't you?"

A smile was struck from the mouth of old Bill.

"Martin?" he said: "Watcha want with Martin, stranger?"

"What do I want with him?" said the boy. "Why, nothing. But everybody's heard about Martin; and I understood that he lived here in the mountains a lot of the time. I suppose you've never seen him?"

"Man can always be hearing about Martin," said the other evasively. "Because after a fellow gets to a certain height everybody can look at him and try to see him, anyway; and talk, always talk. But there ain't nothing in talk," he concluded. "It don't get these here dishes done, anyway!"

And he rose and fell to work.

It was plain that he did not care to continue the conversation, at least if it had to bear upon the subject under discussion. Joe Good, with a sense of depression, decided that he had better give up the quest with words for the time being, at least.

He said: "I'll give you a hand with those dishes, Bill."

"Rather do 'em by myself," said Bill. "I know how to make every lick count, and the way I get through with these here dishes, why, it's a caution. Don't you go bothering about the dishes."

"Well, then," said the boy, "I'll turn in. And I'll be starting along early in the morning. I'd like to know what I owe you for the supper and the bed, Bill."

"Owe?" said Bill, turning with a frown. "You don't owe me nothing. The hay's up there to be slept on, if anybody wants it. And there's more of it out in the shed than our hosses can eat this here season. As for supper, there wasn't nothing extra cooked for you."

He added with a grin: "You kind of paid your way in advance, before supper started."

With that Joe Good said good night, thanked his host, and climbed the ladder.

He had forgotten the Professor during the last few moments, but the Professor had not forgotten him. As the master hung the lantern on a nail that projected from a rafter, he saw the dog appear through the hole after him. The Professor sat down and watched with interest the unfolding of the blankets, and then, when Good was wrapped in them, he curled himself up at the man's feet.

A strange crowd of impressions out of the day's journeying and of all that had happened in Fort Willow rushed through the mind of the boy. But now he heard the wind rising, perhaps the wind of the thunderstorm which old Bill had spoken about; and the song of the wind lulled Joe Good quickly to sleep.

When he wakened he was far from slept out, and the night was still thick and dark about him. But the little dog was licking his face and whining.

"What's the matter, Professor?" said Joe Good, sitting up, and as he reached a higher level of the air he found it filled with acrid smoke; and to his ears came the crackling of burning wood.

25

He lighted the lantern, his head still dizzy with sleep, and he saw that the entire loft was crowded with smoke. The moment he saw it he wondered that he could breathe in that white mist; he began to cough violently; tears streamed from his stinging eyes as he rapidly dressed.

He reached for the head of the ladder to descend, but found the ladder gone, and craning his neck down into the aperture below, he saw the room below him streaked with smoke, also, and illumined by a ragged patch of fire that was crawling up the inside of the wall.

He was stunned by that sight.

He had thought that it was simply a flaw in the stove chimney that had caused the smoke to pour out. But now, by the light of the burning wall, he saw that the three bunks were deserted and the blankets carried away from them. The gear along the walls, too, was gone; or most of it. The weapons no longer leaned in the corners or hung from hooks. Even the fishing rod and most of the pans that had clustered about the stove had been removed as well.

And now, though his mind could not grasp the reality, he was striving to understand that the house had been deserted by the other occupants, who had set fire to it as they departed. It was a mere trap, now, and he was caught in it.

The wind, humming loudly about the old shack, and making it tremble, seemed to confirm him in the thought. It would burn like a matchbox in such a gale!

Why had they done the thing?

It could hardly be because of the flogging that Doc had

received. That punishment had been richly enough deserved—or so thought Joe Good when he remembered how the burly youth had lifted the iron-shod staff to brain him—but some other reason must have worked upon them.

He could not help remembering then what he had said about Martin—merely a question, to be sure, but it might have started a train of thought behind those uncommonly black eyes of Bill.

Even that would hardly have led them, ruffians as they were, to burn a stranger alive. Some other pressure must have been brought to bear, some pressure which assured them that their house was well burned, and the curse of murder well assumed on all their heads to please another person.

And who could that other be, if not Martin himself?

The thought of that name made all clear enough. Martin had come; Martin had swiftly persuaded the dwellers in the shack that his money was worth more to them than the building. Martin himself had pointed out that the flames would at once destroy the victim and act as a funeral pyre to consume utterly all traces of the crime.

Martin himself, then, was somewhere out there in the darkness with the other three, watching, rifle in hand, with a calm, clear eye, the progress of the fire; waiting until the flames ate the man, or drove him at last out of the bonfire into the open, where bullets would finish him fast enough.

It was all perfectly simple, once that name was supplied. And would not Mr. Hugh Alton, at a date not very distant, hear with distinct pleasure of the demise of the star witness, whose testimony was so likely to wreathe a hangman's rope around his neck and tie a hangman's knot under his ear?

He ground his teeth together when he thought of this. The entire scheme was clearer and clearer. He was first struck in Fort Willow. He was drawn away on a wild-goose chase. And now he was cornered, desperate, and done for!

He went about his work methodically.

First he rolled up his blankets and dropped them through the trapdoor. On top of them he allowed the little dog to fall. The Professor landed light, and looking up, barked an invitation for his master to follow.

Then Joe Good hung by his hands from the rim of the trapdoor, preparatory to falling.

What if one of the ruffians, what if the infallible Martin himself were waiting outside the door of the shack, rifle in hand, prepared to shoot at that dangling, easy mark?

He almost felt the rifle bullet break his back in imagination. Then he dropped, and landed without harm done. The fall was not a long one.

He turned to the door and found it closed securely from the outside.

They preferred to close up the means of egress and let the fire take care of their victim, then?

Yes, the flames would either eat him or else, driving him forth, they would be torches by whose light the waiting riflemen could shoot.

Twice he tried the door with the weight of his shoulder; and twice he fell back from the vain effort.

He tried the wall beside it.

The opposite side of the shack was now burning fast, and the wind, striking from that side, blew the flames inward and filled the little room with fierce heat and with intolerable fumes.

So he flung his weight at the wall beside the door, and two badly nailed planks instantly gave way. They were placed running up and down, the cheapest and the flimsiest form of construction. With a few kicks he knocked them flat, and they made an ample doorway for his exit.

Rifles clanged; bullets whirred with a sharp, whining sound through the air about him. Yes, there were watchers on the outside, and murder was the order of the day!

He retreated and looked desperately about him. All was smoke, and flames writhing through it.

And now, throwing himself flat on the floor, he listened to the small voices of the rifle bullets and heard the deep explosions without.

They knew, apparently, that he could not try the opposite side of the house because of the fierceness with which the wind was fanning the flames. So perhaps they had grouped themselves, all of them, in the opposite direction, waiting for his attempt to break out.

It was frightfully hot now, and the fire was beginning to roar. Long sheets of the flame, as the wind broke through the rotting wall, shot across the room and singed the very hair on his head.

So, lying flat, he held the little dog in his arms to shelter it from the heat, and stared out through the improvised doorway. It was true that the fire lighted the way perfectly; but it also furnished a splendid illumination for marksmen who were by no means accustomed to wasting their bullets as they hunted for game through the mountains. If they could hit a running deer in the dusk, they could hit a running man in such a light at such a range.

There seemed one hope. Not ten strides from the house, grass two and three feet high was growing, high enough to cover the body of a man, if only he could get to it.

He set his teeth and prepared to rise, ready at any moment to run the gantlet.

But then he paused and shook his head.

Ten feet seemed a very short distance, but not when such a marksman as the famous Martin was waiting, rifle at shoulder! It was a vast temptation, but it did not hold water for the boy.

He knew it would be instant death when he showed himself beyond the wall.

There was a crash. A shower of sparks rushed through the room. One of the timbers had fallen and still flamed on the floor. A gust of smoke blew out from the house and rolled away across the shining heads of the grass.

If only that smoke were thicker, he might rush out behind it!

The thought gave him a new idea. Desire is the mother of inspiration. Now he picked up the flaming timber by its unburned end and cast it through the aperture in the wall and out among the grass.

It smoldered; all the flames seemed to go out; and a few whiffs of smoke blew away in the gale.

Looking back with fire-seared face, he saw that the windward wall of the house was wavering under the pressure of the wind. At any moment it might spill inward with a mass of burning fragments.

He stretched himself flat. There were bits of pure air circulating still near the floor, for, of course, the smoke tended to rise. As he lay there, wondering how soon he would be tormented into running out of the collapsing shack, to take in place of fire the sudden mercy of the bullets, the little dog, the Professor, licked his face and whined softly.

He could feel the tremor of that small body against his own. He remembered strange things, many of them long ago; the voice of a preacher and the tormented face of the man as he had said in church on a Sunday: "God stands at the side of the utterly despairing. The sick at heart are his children. Why should the children of God despair?"

There was little religion in Joe Good. But now, as he remembered the saying, his own spirit rose in him like a rushing tide and his strength redoubled.

He looked out through the gap in the wall which he had made. But the grass was no longer visible. Instead, there was a wall of smoke and fire receding from the house—smoke so dense from the green tops of the grass that he could see a very little way into the outer night.

He shook his head, bewildered, unable to understand. Then, suddenly, the thing was clear. The timber he had cast outside had not burned out. The fire had sunk, but the coals, breathed on by the wind, had been sufficient to ignite the grass. Once fired, that field would burn rapidly enough.

Before him that receding wall of smoke that obscured his vision would be obscuring the vision of the riflemen as well!

Hope, that had already begun, was instantly a giant in him.

He rose, flung the little dog before him through the gap in the wall, and rushed out at full speed.

Right and left he heard the clanging of the rifles. They had seen him even through the smoke, but they had seen him only dimly, and the bullets, though they sank close indeed, did not bite home.

He raced with all his might toward the central portion of the outward curving arch of the grass fire. The flames were leaping, but they sprang low. Once through that rim of fire, he ought to be able to run on, completely covered by the thick sheets of smoke, and so come to the greater security of the trees.

Poor little Professor! His bare, padding feet on the fire-crisped coals of the burning grass roots, hopped pitifully before him, looking back at his master.

He scooped up the dog under one arm, reached the rim of the fire, and leaped through it wildly, blindly.

He lost his balance and fell forward.

But instantly he was on his feet at once.

All around him were the whirling, shooting funnels of smoke from the grass, a screen far thicker than he needed, promising, indeed, to stifle him before he got to covert among the trees.

Never had he run as he ran then. But suddenly remembering he dropped flat again in the grass. There was air there. The little dog at his side, gasping, coughing, licking his face, took hold of the shoulder of his coat and urged him forward.

But he, turning up his face, sent out a sharp, piercing whistle.

He waited. Beyond the smoke he could hear voices shouting.

"He's out! Look sharp! He's out of the shack!"

That would be Martin.

Then he heard a beat of hoofs. Rifles were suddenly clanging again. But the sweep of the galloping horse came nearer. He repeated his whistle, and suddenly the form of the horse loomed beside him, unsaddled, unbridled, the ragged end of the broken lead rope dangling beneath her chin.

It was Molly, who had snapped her tether to come at the master's call.

26

From the back of Molly, sweeping her head with the guidance of his hand and the mere pressure of heel or knee, he saw the trees loom before him through the smoke, and then, very suddenly, he was among the stark black trunks. The smoke thinned out. He could breathe; and before him he could see the Professor running, jumping up again and again toward the chin of the mare, so great was his rejoicing to find that all three were together once more.

Straight before him, and terribly close at hand, he heard a voice that cried out wildly: "Here! Here! He's come through this way!"

And then a gun roared before him, the brief, heavy bark of a shotgun that carries a big charge of powder and shot. He heard the bullets crash among the branches and foliage, while he himself, totally distraught, feeling that he could not possibly save himself by merely turning to flee, gave the mare his heel and made her leap in at the other.

He made out the flowing beard of old Bill, sitting high on horseback, looking like an evil giant. The loaded butt end of the black snake dashed through the beard of Bill, banged in his front teeth, and rolled him a senseless log from the back of his horse.

Joe Good caught the flying reins of the other horse, and presently it was galloping beside him through the smoke and the entanglement of trees.

Then he heard a crashing of gun shots behind him and a shouting of voices, but he paid no heed. He was out of the trap at last, and riding toward the east, where a rim of dull light told of the coming of dawn.

Would they trace and track him?

Well, that would be slightly more perilous business from this moment forward. For now he had with him in the saddle holsters of the long-striding, dappled gray gelding which he had taken from Bill, an excellent repeating Winchester rifle and a pair of fine Colt revolvers. He was not a great expert in the use of either weapon, but after all, he had knocked over his share of rabbits with a rifle, and had even shot squirrels out of the branches of the big oaks at the home place in Fort Willow. Now, unless his cunning deserted him, he might make it warm for two headlong attackers.

He got up to the top of a long slope, and now, as the trees gave way and scattered out to a clearing, he saw, far away beneath him, the burning of the shack. It was far gone with flames, and as he stared, the roof fell and a vast cloud of sparks and of flame went sailing upward, lighting the stormy sky and throwing floods of rosy radiance over the tops of the pine trees.

The remnants of the fire were now broadly scattered. Rain began to fall, and the sweep of clouds, the tug of the wind, threatened an immediate downpour, quenching the flames and likewise soaking the fugitive who had escaped from that dangerous place.

He ventured, nevertheless, to halt long enough to remove the saddle and bridle from the big gray to the mare. The bridle cheek straps had to be shortened, and the stirrups of the saddle needed much shortening also, before he sat comfortably on the back of Molly again. But there was no sign of pursuit so far.

He had found a well-traveled, although narrow trail, and along this he continued, sending back the Professor to scout behind him should danger come up from that direction.

The dawn was coming up rapidly now.

First it outlined the tops of the mountains, glistening with icy rocks; and then it illumined the lower shoulders, where the pines stood thickly; and last of all it reached to the bottom of the ravines and found the pools and rivers and rubbed them over with gold.

As the morning brightened the storm abated. The rain which had promised for so long did not fall at all; the clouds broke apart, and it was under a sky of brilliant sunshine that Joe Good rode down to the verge of a stream and prepared to ford it.

If he had looked up he would have seen a girl waving a hand at him from the distance, warning him back as she galloped rapidly down the slope, shouting; but she was very far away, and his glance was only down the stream where, just around the bend, he heard the angry talking of a cataract. He would not have dreamed of attempting this place for a ford had it not been that the trail advanced straight down to the edge of the stream and climbed out again on the farther side. That was sufficient proof that this was a much used ford.

So he rode the mare into the water, and the gray gelding came along at his side.

But after sniffing, the big gelding did a very strange thing. It had been following along on the lead like a veritable lamb, but now he sprang far forward into the water, getting halfway across the swift breadth of the current before he dashed into it and began to swim furiously.

That might have been a warning to Joe Good, but it was not. He urged the unwilling Molly in deeper and deeper. The force of the stream staggered her, but the moment she started to swim, the full weight of the running water struck her and sent her slowly turning about and about. The little Professor followed downstream in her wake, barking.

Now at last the boy understood. That current ran fastest by the near shore of the creek; the gray, jumping it as though he were familiar with the necessary tactics here, had got into the slacker stream beyond, though even there he had to swim hard.

Joe Good threw himself into the water and tried to swim to the closest shore; but not for an instant could he shake off the grip of the stream. In spite of his struggling, he and the mare and the Professor were carried in slowly turning circles down to the bend.

Halfway around it the true roar of the waterfall came heavily back to him, increasing every moment.

It was not exactly fear that the boy felt. The danger was too sudden for that, perhaps; but rather he was enraged to think that a life which had been saved from the devices of Martin could be blotted out so easily.

Then, amazed, he saw a rope floating in the water beside him!

He grasped it and glanced down the length of it at the same time to see a rider on the shore in the act of knotting the farther end of the rope to the horn of her saddle.

The noose beside him he drew taut instantly around the horn of Molly's saddle; and the rope tightened with a jerk as the cattle pony on the shore sat down against it.

The Professor next, he dragged from the water and placed astride of the neck of the mare. Then he pulled himself hand over hand along the rope to the farther shore.

He gave no glance to the girl. She was backing her pony up, and Molly was coming in rapidly now until she gained the slack, scrambled up the bank, and stood shaking herself like a dog.

The Professor, jumping down on dry ground again, began to spring up to the hands of his master, licking them in joy and gratitude, as though this rescue were attributed entirely to this lord of men.

But Joe Good, turning, found himself looking into a familiar face.

"Great Scott!" said he. "And what in the world planted you here, Kate?"

"Luck," she said. "I was simply trying out a new pony, and happened to come this way. Thank goodness, it knew how to sit down and hold a rope! Joe Good, don't you know better than to try a ford when the water's that high and running like a mill race?"

"I was a fool," he admitted, looking back to the sweep of the stream.

"You'll be dead yet, before long," said the girl, looking at his shuddering body. "Peel off those clothes and wring them before the wind blows you straight into pneumonia. I'll ride over the hill and meet you on the far side."

She turned the head of her mustang and cantered off up the slope where the gray gelding was running before her, throwing up its heels and frolicking like a colt.

Joe Good obeyed instructions to the letter, stripped, wrung out his clothes, dragged them on again with some difficulty, and then ran up the side of the hill on foot, with Molly following cheerfully behind him and the Professor running before.

He was warmer, and the wind and brilliant sun already were drying him when he came over the crest and found that the girl had caught the gray colt and was holding it by the lead rope.

"How in the world did you happen to know that this horse belongs to Father?" she asked him.

"Belongs to your father?" he said blankly.

"Do you mean to say that you didn't know that? You weren't returning Barley to us?"

"Never knew his name before," said the boy. "Never saw the horse before until this morning."

"Was he a stray?"

"Yes, a sort of a stray," he said, rather uncertainly. And he strove to change the subject by adding: "I knew that you lived up in this direction, but I'd clean forgotten about that when I came into this wild country, Kate. Is this your father's land?"

"Yes, all around here," she said. "Enough acres and enough grass to make us rich if they were any other place. But the Garnets will never be millionaires in this part of the world. But about the horse—about Barley—I don't understand that, Joe!"

He had recovered some composure, finally, as he said: "If Barley belongs to you, you're welcome to him."

"But tell me, Joe, is it your habit to pick up strays wherever you find them along the range? If you don't know it already, I'll tell you that that's an easy way to get yourself shot in these mountains!"

He looked back into her blue, thoughtful eyes and studied the frown she was wearing.

"Do you think that I'm a horse thief, Kate?" said he.

27

She shrugged her shoulders. "I don't know what you are, Joe," she said. "I've seen you playing burglar at midnight, you know. You had reason to do that, I know. Well, I don't think you're a horse thief, but you have to admit that people talk about you as far from Fort Willow as this, and when they talk, they wonder where you get your spending money."

"I'll tell you how I get it," said Joe Good. "By returning stolen horses to their owners and collecting the rewards."

She managed to smile a little at this.

"Sit down, Molly," said he.

The mare sat down, and he stepped into the stirrups as she rose carefully again.

The Professor, tired of walking, or wishing to be nearer to his master, had jumped on the haunches of the mare and now squatted behind the cantle and enjoyed the ride. The girl laughed at this picture. But Joe Good was serious and said: "After I saw you that night in the Alton house, as soon as I found out where you were living, I wrote you two letters. Did you get them?"

"Yes, I got them."

"You didn't answer them," said he.

"Well, they were pretty sentimental, Joe," she explained.

"Of course, they were," he answered. "Because there was a lot of sentiment in me about that time. You hit me pretty hard, Kate. I couldn't sleep, thinking about you. Does that sound silly?"

"What are you trying to get at, Joe?" she asked severely. "Love at first sight and that sort of thing?"

"No," he replied. "I thought it was at first. But I got over it fast enough."

Then he added: "But it makes me hot to think that you wouldn't answer my letters. No matter how foolish they were, I put a lot of heart into them."

"Well, I'll tell you another reason why I didn't answer them," said the girl with an odd smile. "After I got back home from the Alton place—how glad I was to leave that place!—I did a bit of thinking and remembering on my own part. It was a romantic picture, Joe; it was something to remember. I mean, the sight of you rummaging about in that desk in the middle of the night and that terrible giant of a black with you. And then the danger you were in, and your coolness."

"Honest, I was scared to death and shaking all over," confessed the boy.

"You didn't look it. Don't be silly and modest," said the girl. "You took a terrible risk; but what you did that night will make your father's ghost happy, Joe. I understand that. As a matter of fact, I understood so much that—well, I thought I had better not answer your letters because I was feeling a bit sentimental myself."

"Humph!" said the boy, scowling at her. "That would have meant a lot to me—once!"

"Would it?" said the girl casually. "But I remembered what my father always says about love and marriage and such stuff. I remembered and didn't write. And we both pulled through the fog into the clear again."

He nodded. "You're a good clean one," said the boy, looking at her critically. "You're all right, Kate. I'd bank on you. But tell me what it is that your father always says about love and marriage."

"He says: 'Don't, unless you have to. Keep running away till the rope's around your neck. You'll know when you're caught by the choking sensation.'"

They laughed together, looking straight at one another.

"You're a good clean one, too, Joe," said the girl. "I don't care what deviltry you're up to. I think you're a good clean one."

"Thanks," said the boy. "But don't make up your mind so fast."

"I mean," said the girl, "that men can be pretty sappy and silly, most of them. You're different."

"Yeah," he drawled, "that's because you didn't see me in the mooncalf period, when I was baying at the moon and couldn't eat. Betsy said it was the liver; I couldn't tell her it was the heart. Thank God I pulled through that bad time, though. Have to get that stuff over with before a fellow can be friends with a girl."

"Of course," said she. "There's the ranch house."

He looked across the broken, green hills and saw a sweep of trees and the irregular roof line of a large house thrusting up above them.

"It looks like a whale of a place," said the boy.

"Yes, it's pretty big," she answered. "And it used to be filled with servants and punchers, and family, and all that, in the days of my Grandfather Garnet. He built the house chunk by chunk. It had to keep expanding as his business expanded. But now there's nothing left except Dad, me and one hired man. That's all."

He looked about him, puzzled. "But you have a lot of cattle for that many people to handle, and a lot of country to ride over. Only two men to handle this outfit? I should think that you'd need four, at least."

"We could use 'em, but it's hard to keep men up here. Why should they herd your cattle for you when they might as well rustle them for themselves?"

"Yes, everybody calls this a hole-in-the-wall country," he agreed. "But only two men for all these hills!"

He shook his head.

"Well, I work outside as well as inside," said the girl. "I can do most sides of a man's work. I can't very well tail cows out of bogs, or do work like that; I can't very well bulldog a young steer. But still, I get most sides of a man's work done."

"And cook, too, eh?" said he.

"Yes, I cook. You know, I throw some bacon into a pan and mix up some pone. It isn't really cooking."

"Let me have a look at your hand," he suggested.

She caught her glove under her left armpit, pulled out a hand as brown as his own, and extended it for his inspection.

"Yeah. That's all right," he said. "I thought you might have cracked finger nails and stains in the creases of old calluses. But I can see that you've kept on gloves most of the time, eh?"

"Dad won't let me budge without 'em," said she.

Then suddenly: "Joe, where did you get that saddle you're riding in?"

"That?" said he lightly. "Oh, that old thing?"

"Yeah," she answered. "That old thing with all the old gold Mexican inlay all over it, and all that old silver and pearl set in here and there. Where did you get it?"

"I got it to make you a present," said he smugly.

"Stuff," said the girl. "I think you're a smuggler or a church robber or something like that. Here's Dad now. Look at him come sashaying down that hill. Isn't he a Jim Dandy? Oh, there's a man for you, Joe! A regular whale is what he is, bless him! Sixty years old, nearly, and still he never lets up."

It was really a fine picture that the rider made as he swept down the hill on a big horse, taking it quartering along the slope to save the shoulders of the animal. And the wind of the gallop furled back the brim of the hat and showed, as he came closer, a very brown, handsome and composed face.

He exclaimed at the sight of the gray.

As he shook hands with the boy he said: "How did you find Barley? Where did you get him? Great Scott, man, don't tell me that you got him away from Charley Martin!"

"No," said the boy truthfully in part, "I didn't get him from Martin. Just picked him up."

"Martin is half-witted if he lets a horse like that stray around," said the rancher, "even if the rascal can steal more horses from more ranchers. Barley is a grand old fellow. It warms my heart to have him back, and I thank you a thousand times. I haven't your name as yet."

"Why, Dad, it's Joe Good!" said the girl.

The rancher whistled.

"Joe Good?" said he. "The whip expert? The great Black-snake Joe in person? But I thought that you were seven feet tall and had nothing but electric sparks in your eyes. Kate, you've given me an entirely wrong impression. Come along, Good. Come into the house. We'll throw some eggs and bacon together and give you a breakfast. Oh, that Barley is a sight that rests my eyes, the rascal!"

They went on toward the house, the way winding among the huge corrals, now half of them dismantled through disuse and neglect, and the boy saw four huge barns where the winter feed had once been stored. One of them was a crumbling heap; the back of another was broken. Only two were kept in some sort of repair.

Suddenly he stopped the mare and exclaimed: "Look here, Mr. Garnet, if your father before you had cattle enough to cover all these hills, why shouldn't you have 'em, too, and the big barns filled with hay, eh? What's really gone wrong up here?"

Said Garnet: "I have everything in the way of opportunity for raising cattle that my father had before me, and better prices for them once they're raised. But I have better opportunities for losing 'em, too. My father had no Martin on hand, as I've had for fifteen years or so."

"Is it Martin with you, too?" said the boy slowly.

"It's Charley Martin and the rascals who follow him up here in the hills," said the rancher, rather resigned than angered by the thought. "I raise cattle for thugs to rustle. Kate and I live here to work hard and enjoy the climate, as you might say. Come in, Joe Good. Kate, rustle up the fire. I'll get the eggs and bacon."

The big house, as they came closer, showed the signs of wear and tear as well as the barns. It was not actually broken down, but there were eyeless windows filled in with boards, and many broken shutters; paint had not touched the walls for many a year, and a feeling of melancholy came over Joe Good.

28

The size of the kitchen was a fair measure of the scale on which the house had been built. "This is kitchen, dining room and mostly living room, too," explained Kate Garnet. "We haven't much time for housekeeping. And after supper we generally sit here with coffee and newspapers, and drowse and read a few moments before going to bed."

It was large enough for all these purposes. The big range could have furnished forth food for fifty, and the pantries and all of the other adjuncts were on a similar scale. The sink and drain board were as large as a bathtub very nearly. And the whiteness of the big floor, which attested to much scrubbing, made the boy look with sympathetic eyes at the slender arms and shoulders of the girl.

But she was as strong as a man for her poundage, it seemed. The respect of Joe Good for her rose with every moment.

He helped as well as he could while the cookery went on, but he could not disclaim a ravening appetite.

They had coffee with him when he finally sat down to his bacon and eggs and warmed-over pone.

"You've slept too near a fire," said the girl as they sat down. "Your hair's singed, Joe."

"Is it?" said he innocently.

Then he asked: "About Martin—how many times have you tried to put him down?"

"First seven or eight years," said the rancher, "we got

together and tried to corner him—well, once or twice a year, say. There were other ranchers up here then. The roads were kept up. We were able to do a good deal of farming as well as grazing. These bottom lands, you see, are as rich as can be. They'll grow anything—grain, even some kinds of fruit trees, in spite of the hard winters. It was always a hole-in-the-wall country, but in the old days of my father the vigilantes organized and kept down crime. We lost very few cattle. However, crime was put on a different scale when Martin stepped into the picture. The man is a fox. He knows where to step and what to do. We were pretty helpless in front of him, I must confess!"

"And then the other ranchers lost heart finally," added the girl. "We were left alone. Some of the others died out, sold out. The newcomers didn't last long as soon as they had to face the Martin locust plague. The small farmers and the small ranchers simply gave up and quit. There are only a few tucked away in odd corners among the hills. And their profits go every year into Martin's pockets. He doesn't clean us out because he doesn't want to kill completely the goose that lays the golden egg."

Young Joe Good writhed with indignation. "It's enough to make a man boil!" said he. "I should think that the governor would hear about this and send down the military!"

"What good would that be?" asked the rancher. "While they were hunting for him, Martin would be away, a thousand miles off, blowing up a bank safe and getting off with the profits. When the military left, he'd come back and be twice as heavy on our necks as before. Sometimes I think of quitting. It's turning into a wilderness, you see. But Kate, here, wants to stay and pray for a miracle."

"It's only Martin," the girl pointed out. "His hangers-on, they're a worthless lot. It's only this Martin who counts, and once that demon is out of the way, we'll be able to start again. The land is here, we have enough cattle to make a start, and the old place will be as beautiful as ever with him out of the way. Some day a bullet will tag him!"

"He'll die of old age," said Garnet calmly. "The man has too much brains for us. We can't handle him."

Hoofbeats rattled up toward the house and stopped.

A big, gaunt, red-faced fellow rushed into the kitchen, waving his hat, his eyes dancing with excitement.

"There's blazes to pay!" he cried out. "Martin has met his match! Charley Martin has been tagged at last!"

"Dead?" said Garnet.

The girl said nothing, but she rose slowly from her chair.

"Not dead, but almost as good as that," said the other. "I tell you what; this is news. I'll give it to you the way I've picked it up here and there along the hills. Even the squirrels are chattering about it in the trees!"

He laughed, rejoicing.

"Go on, Breen," said Garnet. "Talk, man! Let's hear what it's all about, will you?"

"You've heard of Joe Good in Fort Willow?" said Breen.

The two Garnets glanced at the boy. There had been no time to introduce him. They did not introduce him now.

"Yes, I've heard about him," said Garnet.

"The man with the whip," said Breen by way of quick explanation, if one were necessary. "The one who has the Altons backed up against a wall just now. I hope he hangs the lot of 'em, too! Anyway, this Good was in a saloon in Fort Willow yesterday, and Charley Martin himself, alongside of that crook, Wally Chase, steps in. Nobody knew it was Martin till afterward. Them that recognized his face wouldn't believe their eyes until after he .was gone. But he took his chance and slammed Good with his fist and knocked him down. Didn't dare to pull a gun on Joe Good, of course, in that man's town! Then Martin slid out of the place. And Good followed him.

"I guess it was Martin's scheme to pull Good out of his own happy home, you might say, and get him off on his own ground and then murder him. Maybe there's Alton money behind the idea. I dunno! Anyway, this is what happens:

"Good comes up through the hills, and where does he stop for the night but in old Bill's place!"

"That old scoundrel?" muttered Garnet.

"Yeah, just there. And Martin rides along and finds out where he is, and while the kid is sleeping in the attic, those thugs sneak out of the house with their belongings and they set fire to the place and wait with their rifles for Joe Good to try to break away!"

Garnet looked at the boy with unbelieving eyes, as though he were looking at a ghost, not at flesh and blood. "Are you sure it was Joe Good, and not somebody else?" he demanded of Breen.

"It was Good. You'll believe it when you hear what he done," said the excited Breen. "The door was locked on him, but he busted down a section of the wall, and while they started shooting, he set fire to the grass in front of the house. While it was burning on the gallop, he ran out behind the smoke, and he took his dog with him. Then he whistled through the smoke, and his mare up and broke her halter in the horse shed and come running to him. He jumped on her and he rode through the smoke.

"He found those thugs among the trees, and just with that magic black snake of his, he lit into them and he thrashed the whole gang. He thrashed Bill and Doc and that Dunker, the dirty beast. And he sailed into Charley Martin, and he flogged him, too. Then he took away one of their horses—which it was a fine big gray hoss, I hear. And he rode away and laughed at 'em over his shoulders."

He gasped in a new breath and added: "I've just seen old Bill and Doc, and they look like they'd been through a war; and they can hardly creep, they was so badly licked. And Martin had had the whip for the first time in his life."

"That's a pretty exaggerated yarn," said the boy.

"Didn't I see the black spot where the shack used to be?" demanded Breen furiously. "Didn't I see Bill and Doc with my own eyes? And anyway, who are you to say that it's exaggerated? Whatcha know about it, anyway?"

"Wait a minute, Breen," said Garnet. "This is Joe Good."

"Yes, it is!" said Breen sarcastically, laughing. "It would take two like this one to make Joe Good."

But just then the Professor, not liking the violent gesticulations which had been made in the direction of his master, came around from behind the table, and, standing in front of Good, showed his small, needle-sharp teeth at Breen.

The appearance of the dog was the clinching proof to Breen. He fairly threw up his hands and staggered. "Oh!" he groaned. "It's him! It's Joe Good himself!"

"It's all right, Mr. Breen," said Joe Good, rising and shaking hands. "I'm glad to know you. I said it was exaggerated because I didn't get the whip on Martin. That's all."

"And that's how you met Barley straying, was it?" said the girl.

The rancher went around the table and faced the boy. "What is it, Joe?" said he. "What's the real truth?"

And he answered: "The real truth is that I have to find Mr. Charley Martin. When I borrowed Barley from them I borrowed some guns at the same time. They were in the saddle holsters. And I hope I'll have a chance to use one of those guns on your friend Martin."

"You've come up here alone to tackle Martin?" asked Garnet.

"Yes," said the boy, "I have. You see—"

"He has a reputation, Dad," said Kate Garnet calmly. "And if Martin knocked him down—well, Martin has to pay for doing it."

"Do you mean to say," said the rancher, "that you've come up here without support, without even knowing this crazy country, and hope to find Martin? Have you any plan?"

"I have a plan now," said the boy, "if you'll let me use it, though it may be rather hard on your nerves."

"What plan?" said Garnet. "I'd walk knee-deep through blood to see the end of the scoundrel!"

"I don't think any harm would come to you," said Joe Good. "But speaking of reputations—well, Charley Martin has a reputation, too. And now he has to rub out last night, and rub it out quickly; otherwise all of his adherents around here will take no more stock in him. He'll be a pricked balloon."

"Then what do you mean he'll try to do?" asked Garnet.

"I mean," said the boy, speaking carefully, "that when I left Fort Willow I had to find him. Now the shoe is on the other foot, and he has to find me. I can sit still, and he'll have to come and find me. What I'd like to do, if you'll permit it, is to wait for him right here in your house!"

The girl drew in a sharp breath.

Even Garnet blinked. But then he said: "If you'll stay here—welcome, and God bless you!"

29

His sleep of the night before had been very brief, but he did not attempt to rest again during this day. Instead, he rode out with the Garnets, the father and the daughter, to look over the lay of the land which made up the ranch.

As for Breen, by the special request of Joe Good, that puncher galloped off to spread the news wherever he could that Good was waiting at the house of Garnet for the coming of the outlaw, and that he would there fight the battle out with him hand to hand.

"You think that he'll have to come?" asked Joe curiously.

"Have to come? He'll never dare to show his face in this part of the world again if he doesn't come," said Breen. "It ain't public opinion that he minds, usually. He wouldn't care what the folks in Fort Willow or any other town thought about him. But the thugs that foller him up here in the mountains would laugh in his face if he didn't come to fight you man to man. Besides, I got an idea that he'd like to take you single-handed. He ain't one to dodge a fight. He's a bulldog, and loves to sink his teeth in!"

And he went off on his mission. What he had said, or rather the last part of it, remained for long in the mind of the boy, and hummed through his thoughts all the rest of the day like the haunting refrain of a song.

Half of his mind was given over to what he saw and heard as he rode the rounds of the ranch with Kate and her father. The other half dwelt on that approaching battle with the great Martin.

He felt now that he had given way to a vast and foolish temptation in sending such a challenge. It was like the impulse a climber feels after he has scaled a huge and perpendicular height.

Martin would come. There was no doubt of that. And when he came, his guns would be with him! As for the weapons which might be in the hand of the boy, he knew perfectly well that he was master of the black snake alone. It had served him well in the past, but unless he could stand within ten feet of his target he might as well be equipped with a paper knife for storming a fortress with barbed-wire entanglements in front.

No, he had been rash; but he saw that he had taken a step so definite that he would have to intrust himself to chance. He strove to close his eyes. The future would have to take care of itself.

In the meantime he was shown all the acres of the ranch, and the farther he rode the more he realized the possibilities of the place.

No matter how white and stern the winter months might be, there was grass and water here to accommodate the needs of a host of cattle. All about the circle of hills rose the higher mountains, looking impenetrably rugged and grand, but these lower lands were a long succession of smooth waves of green.

Wood, water and endless acreage—what more could a man want in the making of a home? It enlarged the mind of the boy.

They came back as night was falling toward the house, near which the great outlaw might even now be lurking in wait for him. As they rode, the girl drifted her horse close to the side of Molly, saying: "Can you tell me frankly what you think that your chances would be against that man?"

He said, with all the frankness she could have desired: "If I can get close to him—three or four steps from him— I think I have better than an even chance. But he knows that, too. And if guns start at a bigger distance than that —well, I imagine that my chances are about one in four or five."

She looked earnestly at him, saying: "Isn't it suicide to try such a fight?"

"Everything is partly luck and partly skill," he said. "I'm going to put most of my trust in blind luck."

Still, she was curious in an odd, rather impersonal way,

as though his were a distant problem—a picture to be looked at as it hung on the wall, so to speak.

"Do you feel steady about it?" she asked him.

"I'm badly scared," said the boy. "It's worse than the first day of school."

Then she nodded with a faint smile.

"But not much worse," she suggested. "I know what men with courage are. They'll be frightened like the rest of us, but only a little frightened. Their hands and nerves are never paralyzed."

All three checked the speed of the horses, and they came up toward the house with their animals walking. They said nothing to one another, but there was only one thought among them all.

Yet nothing happened; Martin did not appear as they put up the horses and went on toward the house. Then a wild thought came to Joe Good and was embraced eagerly by him.

What if the nerve of the great Martin himself had failed under the strain of waiting to fulfill the challenge? What if Martin himself had found that he could not venture himself with any equanimity against the danger which Joe Good might prove to him?

In the early morning of that day the outlaw must have seen that luck was no stranger to his enemy. Superstition, if nothing else, might have raveled his nerves!

No sooner had the hope appeared than a cold weight lifted from the heart of the boy, and through the supper he became actually gay and hilarious.

He could see that Garnet and the girl marveled at his steady nerves; he could not, however, tell them the hope that had come to him; for the thing would appear too totally foolish and vain.

He helped with the washing of the dishes afterward. And then he saw Garnet frowning through the wreaths of smoke that arose from his pipe.

The rancher said: "I'll tell you what, Joe. You're a good game one. But, after all, if you make this fight and win it, I'll be the great gainer. This land of mine will be freed. All the grazers in the mountains will bless you, Joe. And I don't see how I can let you go through the thing without my help. I've got to stand beside you."

Joe Good shook his head, smiling as he did so.

"I know what you feel," he said. "But if you help me,

he'll have men to help him. And we know what will happen if it turns into a gang fight."

Garnet was still not convinced, but his daughter said gravely: "It all seems a pretty crazy business. But I'll tell you what. There is no way to look at it except as a fairy tale. There are people in need in a gloomy castle, with a cruel enchanter holding them—that's the Garnets, and Martin is the enchanter. Along comes the brave prince. Well, it sounds pretty silly, but I don't see any other way of looking at it. We haven't been able to help ourselves. So we have to look to him!"

Garnet sighed.

"This is an ugly—" he began.

But here the girl held up her hand suddenly for silence. Then distinctly they heard it: a softly creaking sound that moved toward the door that was on one side of the kitchen!

There were three doors to that room.

One was that which opened over the back porch; one communicated with the dining room, and one led to the room in which the cook, in the old days, had slept.

From the dining-room side it was that these steps now appeared to be approaching.

Garnet, his face twisted with sudden fear, his jaw muscles bulging with sudden determination, stepped to the lamp and blew it out. The darkness did not seem to come at once over the eyes of the boy, but in a slow wave, growing thicker and thicker.

The window glass, which had been an 'impenetrable wall of black, polished rock, now became again translucent, and through it dim objects in the outer night appeared.

A man whistled outside, on the back porch or immediately beneath it.

That whistle was repeated almost immediately inside the house, not from the dining room, but from the opposite bedroom.

"He's come!" said Garnet bitterly. "But he hasn't come alone!"

And the girl said: "It's murder that he means. Oh, the cowardly scoundrel. Joe, he doesn't mean to face you like a man!"

Joe Good said nothing.

The full realization of the disaster was gradually sweeping over him, and still he used his eyes more than his mind, which appeared to have been struck numb.

He saw the thin, curved line of red on the top of the stove, where one of the surface plates had been pushed a little to one side. And the door of the ash box, being open, allowed the red coals to shine dimly down upon the heaping ashes in the box.

Those were the only points of light in the room. Beyond the window he saw two big stars, blurred by the glass of the pane.

And now, down the chimney came the odd, muffled, howling sound of the wind. He had heard it a thousand times before, of course, but never had it seemed the very token of evil doom as it seemed now!

A voice said, close to the back porch, shouting out the words as though through a funnel of cupped hands: "We want only the kid. Throw out Joe Good and the rest of you we'll let alone."

Another voice joined in with an odd, thick enunciation: "Yeah! We want the kid! Give us Joe Good!"

It sounded very much like the voice of old Bill; the same voice, and the enunciation thickened, as it well might be since his front teeth had been knocked out that morning.

A very odd and totally unexpected thing happened then, before either Garnet or the boy could prevent it.

Kate Garnet stepped to the window and threw it open with a crash of breaking glass, and leaning far out into that perilous night, she shouted:

"Charley Martin! Charley Martin! Where's that coward who has to have a crowd and doesn't dare to fight a fair fight man to man?"

30.

It was Joe Good who reached her first, and catching her arm, started to draw her back, exclaiming:

"Kate! Kate! You've lost your wits! They'll—"

"They're Martin's men," she said, "but even they won't shoot a woman."

And she struck his hand away from her arm, adding: "Let me do this. I know what I'm about. I know how to sting these fellows."

An unseen watcher by the porch was drawling: "I dunno, Kate, what kind of fools you think we are! There's your old man and Breen in there, and you talk like it was a one-man-against-one-man fight. It ain't such a thing at all!"

"Breen is not here," said the girl. "He's gone to tell people that Joe Good is willing to fight your Charley Martin hand to hand. My father is here, but he knows that we haven't a mob to fight at all. Joe Good is here, too, and he's only asking for Martin to stand by himself."

The drawling voice called out: "Come on, Martin! Come out here and stand in the starlight, because there's a gent inside that wants to have a good shot at you!"

Other voices laughed; the same laughter echoed and rumbled and thundered through the rooms near the kitchen. The place seemed to be literally filled with men!

"Jemmy," said another voice outside, "it ain't no way to mock a lady like this here. I'm gunna make a truce for a minute. I'm gunna step out and talk to her."

"You'll make a truce with a slug through your brain, old fool!" said Jemmy.

"Hey, Miss Kate!" said the other voice. "Look at here —you can see for yourself that there ain't any way that

161

we can make a go of this. There ain't any way that we can put 'em together and be sure that neither side will join in."

"Is that you, Baldy?" demanded the girl.

"This is sure me," said he.

"Fine, and ashamed you ought to be of yourself!" she cried down at him.

"Charley Martin is my boss, and a good boss he's been to me," said Baldy. "I don't care what other folks may have to say about him, either!"

"Baldy," said she, "at least you're man enough to want to see fair play. They've already tried to murder Joe Good inside of the last twenty-four hours."

"Well," said Baldy, revealed by starlight as he pushed his hat to one side and scratched his head over the problem. "Well, Kate, it's this way. Joe Good is a bright young feller, and he's done pretty good by himself. He's gone and got himself a big reputation here and there. But men have gotta die some day, and it looks like this is Joe Good's day for dying. Martin wants him!"

She burst out: "If Martin is half a man, he'll send the rest of you away, and he'll step out between the barn and the house. Joe will meet him there!"

"Well," said Baldy, "there ain't anything better than a clean, open, fair fight, I gotta say."

"If Martin does a murder instead of fighting fair," said the girl, "the world will simply despise him as much as it's feared him up to this day!"

"Look here, Miss Kate," said Baldy, while other voices murmured inside and outside the house as though in agreement, "there's nothing better than a square fight would be. But you can look from the house to the barn. You can't see very clear, but you can see. There's enough light for that. And suppose that your old man stays inside there and rests his rifle on the sill of the window and takes a good aim and picks off Martin before the fight begins? What if that should happen, now?"

She answered unexpectedly again: "The only other way is to murder all three of us, because we'll stand shoulder to shoulder. I can use a rifle, and I'll use it to kill, you cowardly dogs!"

"Them are pretty mean sentiments," said Baldy. "I wouldn't like to hear you talk like that, Miss Kate. Hey,

Charley! Hey, Martin! Have you heard what's what so far?"

And the voice of Martin answered, close to the dining-room door: "I've heard. The rest of you be quiet, will you?"

The murmurings ended at once. Only one fellow cried in the extreme distance: "Take him on for a square fight, Martin, and cut the heart out of him!"

Martin's voice rose like the roar of a lion.

"Be quiet, the rest of you!"

And quiet there was, a sudden drawing of a veil, as it were. It was at this command that the heart of Joe Good stood still.

Had he hoped that there might be nervous fear in this man?

No. In the mere sound of the voice there was ample as-surance that the nerves of Martin were, as ever, the nerves of a destroying machine.

When silence covered the house and all around it, Mar-tin said: "Where's the man I want? I'd like to hear his voice?"

Joe Good cleared his throat.

"I'm in here, Martin," said he.

"Glad to hear you speak up," said the outlaw. "Kind of had an idea that you was gunna let the girl do your fighting for you. Now, young feller, the time's come for you. Step out and take your medicine."

"I'll step out with you, Martin," said the boy.

"Will you?" said Martin with a snarl. "I dunno how long that stepping out of yours will wanta last. But where d'you suggest that we step, where neither side can cut in on the deal?"

"You got any suggestions, Charley?" said Joe Good.

He was exceedingly grateful for the chance to talk. The opportunity to use his voice was steadying all his nerves and making his breath come and go easily.

It seemed to him that he was almost less afraid of the great Martin than of fear itself, the cold ghost that freezes the hearts of men.

"I've thought it over," said the other. "I'm not gunna step out into the open where a rifle from that kitchen window could cover me. I know what old man Garnet would give to send a slug through me!"

"Garnet's a gentleman," said the boy, "and he'll give you his word of honor."

"Oh, word of honor!" said the outlaw contemptuously. "That's only talk to fill up the time!"

A sudden wave of emotion, a sort of gust and storm of hysteria came over Joe Good.

"Martin," he said, "crook and thug that you are, I'll trust your word and your honor!"

There was a snarling laugh unlike any human sound that the boy ever had heard.

"How'll you trust me?" asked the other. "Go ahead and tell me how you'll be willing to trust me, kid!"

"I'll trust you," said the boy, "to clear out that room you're standing in. And when you say it's empty, except for yourself, I'll go in there and have it out with you."

"Hold on," said the other. "There's precious little light in here."

"That's all the worse for me," said Joe Good. "I'm not a wild cat that can see in the dark well enough for killing. But you are!"

Martin laughed again, as though he took this for a compliment.

Then he said: "I think the kid means it. You fellows clear out of here."

This was followed by a rapid murmuring of voices; footsteps sounded, but slow and dragging ones.

"Don't go in there, Joe," urged Garnet. "We'll stay here and face it out together. If you go in there it's a murder trap."

"If we stay in here," said the boy, "they'll simply burn us out. They've tried the burning trick once with me and failed, but they wouldn't fail this time. Kate, where are you?"

"Here, beside you," said her low, troubled voice.

"Tell me—whisper it—the layout of that next room. I've never been in it."

"It's the dining room. Joe, do you really think that it's the best way? To meet that fiend in the dark!"

"It's the only way," he said. "It's the only way that can be thought out. Now, quick! Tell me the layout of the room!"

She stood close to him, gripping his left arm with both her hands, her lips whispering close to his ear. "The door from the kitchen opens on the width of the room. It's long and narrow. Forty feet long, because of the number who used to have to eat in there."

"Forty feet long," he muttered in answer. "How wide?"

"About eighteen or twenty feet. I'm not sure."

"Is there a table?"

"The old, long table is in there, too. It must take up twenty-five feet of the length and about four feet of the breadth."

"I have that. Is it centered?"

"Yes."

"Chairs in the room?"

"Yes."

"Where?"

"Most of them are along the sides of the wall. But I think there are a few pulled up to the table. Heavens, why can't I remember?"

"It's all right. And the windows?"

"Two big windows, one fairly close to this end of the room, and the other a little past the center of the room."

"This will be the brighter end, then—"

"Yes, whatever starlight or moonshine gets in. It will be as dark as this kitchen, though!"

He looked about him! Yes, it certainly was dark enough! It would be like swimming through murky water.

A voice called at a little distance, as though from about the middle point of the dining room.

"Are you ready, Joe Good?"

"I'm ready."

"The deck's cleared and the table's laid. Come and get it!"

It was the cook's familiar call to a meal. Joe Good shuddered a little. Then he turned toward the door.

31

As he reached it he paused to think. Once inside that doorway he would have no time for thinking. He would be in the center of a maelstrom. In the meantime, he must try to fathom the probable purposes and plans of the other.

What would the great Martin conceive?

To stand close by the doorway, perhaps. No doubt for that very reason he had spoken from the center of the chamber, immediately afterward creeping toward the threshold to be in readiness.

That would be an obvious trick. Standing squarely before the opened door, the trained eyes staring through the muddy dimness might be able to make out a form that stepped through that frame. And the frame of the doorway itself would help to make the shot strike home.

He turned the handle of the door and thrust it wide open; then he crouched into the attitude of a sprinter about to leave the mark, except that the right hand was raised and in it was the black snake prepared.

As the door swung open with a ghostly, whispering sound, he heard a faint moan of dread in the room behind him.

That was Kate Garnet. He had time to wonder if it were merely the dread of this horrible moment that had brought the sound from her throat.

But there was no sound, no sight in the next room.

He could see the faintly lighted square of the nearer window. The second window was a mere gray streak from the angle at which he looked toward it.

With the reaching, knifelike lash of the whip he cut through the space within the door.

He felt the lash strike—it seemed as though his own nerves ran down into the senseless skin that covered the black snake!—and then he heard an oath; a gun flashed, a bullet darted with a whir above his head, and by the glancing illumination, he was able to make out the form of a man standing exactly as he had expected, near the door.

But already the form was in instant motion, backward and to the side.

Young Joe Good sprang in pursuit, the whip reversing like a living thing in his hand, the heavily loaded butt end now driving at the shadowy target.

It struck; another spark of light spouted from the mouth of the revolver; and again the great Martin missed, for Good was inside the room by this time, and had sprung noiselessly to the side.

He thought he heard a sound like the gritting of teeth. But that was all. An odd feeling of safety and of exultation came over him. He had read the mind of Martin in the first instance. Perhaps he would be able to read it a second time.

Now he strode forward, his revolver in his left hand, the whip ready in the right, like the antenna of a huge insect, ready to probe the gloomy spaces before him.

Could he ever be able to make his weapons count against the two guns, the inhuman accuracy of the great Martin?

He touched something—the top of the table. He moved to one side, and before he knew it, a chair had been pushed by his weight and scraped slightly on the floor.

Instantly a gun spoke, terribly close at hand and behind him.

He whirled, leaping frantically to the side as he did so, but he was too late to see the flash of the Colt and to gain from it any true sight of the position of Martin.

A breathless silence closed over the room again. Outside of the house, however, there was a muttering of voices. Some man yonder was cursing fiercely and rapidly, though in subdued tones.

It must have been a weird thing to listen to, that battle

in the coffinlike dark. But the dark was not so entire as he had expected.

He retreated to the farther wall, away from the windows. And there he crouched very low. Looking up, his dilating eyes could make out not only the comparatively brilliant squares of the windows, but he could see, as well, a vague outline of the table and the huddling forms of chairs here and there. But everything within the room was only to be guessed at.

A sharp, scraping sound reached his ears, followed by the flight of a fiery streak that landed on the floor not far from him; it was a bunch of sulphur matches, and the heads flared out with a blue blaze of phosphorous-fed light.

He felt that dull light on his face and body as though it were a flood of living fire itself; at the same time, as he sprang to the side, he heard a gunshot. There was the great Martin, lying flat on the table, firing!

A sharp twinge came in the side of the boy. He had been hit; how badly he could not guess; and now the curling lash of the whip found the bunch of matches and flung it far away, where it lay spluttering in a corner.

Again, and yet again, bullets flowed from the guns of the outlaw; but the body of Joe Good was wavering back and forth like a snipe in full flight down the wind as he darted in to close with his enemy.

Martin would be rising now from his sprawling position. And the butt end of the black snake flung out in full circle. It struck heavily against something—something soft and padded; not the skull, not the more thinly covered bones of the arms or the lower legs.

Could such a stroke go home, a broken bone or a fractured skull would be the result.

But the cudgel stroke brought again the snarling curse of rage and pain from the lips of Martin, and another shot in that darkness. It clipped the ear of Joe Good; only a scratch, but that scratch was a half inch from death!

He struck at the sound, at the flash, and felt the loaded handle beat home again.

What followed he was not prepared for.

It seemed as though Martin, maddened by that constant beating, had lost his wits, and in a brain-numbing flare of rage, he sprang from the table.

Joe Good heard the whole structure of the big table groan, and vaguely was aware of the form that hurtled through the air.

A clubbed revolver missed his head and bruised his shoulder; then the flying weight of the monster hit him and knocked him headlong back against the wall and the floor.

"And now—" he heard the snarl of Martin.

The revolver was still firmly clutched in the left hand of the boy. He had not risked a shot at any distance, but now, as he was still falling, he was firing.

As he lay, more than half stunned, the weight of Martin turned limp and sagged loosely off him, rolling to the floor.

He reached out and felt the face of the man. He reached lower and put his hand into a soggy, warm place. The heart should have been under that, but the heart no longer beat.

He rose to his feet and went slowly, fumbling his way, to the door of the kitchen.

"You can light that lamp, Mr. Garnet," he said. "I think that Martin's dead."

Only hysterical sobbing answered him.

That would be Kate, he decided with dulled brain. But now Garnet had lighted the lamp. Very strange his face looked above it, as the light flared, a green-gray color, with the eyes thrusting out and the lips compressed in a hard, straight line. His hand was trembling so that the chimney chattered against the guards as he pressed it back into place.

Then he ran past the boy and into the next room.

He heard the voice of Kate, the sobbing checked, coming toward him through this new darkness, somewhat lessened by the light that was reflected now from the doorway of the dining room.

"Joe," she was saying, "I saw blood on your face. You're hurt. You're dying!"

"I'm barely scratched," said he. "But see about Martin, will you?"

The lamp came back to him, but Garnet said nothing to them.

His face was altered, but as grim as ever. One of his hands was crimson. He closed the door behind him, blew out the lamp, and went to the window. Through it he called:

"Baldy—and any of the rest of you who are out there— you can come inside, now. Take the side entrance. Martin is lying dead in the dining room!"

32

Hugh Alton was never a rash or a too forehanded man, but he felt, as he sat in the office of his lawyer in Fort Willow, that he had reason to congratulate himself, and his lawyer felt the same way about it.

The lawyer was one William J. Wisner, not an old-timer in the town, but a young man who looked like a hawk, and, like the same bird, had learned how to fly higher and higher even in a small community like Fort Willow.

His trade was criminal law. He sometimes prosecuted with fearful keenness; but he preferred to defend, and the more desperate the case, with all the more desperate cunning did he wage his war. Mr. Alton had patronized him long before he had an actual need of such a man; by a sort of prophetic insight, he had seen that William J. Wisner, in spite of his little eyes, might be one day both a sword and a shield. He had given the youth a start, and Wisner needed no more than a hand grip on the ladder in order to mount both high and swiftly.

He felt a certain gratitude toward his benefactor. But he felt still more interest in this case because he felt by the time he had saved the ample neck of Mr. Alton from the hangman's rope he would also have a very fair and deep claim upon the fat Alton estates.

Now he spoke with words of flattery to the rancher.

"What gave you the idea of going to Martin?" he asked.

"By lying awake at night and thinking things over," said Alton. He had discovered that absolute frankness was the only way in which he could deal with the younger man. Mr. Wisner asked nothing except the complete confidence of his clients. This he had to have before he could accomplish anything in the law courts.

"I thought things over until the darkness spun in front of my eyes," said Alton. "Finally I thought of Martin."

He did not lower his voice, because the walls of the lawyer's office had been carefully sound-proofed, as he said:

"It was reasonably clear. You're a bright fellow, Wisner, but it was clear to me that the boy had to die—or else I would certainly have to hang."

He raised a finger and delicately brushed the impeccable mustache higher from his upper lip.

Wisner looked at him with his narrow eyes bright with admiration.

"There's a kind of pity about it," said he. "It's kind of a pity that you didn't take to the law, because you see what has to be done and then you do it. That's the way to deal with cases. It was going to be a hard rub to save you; now you've saved yourself. Martin! You may hear from him again, though. Twenty thousand dollars is a great deal of money, but he won't be above blackmail in excess of that figure, I'm afraid."

Alton shrugged his shoulders. It was raining, and he walked over to the wet, dripping windowpane. "A man has to take his chances," he said. "The foolish boy actually followed Martin into his own country, it appears. In other words, Good walked into a lethal chamber, deliberately closed the door behind, and locked himself in! One doesn't expect that sort of thing except from heroes!"

"When his death is known," said the lawyer, "people may make certain suggestions. You may have to leave Fort Willow, no matter how your actual trial comes out!"

"Public opinion," said the rancher, "is nothing to me. I have my work and my family, and that is enough for me!"

He clicked his teeth as he said this, and then he laughed, pleasantly amused. "They're still on the spot, Wisner," he said.

"The big black?" asked Wisner, laughing in turn.

"Yes. The black and his wife, now. And old Zeke Stevens, that scoundrel of a miser, has come to speak with them."

Wisner got up and walked to the window. Across the rain-darkened street he saw a buckboard drawn up in front of the post office, where also the telegraph, that was preceding the railroad by some weeks, was housed.

There, ever since his master's disappearance, huge Budge Morrissey had taken his place, sitting in the buckboard and waiting for the first word that might come to his ears. His great bulk had stooped more and more, but in spite of weariness, his reddened eyes never blinked or even closed, and he outstared the hours.

At his side now was the small form of his wife, as erect as her husband was stooping. She wore a gay, yellow-colored slicker. But he sat without any real shelter, allowing the beating rain to soften and bend the brim of his hat and the wet to blacken his coat.

Twice she had thrown the slicker around his vast shoulders, and twice he had allowed it to slide down again.

Time had ceased for Budge Morrissey; it would not begin again until he received the word that would start him off, at the full gallop of the horses, to go to the help of his employer.

Old Zeke Stevens, protected by a ratty umbrella, had paused near them, and in the course of his chatting he turned and raised a fist and shook it in the direction of Wisner's gold-labeled window.

"He knows that I'm in here," said Alton, "and maybe he knows what we're talking about, you and I. I really hope that he does. The more misery the better for the old rascal."

"It's a rather strange thing," murmured the lawyer, "that that old miser should have become so interested in Joe Good."

"I'll tell you why. Stevens has always hated the established families of the county," said Alton. "And he's delighted to see a man like me put in jeopardy! That's the inside history of the attitude of Zeke Stevens."

"They all are devoted to Joe Good," said the lawyer, shaking his head. "I don't understand it. Young worthless idler, with a certain amount of natural courage. Nothing else. But we've heard and feared him for the last time, Mr. Alton, thanks to your own strong measures!"

Alton nodded.

He had turned to speak when there was a wild outburst of cheering farther down the street.

"More rioting cow-punchers come to town," said the lawyer.

"They wouldn't be rioting in this sort of weather," said Alton.

He shook his head.

"Not in this sort of a driving rain, I think."

"It's getting louder," said the lawyer.

"What in the world is happening?" asked Hugh Alton. "There's Judge Tomlinson running out into the street to look; there's the blacksmith and his apprentice; why, the whole town is crowding out, and paying no more attention to the weather than if it were bright sunshine falling! What can it be?"

He jerked up the window.

"There's the black coming to life, too," said the lawyer. "Why—"

He also leaned out of the window, and then they saw that a single horseman was jogging on a small horse down the center of the street, occasionally turning to wave to a friend or to answer to a friendly hail. His rain-polished black slicker flowed down from his shoulders like steel armor.

As he came closer, big Budge Morrissey, who had galloped his ponies suddenly up the street, halted them, flung himself out of the buckboard, and ran to the side of the horseman.

It was then that the wind blew back the brim of the rider's hat, and the two men in the window saw the face.

It was somewhat hidden by a broad white bandage that ran around it from the back of the head and across the forehead, but they could make out the features well enough.

Alton said not a word.

But the lawyer went reeling back into the room as though he had been shot through the brain.

"He's back! It's the boy! It's Joe Good!" he exclaimed. "And what's he done to Martin?"

"He's been scared off," said Alton savagely. "That's the only possible explanation. Martin never fails; Martin never fails! Never!"

William Wisner came running back and leaned out of the window again, and as they did so, they could hear from a neighboring window the exclamation: "Did you hear? He's back. There he is now. I've just got the news. You won't believe it. It wasn't the whip this time. He met

Martin on the Garnet ranch and shot him to pieces! Martin's dead at last!"

"A man like that fellow Good," said an answering voice, "is worth his weight in gold; and set with diamonds, you can take it from me!"

Hugh Alton slowly withdrew from the window.

"Help me to a chair, Wisner," he said. "I'm a little sick!"

33

His age was just thirty-two; his full name, Vincent Lafayette St. Ives Jones; he was black; his residence was here and there; his occupation, go as you please. Now he waited until the master of the little white house had ridden away. Then he rose from the brush and dusted himself with his yellow gloves, arranged his necktie as precisely as though he had been standing in front of a pier glass, pulled his hat at a striking angle over one eye, and spun his walking stick once or twice to give himself confidence.

Then he walked to the rear of the little house and knocked on the door.

It was opened by a slender woman, rather pretty, with eyes that were as brilliant as black glass.

She looked him over from his hat, which was now in his hand, to his spats; she considered his smile, which was enriched with goldwork on the front teeth, and the little, close-set eyes of V. L. St. I. Jones, now disappearing behind the wrinkles of his smile as the prow of a ship is covered by its own bow waves.

"Mrs. Morrissey?" said Mr. Jones. "Mrs. Morrissey, if I ain't mistaken?"

"What you want here?" said Betsy Morrissey at last.

"My card," said Mr. Jones, and held it forth.

Betsy disregarded it. In the corral near by, the burro began to bray.

"This is my busy day," said Mrs. Morrissey, and started to close the door.

"Ma'am," said Mr. Jones, "I got a desperate need to see—"

She slammed the door hastily in his face as he moved forward.

Then she went back to the kitchen stove, whispering savagely to herself: "Worthless, no-account, dressed-up black man!"

From the sizzling frying pan she lifted four eggs, together with the nest of strips of crisp bacon in which they reposed. She laid this white and golden and brown delicacy on a warmed platter which she had previously decorated with a fringe of lettuce leaves. From the oven she took out a pan of corn bread, baked deep, a delight to the eye and a temptation to the palate.

These she bore into the dining room and laid them on the table before Budge. She herself had breakfasted at dawn upon the heel of a loaf and a sip of black coffee; Joseph Good broke his fast a good deal later; but when he had ended his meal and was off for the day, then came the turn of her husband.

Budge Morrissey, conscious of food near by, slowly lowered his newspaper and looked over the rims of spectacles, which he wore not to help his vision, but to grace himself with a more studious and philosophic air.

He found that food was indeed there, and turning his vast shoulders more squarely toward the board, he handed the newspaper to his wife. She folded it and laid it carefully near his right hand. She picked up the napkin, flawlessly white, shook out its folds, and tucked a corner of it under the top of his waistcoat. For the vest was white, and so was the jacket which Budge Morrissey wore when he was appearing as the house servant of Joseph Good. On other occasions he was the bodyguard, the field lieutenant, the scouting companion, or the marketing agent of the same young gentleman. He had appropriate clothes for all these occasions.

Now, as he considered the platter before him and prepared to attack it with caution, but with confidence, his wife brought in a large pot of coffee and a pitcher of cream, then mixed, sweetened, and stirred the drink for her spouse.

He raised his enormous head, which would have appeared unsupportable on any neck less columnar than his own. He smiled upon his wife, and in a voice of gently bubbling thunder, he said: "Thank you, Betsy. You is a good gal."

Then he removed his spectacles, and still smiling a little, he submitted to a caress which touched the huge, dark crag of his chin.

Next he laid the spectacles on the table, and was about to begin eating when a rap came at the dining-room door that opened upon the rear veranda of the little house.

Budge raised his eyes and one finger toward his wife.

"It's nothing but a worthless, dressed-up black man," she said. "Big and useless is what he looked like to me. He's got a walking stick, and he give me his card."

Budge frowned. It was only a slight wrinkling of that backward slope of brow, but it indicated a sort of displeasure.

"Black or white, Betsy," he said, "a gentleman's a gentleman. I've gotta tell you that too many times."

"This one's not a gentleman," said Betsy. He's just an ape!"

It was the wrong word. It was a most unfortunate word, indeed. For it might have been used appropriately in describing the face of Budge Morrissey himself.

Now the frown deepened to a terrible, black, hurricane danger; the nostrils flared; appropriate lightning gleamed in the eyes of the monster.

He raised his left hand, adorned with a dripping fork, and pointed it toward the door.

"You hear me? Let 'im in!" said he.

Betsy hesitated.

Under ordinary circumstances she was able to handle her gigantic husband with perfect ease. A little wheedling, a touch of admiration, and then another of appeal were generally enough to wind him around her finger, but she knew the moments when he was totally intractable. By a single word she saw that she had roused the blind bull of his passion; and reluctantly she gave way.

She crossed the floor, opened the door, and sneered in the face of the tall young man who was again smiling and bowing before her.

"Come in, Mr. Jones," she said, in a voice whose good cheer and courtesy were entirely for the benefit of her husband's ear.

Jones stepped in, bowing again to her as he passed by. "Good morning, Budge!" said he.

Budge Morrissey turned his immense torso with dignified slowness. He prepared a gentle and friendly smile;

but when he saw the gold-toothed smile of the other he rose suddenly from his chair, wonderfully light in spite of his bulk.

Jones did not permit his host to speak at once. He widened his grin, made his eyes shine with friendliness, and held forth his hand.

"It's fine to see you, Budge," said he.

Budge Morrissey extended his own hand slowly; and when it closed over the fingers of Jones, a considering look appeared in the eyes of Budge, as though he thought of exerting a trifling part of his incredible force and smashing all the bones in the hand which he clasped.

But he thought better of it, merely saying: "What you doing out here so far from home, Vince?"

"Most important reason," said Vincent Lafayette St. Ives Jones, "was to see you, Budge. I heard what some low-down black men had been saying to you about me and a double-cross. I come clear out here mostly to tell you that they lied. I don't bother much the way I treat common men, Budge, but God gave me sense enough to know a gentleman and a friend."

Budge was pleased.

He knew perfectly well that Jones lied. He knew perfectly well that Jones had tried to sell him to the police on a certain memorable occasion during the days when Morrissey rested much of the time behind bars. Still, Budge was pleased with this present lie because it was fluent and because it contained a gentle tribute.

With a magnificent gesture he scattered the shades of the past and cleared the storm from his face.

"Sit down, Vince," said he. "This is my wife, Betsy. Ask the gentleman if he'll have some breakfast with me, Betsy."

Jones was hungry. The golden gleam of the eggs struck him to the very soul, but he felt that it would be most undiplomatic to cause Betsy any trouble on his account. He protested that he had eaten a hearty breakfast, and all he wanted now was the pleasure of sitting a moment in the company of his friend. He was accorded that privilege; he was given a chair facing Morrissey, and he sat down at ease, with his cane between his legs, his gloves on the head of the cane, his hands folded on top of the gloves. His hat rested on the seat of the next chair.

"Mr. Jones is an old friend of mine, Betsy," said the magnanimous Budge.

"Where'd you get to know him?" she asked. "In Sing Sing?"

Jones rolled his eyes savagely toward her, but he said nothing. However, Morrissey was indignant.

"Don't you be smart, Betsy," he cautioned. "You go on and get about your work in the kitchen and leave me alone. I ain't going to have my friends insulted in my own house!"

"Who made it your house, Budge?" she ventured to ask. "What would Mr. Joseph say to that?"

The glare she received sent her hastily into the kitchen, but she gratified herself by slamming the door noisily behind her.

Budge was much annoyed, but with delicate tact Jones smoothed over the situation, saying: "These here little fusses and rows at home, every married man has gotta have them, Budge."

"I guess he has," said Budge. "Now, Vince, what you want out here?"

"I want a chance to make you a rich man, Budge," said the other.

"That's mighty kind of you," said the giant, not greatly moved.

"I mean fifty grand!" said the other.

"To split how many ways?" asked Morrissey.

"All for your share," said Jones.

Morrissey lifted his eyes toward a corner of the ceiling and considered.

"Fifty thousand dollars," he said at last, "is fifty thousand dollars of any man's money. But—"

He paused and shook his terrible head.

"I couldn't leave this house, Jones, without permission."

"Who's goin' to keep you from leavin' it?" asked Jones, somewhat incredulous.

"Mr. Joseph Good," said the other.

34

Jones was surprised. He said: "I dunno that I make this out, Budge. Here you are, one of the most important men I ever had the pleasure of knowing; a name that's caused a buzz in the world, a name that's known in every big city of the country pretty near"—he did not say that he referred chiefly to police circles—"and yet here you are, settled down as the slave of a little white man that you could bite in two and swaller both the halves of him! I don't know that I make it out!"

"Maybe you don't, Vince," said the big man. "But that's because you don't know Mr. Joseph the way that I know him. The first time I met up with him I didn't try to bit him in two, but I tried to shoot him in two and to cut him in two. But I didn't make out very well!"

"What did he do, a little runt like that?" asked Vince Jones.

"You try him, brother," said Budge out of the superiority of his knowledge and of his certainty. "You try him, Vince, and in about five seconds you'll see what he can do."

Jones stirred uneasily.

"I don't mind taking your word for it, Budge," said he. "Only, it's an amazin' thing. And then, when I think of the way that you could be rakin' in and haulin' in the money in the old business—"

He paused and shook his head.

"There ain't many folks," he said, "that'll believe when they hear that you're a house servant, Budge!"

Budge stirred in his turn, as though he had been stung.

"What folks is saying about me I don't care," said he untruthfully. "I done got enough. I tried it, and I did

181

pretty good at it. But now I'm working for Mr. Joseph Good, and don't you forget it!"

"Well, Budge," said Vince, "I'll tell you one thing: you ain't gunna be working for him long; not if you stay in this here house with him!"

"Ain't I?" echoed Budge, calmly, full of resolution.

"No, you ain't! I tell you who I seen in this man's town."

"Who did you see?" asked Budge disdainfully.

"That little, cockeyed, crippled detective from Pittsburgh. I mean Flash Kennedy."

Morrissey grew very attentive.

"You seen Flash Kennedy here?" he demanded.

"I seen him here in this little old town," said Vince Jones, and settled back in his chair as though willing to wait while the full importance of this information soaked into the mind of Morrissey.

The latter was plainly worried, but finally he said: "Flash is a mighty smart man, but he's got nothing on me!"

"He didn't use to have," agreed Jones. "But times has changed. The way I got it, you once did business with a black man by name of Lew Tucker. Ain't that right?"

"Tucker? Yeah, I remember him. It wasn't much of a job. What's become of Lew?"

"Lew they got for a little second-story job, and when they started to roll him he broke down and begun to tell everything he knew. He didn't know much, but he knew something about you!"

"He didn't know much about me," said Budge. "I wouldn't work with a low-down third-rater like that Lew Tucker. It was only a little hundred-and-fifty-dollar job that he got a split on. It wasn't nothing at all!"

"It was burglary, wasn't it?" said Vincent St. Ives Jones, thrusting out his jaw while his eyes narrowed and twinkled.

Budge Morrissey did not directly answer. He cleared his throat.

"They been wanting to get their hands on you for a long time, Budge," said Jones. "You know that all they could do was to grab you for disturbing the peace, or vagrancy, or something like that. But all the while they was hoping that they could get a grand big charge agin' you. And now they got one. Lew Tucker's turned State's evidence."

"How'd you come to know all this before I was put in jail?" asked Budge Morrissey, sitting forward in his chair as he swallowed the last of his breakfast.

"The dick come to me and tried to pump me," said Jones. "But he couldn't get nothing out of me. I ain't the kind that would blow on a partner like you, Budge."

Morrissey made a cigarette, lighted it, and consumed a third of it in one tremendous inhalation.

"Flash Kennedy is a smart man," he said. "He knows where I am, does he? He knows that I'm out here?"

"Everybody in this man's town knows that you live out here," said Jones. "Flash might be along any minute. I hurried out here to tell you about him. But I had a hard time getting in to tell you."

Morrissey went to the window and looked anxiously out. He began to pad up and down the room with the soundless but heavy stride of a lion.

"I got to see my boss!" he said.

"What good is your boss now?" snapped Jones. "This is the law that's after you, Budge."

"Joe Good can do anything that he wants to in this town," said Morrissey. "If he winked once, a hundred cow-punchers would take Flash Kennedy and run him out of Fort Willow so far that he'd never see it again if he came back a thousand miles. My boss owns this town, Vince!"

"It's a kind of a funny thing," commented Vince Jones. "He ain't big; and he ain't rich; and he don't look very mean!"

"Listen. A few months back he was poor as a baby," said Morrissey. "He was just a loafer. He was taking things easy. Then the rich Altons wanted this land on the Good place, and they murdered his father and tried to run him out of the county. But they only woke him up, and he's kept on waking ever since. Wally Chase, the gunman, he broke up into little pieces that even a kid could handle; and he killed that Charley Martin.

"He went into the Alton house, and there he got the evidence that's going to hang Hugh Alton when his trial comes; and his trial, it comes in three days, now. This Joseph Good, when he wanted somebody that he could trust to take care of him, he went and found me in jail, and he took me out and he made me his butler. He trusted me right from the start. He treats me like a brother, pretty near. Those are some of the reasons that this black man won't ever leave him."

"I never heard so many reasons that sounded half so good as them do," declared Vince Jones, his eyes fairly starting from his head. "But I wouldn't wait here, if I was you, to see Flash Kennedy."

Sweat beaded the face of the giant. He looked desperately from one side to the other.

"My boss would get me out," he declared.

"Oh, maybe," said the other. "But if he didn't, twelve, fifteen years is a pretty long spell to stay behind the bars!"

The mention of the long term made the giant groan again.

"I dunno——" he began.

"You better know this," said Jones. "There ain't anything for you to do but to slide out for a few days, man. You say your boss loves you like a brother. Then he wouldn't mind your leaving his house for a spell like that—just a few days to let the dust settle down."

"Betsy," muttered Budge Morrissey. "She'll leave me if I leave Mr. Joseph."

His terror was so great his body was convulsed. He could not remain still.

Said Vincent Jones: "Now you listen at me, Budge. I've got a job planned that I told you about. It'll only take three days. It's right here in Fort Willow. All that you need to do is to write a letter to your boss. Tell him you're gone for three days. While you're away, you and me do this job. Fifty thousand dollars can get into your bank account before you come back here, Budge. You don't need to be a servant no more. You can hire a butler of your own if you want to!"

Morrissey actually dropped his elbows on the table and buried his huge, grotesquely ugly face in his hands.

He groaned faintly as he sat there, and over the face of Vincent St. Ives Jones passed a gray shadow of fear, mixed with disdain and hate, as of a trickster who has managed to baffle and bind the king of beasts, but who trembles lest the monster should manage to snap the cords that hold it.

So Vince Jones looked down on the bowed head of the giant.

At last Morrissey, without a word, went into the front of the house, beckoning to his companion to follow. In the little living room, painted clean white and cream, Morrissey sat down at a desk, took out writing paper, and inscribed with heavy labor:

DEAR MR. JOSEPH: They's closing in on me, and I have to move along.

I am sorry, Mr. Joseph, for leaving without your say so, but I couldn't wait till you come back today. The police is coming!

As soon as things quiet down, maybe in a few days, I'll be back again, and ready to serve you the rest of my life.

Mr. Joseph, I mighty well wish that you'd been here to give me your advice. I'm doing the best that I know how.

BUDGE MORRISSEY.

He folded this paper with uncertain hands, inclosed it in an envelope, wrote on the envelope: "Mr. Joseph Good." Then he stood up.

"I don't dare to tell Betsy," said he. "She'd a lot rather see me in jail than away from Mr. Joseph!"

"Don't tell Betsy, then," said the other. "Just change your coat, and then you come out with me and we'll slip away. It ain't far to the place I know where we can den up, and nobody in Fort Willow will think that you're closer than a thousand miles away. Not your boss, nor Betsy, nor even Flash Kennedy."

The last name was used at just the right moment.

Budge Morrissey, with a roll of his desperate eyes and an upward wave of his arms, surrendered to the tempter.

35

Into the offices of William J. Wisner, criminal lawyer extraordinary, Mr. Hugh Alton burst like a storm, exclaiming: "It's a plot against me, Wisner. It's a damnable plot against me! Something has to be done at once."

Wisner looked at his client with concern and banished his former happiness from his thoughts. For he had been very contentedly reflecting on the case of a certain murderer whom he had just finished defending. There never had been a man caught more red-handed in the commission of a crime, and yet, beginning with clever fencing, Wisner had finally reduced the conviction to one for manslaughter, and the appeals of Wisner had finally brought from the mercy of the judge a sentence of only a few years. That client would have been very happy, in this first place, to have changed a death sentence for one of life imprisonment. And he regarded the handling of his case as a miracle. His check for ten thousand dollars had just accompained his letter of gratitude.

However, Wisner wiped out all smiles as he faced the rancher.

The magnificent Hugh Alton was a sagging and wrinhad just accompanied his letter of gratitude.

Lines creased his face. He had grown ten years older in the last week; his eyes were haunted with suspicion and fear; those eyes which had once looked out securely upon the whole world.

He had lost so much weight that his shirt collars no longer fitted him; and his coat hung sadly from his shoulders. His very mustache was no longer an example of neatness and of personal care. It drooped wretchedly, and, in fact, Hugh Alton looked no better than the invalid other brother of the brisk fellow who, a little while before, had the county and its affairs in the palm of his hand.

"You'll have to take things a little more easily," said Wisner.

"How can I take things more easily?" said Alton. "Judge Tomlinson used to be one of my best friends. This morning the infernal ingrate and scoundrel would hardly speak when I passed him on the street. The case is lost to me, I tell you! You may save my neck, but you can't keep me from going for ten or fifteen years to prison, and that's really worse than death to me."

He beat his fist against his forehead.

"I wish," he groaned, "that I never had laid eyes on the Good family; I wish I'd never had a friend who was willing to tell me before the public knew about the probable course of the railroad when it was constructed. My life was one long triumph before that moment. Then greed got the better of me. I tell you, Wisner, I didn't want to actually have old Vincent Good killed. I honestly didn't. And on that evening I really did believe the rumor that Good had shot down my boy, Harry! Besides, it seemed to me that even God in heaven could not care a rap whether such a fellow lived or died!"

"You played in bad luck, that's all. Your scheme was all right," said Wisner. "If it had worked, you would have been twice as rich as you are today! Because you were right; and the railroad will come where you were told. The Good land, which is hardly worth five hundred dollars for the entire hundred acres, is already worth a thousand dollars an acre of any far-sighted man's money this minute. It will all be cut up into town lots. And within another two years those same acres will be selling for two or three thousand dollars each. There's no doubt of it!"

"I don't doubt it," said the rancher. "But why drive me mad by telling me such things? Joe Good is going to be a rich man for what reason? Because he's spent his life as an idler and a wastrel? Because he happens to be able to play tricks with a loaded black snake? I've spent my life building up my ranches, establishing a fortune for a decent family—and now I am to be ruined, while that puppy of a nameless boy becomes famous and well-to-do! Do you know what I heard?"

"What? About Joe Good? There's a hundred new rumors every day. Which is this one?"

"The rumor I heard is that Zeke Stevens, the miser, the scoundrel of a millionaire beggar, intends to make Joe Good his heir and leave him every penny of his filthy blood money!"

He raved and struck his forehead again with his hand.

Said the lawyer: "The boy's playing in luck just now. Big luck, deep luck! I heard that the First National Bank, which wouldn't have loaned him fifty cents if he'd mortgaged his soul ten weeks ago, now wants him to enter the bank—an honorable position, with nothing to do except spend an hour or so in the morning chatting over profitable big accounts with the president of the bank. They want that brat of a boy, mind you, they want Beggar Joe Good to be attached to the bank because he'll be able to bring them in so many big accounts through his influence! Doesn't that stagger you, man?"

"People are driveling idiots; men are fools! In a bank, is he? In the First National? And I've just been asked to resign from the board of directors. Yes, sir, by a unanimous vote they asked me to resign, the largest single rancher in this county, with more cash on hand than any soul on the range, with the exception of Stevens, and yet I've been asked to resign!"

Alton hurried up and down the room, still storming.

Then he checked himself suddenly.

"In three days," he said, "do you realize that I'll face the jury?"

"I certainly realize it," said the lawyer.

"Then what are you going to do about it? Can you hang the jury, do you think?"

"I can't hang the jury," said the lawyer. "No juryman picked from this town would ever dare to vote 'not guilty' against you. He'd be lynched by his brother jurors at the end of the case! I understand what I'm talking about!"

The rancher turned greener gray than before. "Very good," he said. "I understand what you mean. Every juror picked will long ago have made up his mind that I'm guilty!"

"He will."

"Then the rope's around my neck, or else I die in prison. My family disgraced! Wisner, I'm paying you to have brains! What are you going to do?"

"Kill Joe Good."

That short answer sent a hot wave of color into the face of Alton, and his eyes sparkled for a moment.

But the darkness descended upon him again almost at once.

"We've tried before," he said. "We've tried all that money could do. But it's hopeless. No hand can be lifted against him in this town, because the entire population of Fort Willow would rise up to lynch the killer. Nothing can be done against him in his house, because the two servants who take care of him watch him like a baby night and day. He has to be taken by surprise if he's to be killed. He can't be surprised except where he doesn't expect danger. And where would that be, except in this town or in his own home? As for taking him away into another part of the range, even the great Martin tried that; and Charley Martin is dead!"

"Wait a minute," said Wisner. "I think that I've changed the situation a little since I last talked to you. There's a man waiting to see me now. Suppose that you step into the next room and leave the door ajar a little?"

Hugh Alton followed the suggestion, and presently, into the office of Wisner stepped Vincent St. Ives Jones, pausing in the doorway to take his gloves and stick in one hand and his hat in the other while he bowed at the lawyer.

"What have you done, Jones?" asked the lawyer peremptorily.

"Mr. Wisner," said Jones, "I done gone and turned the trick for you."

"The mischief you have!"

"Yes, suh!"

"How did you manage it?"

"I'll tell you, sir, it's a long story. But the thing that turned the tide for me was a little remark, sir, about a gentleman from Pittsburgh being in Fort Willow."

"Who is he?"

"It don't matter. He really ain't here, but Budge Morrissey thinks that he is, and now Budge is down in the cellar of a shack on the edge of town, scared, and ready to fight for his life. He won't go home till I tell him that the coast is clear, and the coast ain't gunna be clear, Mr. Wisner, till Morrissey's boss is out of the way.

"But it ain't an easy job. If Budge dreams that I got a

scheme agin' his boss, he'll kill me with them big hands of
his. He loves that white man, suh. And it looks like the
white man loves him. But for a coupla days I can keep
Budge safe, I think. Only I'd rather be trying to keep a
grizzly bear safe and quiet. It's mighty hard on my
nerves!"

"You've had money," said Wisner, "and when the job is
finished you're going to have more money. There won't
be any doubt about that."

"There oughtn't to be no doubt," said Vincent Jones
cheerfully, "if Mr. Hugh Alton knows what this man is
doing for him!"

"Hugh Alton?" exclaimed Wisner. "Who brought his
name into the story?"

"I ain't a blind man, and I ain't deaf, neither," said
Jones, grinning. "Is they anything else you want, Mr. Wisner?"

"Nothing but to keep Morrissey safe. That's all. The
instant you lose control of him, let me have word! Good-
by for today."

Jones left, and Hugh Alton, crimson with excitement,
came back in by the other door.

"If you've got Morrissey out of the way, then we've a
fighting chance to finish off Joe Good!" he exclaimed.

"That's the way I looked at it," said Wisner compla-
cently.

"Man," cried Alton, "you're a wonderful fellow."

"I hope that you'll find me a friend worth having," said
the lawyer. "And as for Joe Good, I think that he'll curse
the day that I took control of your case. As a matter of
fact, I don't think that Joe Good will have long to live,
either for cursing or blessing! His time has come!"

"You have made the whole plan?"

"The whole plan," said the lawyer solemnly.

He opened his hand.

"I have his life here!" said he.

And he closed the fingers one by one against his palm.

36

A little later in the day, when the sun was high enough to strike with its full burning intensity, young Joseph Good sat under the shadows of the oak trees on his front veranda just in the center of the porch, where he could look down the pathway to the white-painted picket fence and beyond the old, sagging gate, across the barbed-wire fence on the farther side of the road, down to the hollow beyond, where gangs of laborers were toiling. Now and then the light flashed on a swinging pick or on the blade of a shovel as its load was pitched onto a wheelbarrow.

The boy was content, for every stroke of that labor was turning the new railroad station from a dream into a reality. The cut had been made through the low, sandy hills; the main tracks would soon be here; and in the meantime these workers were laying out the siding. It was not strange if Joe Good was pleased to watch the workers, for their picks and shovels were digging buried treasure, as it were, for him. Already the price of his land had soared amazingly, and when the walls of the station house and the big warehouse began to rise, then the price of his acres was sure to soar again. He would not be staggeringly wealthy, but he would be very well off for the rest of his days.

The thought of prosperity was exceedingly sweet to him. He could remember the bitter poverty of the old days, though there had been a certain happiness in the haphazard, shiftless life of which his father had been so fond seemingly. But he did not have to close his eyes in order to call up the visions of the first of the month and the stealthy dodging of creditors. That wretchedness was already behind him. The bankers would lend him almost

191

any sum he required. But just now he required nothing. He could afford to sit and to wait.

That was what he was doing now, tasting the new life over and over again, contented, when a buckboard drawn by a staggeringly old horse stopped at his gate and the driver, a bent, old, red-faced man, dressed in tawdry rags and patches, threw down the reins and climbed slowly to the ground.

He pushed open the gate and came down the pathway, waving his hand. The boy went hastily to meet him, and accompanied him back onto the porch. There they sat down.

"It's hot as Hades," said the man in rags. "All right for you gentlemen of leisure to set around in the shade, weather like this, but us working men have gotta keep stirring. Any water to drink on this confounded place of yours, Joe?"

"Betsy!" called Joe Good, and as the slender little woman appeared he said: "Bring out a bottle of whisky."

"There, now," said Zeke Stevens. "There's whisky and whisky, but this is what I call an honest man's drink."

The black bottle appeared, and Zeke's glass was poured brimming full; the boy barely covered the bottom of his own glass.

"That ain't a drink; that's only a taste that you have there," said Zeke Stevens.

"I don't drink whisky any more," confessed Joe Good. "I can't afford to."

"How much you pay for them boots?" asked the other, pointing an accusing forefinger.

"Forty dollars, I think," said Joe Good.

"You talk about not being able to afford, do you?" asked Zeke Stevens fiercely. "You can't afford whisky, but you can afford boots at forty dollars a pair, eh? Blasted talk! I paid a dollar and a half for these two years back. They was second-hand and wore a bit lopsided at the heels, but they've kept my feet covered for two years. That's why I can afford a drink now and then."

"I wasn't talking about money, Zeke," said the other. "I was talking about something else. You can guess what. The trial's due to come on in just a few days."

"I know what you mean," nodded Zeke. "You think that they're gunna try to choke you with lead so's you can't say the words that'll hang Hugh Alton. Is that it?"

"That's about it," answered Joe Good.

The old man took another swallow from the glass, shuddered, blinked his red-stained eyes rapidly, and then took in a gasping breath.

"Good, but hot!" said he. "Well, son, they can't touch you. Not around this town. Folks is too fond of you. They'll take care of you. I've heard 'em talk!"

"The only kind of talk that counts in cases like mine," answered Joe Good, "is the kind that comes out of the mouth of a gun with fire and smoke. But I'll take care of myself, I hope. Zeke, you're too hot. The water from that windmill is as cold as ice. I'm going to get you a pitcher of it!"

The trembling old crimson hand rose to thrust the idea far from him.

"I don't want no water," said Zeke Stevens. "Seventy year, pretty nigh, since I've had water inside of me to speak of, and I hope it'll be another seventy years before I taste it ag'in. There ain't anything that raises Cain with my stomach and puts my teeth on edge, gives me the heartburn and favors colds and rheumatism like plain water. I've tried it out all these years, and I know. But you take a lazy, worthless gent like yourself, always setting around and doing nothing, and water is about all you can stand. Me, I'm a hard-working man!"

"You ought to give yourself a vacation the rest of your life, Zeke," said the boy.

"And what would I live on, air?" asked Zeke.

"Hello, Zeke," said Joe Good. "Everybody knows that you have a couple of millions tucked away."

"A couple of millions! Everybody's a fool, then!" exclaimed Zeke Stevens. "A couple of millions? I never heard such crazy talk in my life! Look at me! Do I look like a couple of millions? Son, I never heard you talk so ratty and plain crazy before in all my born days!"

But young Good merely laughed.

"It's all right, Zeke. You're poor as can be, but you were able to lend me several thousand dollars when I needed it."

"I borrowed that money," said Zeke instantly, his eyelids fluttering rapidly, more rapidly than when the whisky had burned his leathery throat. "The only way that I got it was borrowing!"

"I'll have it ready for you again in a few days," said the boy.

"Stop talkin' that way!" exclaimed Zeke. "There's plenty more money where that come from. There's people that trust me on this range. Well, I gotta be starting along. I see some more folks coming to visit you. You've gone and got yourself popular, ain't you?"

And cheerfully he slapped the boy on the shoulder.

At this the little mongrel dog that had remained until this moment curled up beside the chair of Joe Good, suddenly bounded to its feet and stood snarling, bristling, ready to leap at Zeke's throat.

"Hold on, Professor," said Zeke, somewhat alarmed. "I ain't an enemy. I'm a friend of your boss."

The Professor was not reassured, however, until he heard a word from his master. Even then he was reluctant to give over his hostile attitude, but followed, sniffing suspiciously, at the heels of Zeke's boots, while the old man went down the steps, pausing at the bottom to say: "You bank on me, lad. I'm gunna help you ag'in whenever you need it. You've pulled the Altons down off their high hoss. A common, ordinary gent like me can walk and live and breathe in the same county with 'em now. Go on and throw Hugh Alton in jail. And that's where Harry Alton belongs, too!"

He waved and went on down the path to his buckboard.

In the meantime five more men had walked to the gate and passed Zeke on their way to the house.

They were equipped in motley clothes, and they looked the full part of what they seemed to be, railroad laborers. The round, brown face of a Mexican, the dark features of a full-blooded Indian, the starved cheeks and savage eyes of a half-breed, a burly, red-headed monster; all of these carrying picks or shovels, and foremost a short and powerfully built man with the sallow skin of an Italian. His air was a weird one which mingled sullen sneering and an attempted pleasant cheer.

He gave a half salute to the boy. "Mack sent me up with this here gang," said he, "to start work on the foundations."

"Mack who?" asked the boy.

"MacFarlane."

"He has the contract for moving my house back farther

into the hills," agreed Joe Good, "but he doesn't start for a couple of weeks, and he said nothing to me about working on the foundations."

"All right," said the other. "I'd rather walk back to town than start working in a dark cellar. Come on, boys." He turned about.

"Wait a minute," said Joe Good. "What's the idea of starting on the foundation as early as this?"

"Oh, we ain't gunna wreck your house," said the man half angrily. "But we gotta free the foundations, don't we? We gotta take and cut 'em away at the sides and corners, and see how she rides. Maybe there's gotta be work done in bracing the house inside and out before it'll stand moving. Looks like an old shack that'd fall in a heap," he added, his sneer coming out more prominently.

Joe Good considered him without a frown.

Not since the evening when he flogged Gunman Wally Chase on the veranda of the Fort Willow Hotel had any man talked to him so carelessly and rudely. But still, he had fought too many battles recently to invite trouble. There was still a plaster over the bullet wound on his left side.

"Well, go down in the cellar and start, then," he said. "I suppose that MacFarlane knows his business."

"All right," said the foreman of the gang. "Come on, boys. Let's get at it."

"What's your name?" asked Joe Good.

"Shorty," said the foreman, and led his men around the corner.

Very keenly the boy watched them go.

They were perfectly dressed for their parts, and they had the faces that might have been expected in a gang of haphazard laborers; but it seemed to him that their steps were singularly light and their heads carried wonderfully high for men of such an occupation.

He was about to follow them with more questions when he saw three riders come to his gate, and at the sight of one of them he forgot all his cares and suspicions.

37

There were two men in the party; one gaunt, tall, with wide, flat shoulder; the other more heavily built, wearing a sombrero with a flopping brim; that was Garnet, of the hole-in-the-wall country. And the third rider was Kate Garnet.

Because of her, Joe Good did not move in pursuit of the ostensible laborers. Because of her, he hurried down the path and was at the gate as they entered, the girl was first.

He was a little shocked at the first sight of her. He had pictured her as always blooming, young, gay, forever fixed in life at the age of twenty. Men have that foolish way of regarding women with whom they fall in love. And for years they look on wrinkles as a sort of illness from which the loved one will recover. Only after much length of years do they understand that time leaves for the careful mind as much as it takes away from the foolish.

Joe Good saw that there were blue circles under her eyes, that her cheeks were less rosy, that the suggestion of thin lines ran past the corners of her mouth. She had a graver air, too, and when she met him, he thought there was something almost melancholy in the lift of her eyes and in her smile, fixed steadily upon him. He shook hands with her father.

"This is Bill Dixon, Joe," said Garnet. "He rode down with us from the hills. We couldn't leave him behind."

Professor began to dance and bark furiously around the girl; she ran ahead with him, and the three men followed slowly, making rather sidling steps.

Dixon, as he shook hands with the boy, showed him a

rather sour face. He did not smile. He spoke with a slight lift of the upper lip as though he were saying cutting words.

What he actually said was: "I've got some land up there in the hills, too. I quit the country because Martin was too much for me. But I paid my taxes, anyway. I've been punching cows and playing poker to pay for taxes. When I heard that you'd put Martin away I went back. I'm going to open up again. Even the banks know that Martin is dead. They'll lend money on that land of mine now. Six months ago I might as well have had the same number of acres of sea water for all they cared about it! Then I heard that the pinch was coming for you, and I thought that I'd ride down with Garnet to see you and thank you and hang around for a few days."

"What pinch do you mean?" asked the boy.

"Well, the trial comes in three days, doesn't it? Inside of those three days I suppose that the Alton crowd will try something or other. You may need to have some friendly guns around."

He grinned.

"I've got one pair; Garnet has another. But Garnet never hits anything."

Joe Good thanked them both; and so they came to the veranda. They were not hungry; they were not thirsty. Their host could do nothing for them except to show them through the little white-painted house. He pointed out the care of Budge Morrissey and Betsy, who had done so much to make the house habitable.

He found a chance to say to Garnet: "Has Kate been ill?"

Garnet looked sharply at him, frowned a little.

"No, she's been worried," he said.

He spoke in a way that forbade more questioning, and Joe Good, flushing, realized that the worry might have been on his account.

They went back to the front veranda.

"There are two more things that I'd like to see—I've heard enough about 'em" said tall Bill Dixon. "The black snake and the mare, Molly. Could I see those things?"

The boy hesitated; then Kate Garnet said: "Show him, please, Joe. He really wants to see."

She spoke with a certain air of authority, as though she had a right to command, and Joe Good thought that he never had seen any mien become her so well. Whom should she command, if not him?

He shook his right arm a trifle, and into his hand came the coil of the whip, more supple, more slender than the body of a snake, more filled with poison for fighting men than the fangs of any cobra, too.

"This is the thing," said Joe Good. And he explained. "I thought that most black snakes have too thick a body. Makes too much air pressure. So I loaded this not in the handle only, but almost all the way to the tip. That gives it weight, but makes it slender. It cuts the air like a knife, and you can hit a target with it."

Bill Dixon held out his hand and received it. He made a few passes in the air; the lash tangled.

"It's too flimsy in spite of the weight," said he. "I don't see how you manage to do anything accurate with it."

He handed it back.

"It takes practice," said the boy. "Lazy men like to do things they can manage while they're sitting still, and I'm lazy. You see?"

A big wasp had come hovering around the head of Dixon, and from the hand of the boy the fluid line of the black snake darted out, the lash snapped, and the wasp disappeared from the air.

"You mean you scared that away or hit it?" asked Dixon, unbelieving.

"I think I hit it," said Joe Good. "It's just a trick."

"I hear that you can take a knife out of a man's hand or his belt," said the doubting mountaineer. "Well, there's a knife, if it interests you!"

And suddenly drawing a big bowie knife, he flung it so that it stuck in the boards of the veranda, trembling, humming.

"Perhaps I could pick it up," said the boy.

He was eight or nine feet from the spot, but the lash jumped as a snake strikes, and the supple tip of it curled around the knife handle, jerked the knife loose from its grip, and brought it shooting through the air. Out of the air Joe Good caught it and handed it back to the owner.

Bill Dixon was staring and agape.

"That's enough for me," he said. "You could cut out a man's eyes. I'd rather face two guns than that whip with you behind it—providing that the range was right! But what about the mare that understands talk and the dog that speaks English?"

Joe Good laughed.

"Kate's been talking," he said. "She's like a gang, and always giving me a boost. But I'll try to get Molly for you. Here, Professor," he added, "go bring in Molly, will you?"

The dog canted its head to one side; then, with a little yelp, it fled.

"He's run away, eh?" asked Bill Dixon.

Kate Garnet sat in a chair in a corner, her face oddly sober.

"You watch the results now," she said.

Through a small gap in the corral fence the Professor slid and shot away across the corral, raising a little windy trail of dust, then on into the pasture. There he disappeared behind the barn. His excited, yapping voice came back to them, then the snorting of a horse and the beating of hoofs.

"Come, come," said Bill Dixon. "Well," he added, "other dogs have been taught how to drive in horses from the field."

"Now wait and see what happens," said the girl, still grave, almost wearied as she looked confidently toward the corral.

Then Bill Dixon saw a chestnut mare with black points all around come sweeping up from the pasture, a small horse, not more than fifteen hands high, but she took the pasture gate with sweeping ease, while the barking dog shot between the lower bars and hurtled on in pursuit.

"Now watch," said Kate Garnet.

Halfway across the corral, outdistanced by the mare, the Professor suddenly sat down and lifted his voice in a piercing wail. Molly, the mare, heard, swung about, and cantered back to him.

"She's going to run him down!" exclaimed Dixon as the mare lowered her head.

Instead of running the Professor down, she allowed the little dog to spring onto the flowing mane that clothed her neck, and she dog-trotted until he had arranged himself across her withers.

Then she cantered forward again, increased her pace, reached the picket fence that surrounded the yard of the house, and went over like a bird, with the Professor flattening himself against the jump!

Down came the beautiful mare and danced forward to the veranda, reached it, reared, and with her forehoofs on the edge of the floor boards, nibbled at the coat sleeve of her master.

Bill Dixon could not keep his hands from her.

"It's all true," he said. "It had to be true, or you never could have beaten Martin, to say nothing of killing him. Man to man, without help—that's what I couldn't believe. Good, you've done miracles, that's all. And now, all through those hills the Martin men have been run out. Some of them needed a little urging, but after we'd helped a few of 'em on their way, the rest of 'em followed their good example. The hills are clean now. They're as clean as a whistle, thanks to you and Molly and the Professor!"

Garnet made a serious proposal.

He said: "We think that you're going to be in danger. And Dixon and I want to stay with you every minute of the time between this and the trial. It was Kate's idea, to be frank. But we think that it's a good one. What do you think?"

Joe Good hesitated.

He looked down his front path and across the field to the hollow, where the men were working more or less on his behalf, and from the cellar of the house he heard the noise of picks begin driven solidly home.

He had an odd sense, as he was aware of these things, that a fate quite beyond his control had taken charge of affairs.

Then he said: "I thank you all a lot. But the only luck I've ever had in the world has been when I fought out the hard things on my own hook, alone. When I leaned on my father and my friends, nothing ever happened. I'm going to keep to the new idea. I think my luck's tied up in it!"

38

Garnet started a long argument, but the girl broke in to say: "He's made up his mind. All you can do now is to bother him if you insist. He doesn't want you."

They were gone with breathless suddenness, as it seemed to Joe Good. They would stay in the hotel in Fort Willow for the three days and until the trial was concluded. They wanted to be on hand.

As they walked out to the gate together, the rancher said to the boy, lingering behind with him: "You've made Bill Dixon's little place worth while again; and you've made me a rich man, Joe. I've borrowed money; I'm buying cattle. I'll have those hills stocked as they ought to be, and I have you to thank for it.

"Now that Martin's gone, I wonder how we could have let that demon tyrannize over us for so long. But that's what he did, and we stood still and surrendered till you came along. I think you'll beat Hugh Alton and his money and his hired guns, too. But watch sharply every step of the way, because he'll kill you if money can buy bullets."

Then they rode off.

He hoped, as he held the stirrup for the girl, that she would have some special word for him, but she said nothing, and only from the saddle looked long and steadily down into his eyes.

Then she trotted down the road with the others and left him feeling seriously disturbed.

When he got back to the veranda Betsy was waiting to speak to him.

"What is it, Betsy?" he asked her.

She pointed downward. Her eyes were big as she stepped closer and whispered: "They're not right!"

"The men in the cellar?" he asked her sharply.

She nodded. She had overheard one of them exclaiming, "It's like digging a grave!"

Another of them had answered in Mexican: "It's his grave, not yours, brother!"

She understood Mexican; she understood it well enough to wonder whose grave they referred to, and it was of her master that she necessarily thought.

"If Budge was here," said Betsy, "he'd be down there in a minute and give them a look. He knows a rascal when he sees one, because he's been a rascal himself! But he ain't here, Mr. Joseph, and I'm sick thinking what may be happening to him!"

"Why," said Joe Good, "I showed you his letter when I got back. Didn't he tell you?"

"He didn't tell me nothing," said the girl, "and I seen the man that persuaded him away. That black man that called himself Jones, there's nothing good will ever come out of him. And Budge is in a mighty lot of trouble right this minute, I'm guessing. Oh, my fingers are itching and there's a dizziness behind my eyes."

Joe said: "This fellow Jones who came this morning— you think that he's a bad one, Betsy?"

"I don't think, I know, Mr. Joseph. I've seen good men and I've seen plenty of bad ones, too," said she. "My Budge ain't been a good man all his days, sir. And that Jones is plain bad. I could've told it by looking at him from behind by the way that he carried his head."

"You've no idea where Budge is?" asked the master.

"I got no idea in the world," she answered, with a mournful sound in her voice. "I'm afeared that I'll never see him again."

Then she broke out: "They wouldn't want to leave him here because they knew that he always had one ear and one eye open, day and night, to look after you, Mr. Joseph."

"If you don't know," said Joe Good, "maybe the Professor will be able to spot his trail for me. I'll see what we can do. Don't worry, Betsy, but call up the foreman of that gang and tell him that I want to speak with him about the digging."

She went hastily. He heard her voice calling at the cellar door: "Hey, boss! Come up here, will you? Mr. Good wants to talk to you a minute!"

Murmurs answered.

Then a step came around the corner of the house and there was Shorty, with his sallow face, knocking some dust off the wide shoulders of his coat.

He came to the steps and put his foot on the first one, looking up to the boy who stood above him. He had calm eyes, and they studied the face of Joe Good as a practiced boxer studies an opponent.

But that might mean nothing, for some men do not understand how to meet the glance of another except by an insult in their own faces.

Said Joe Good: "Shorty, when did you see Mac-Farlane?"

"Him? Yesterday evening," said Shorty.

"That's wrong," said Good. "MacFarlane was out of town."

He had made the guess at random; he was glad to see that Shorty turned not red, but pale with excitement and anger.

"Are you calling me a liar?" asked Shorty.

"Not yet," answered Joe Good. "I intend to lead up to that."

Shorty glanced once rather anxiously toward the corner of the house around which he himself had just walked, as though he expected that others might at any moment come to his aid.

Then he shrugged his strong shoulders and looked back at the rather frail body of the boy.

"You can't talk like that to a man like me," said Shorty. "These cheap skates and fakes that live around this neck of the woods—you can bluff them, but you can't bluff me!"

His voice rose in pitch into a whine like the whine of a bull terrier. Curses spilled from his lips.

Joe Good shook his right arm a little; a supple weight, unperceived, slid down into his ready fingers.

"And I'm gunna show these gents what a man does when he's called, the way you tried to call me. I'm gunna get you, you—"

He could not finish the next curse; his own hasty action supplied the lack of a word as he started to draw his gun.

Under the house, Joe Good heard running feet rush-

ing up the back stairs of the cellar, and he knew that he
must act quickly.

As the right hand of Shorty moved, the lash jumped
from Joe's hand and slashed straight across the eyes of
Shorty.

Blinded for a moment by what seemed a wall of crimson fire, Shorty screamed at the agony and fired twice
without aim.

Joe Good stepped nearer, and with the loaded handle
of the whip, tapped the other just hard enough across the
wrist; there would be no broken bones following such a
stroke, but from the unnerved fingers the heavy gun fell
to the ground.

The boy scooped it up. He was holding it in his right
hand, and the whip gathered again magically into the
fingers of his right as he sprang to the corner of the
house.

The round-faced fellow with the look of a Mexican
about him was rushing around it, a gun extended before
him, as the weighted handle of the whip crashed into his
face. He fell sidelong; his gun lost as well.

But he was only partially stunned, and rolling on the
ground, he staggered to his feet, yelling: "Shorty's got
it! The devil's loose! Get back!"

There was a great rushing of footsteps, but no more
armed men appeared around the corner of the house.

Joe Good turned to pick up the second weapon he had
secured in this brief scuffle only to find that Betsy, her
face wrinkled with determination, already had the gun in
her hands and was holding it under the chin of Shorty,
muttering: "White man, what did you do with Budge
Morrissey? Where's my Budge, I want to know?"

The sight of Shorty was clearing, though tears and
blood still flowed down his face. He had not been
blinded. It was almost by the grace of kind Providence
that he had escaped such a fate.

"Keep the gun on him, Betsy," said the boy. "He may
have a few more things of interest on him."

So she held the gun close under the chin of the gunman and listened to the curses which he whispered.

In the meantime, Joe Good found on the second man
some singular possessions for a hired day laborer.

He found a second full-sized Colt and another five-shot
revolver of an old style, a weapon with a large caliber and

a very short nose, convenient for being carried in the pocket, as this gun was carried. There was also a stiletto, such as desperados of a certain type are likely to love on account of the smallness of the wounds they make and the readiness with which death follows.

There was a wallet, and in the wallet seven hundred dollars in crisp, new bills.

That was all that was found worth noting.

Said Joe Good: "Shorty, they hired you to get me, eh?" Shorty said nothing. "They hired you, eh, Shorty, for that seven hundred?"

"I ain't talking," said Shorty, his handkerchief pressed against the cut, which still bled profusely across his brow and temple. "And if you hadn't been lucky enough to hit me over the eyes, you'd be rotting now!"

"It wasn't luck," said the boy. "And I didn't hit lower because that would have blinded you, and I need your eyes, Shorty, I need 'em, and I'm going to use 'em."

"You need my eyes?" snarled Shorty.

"I need 'em to find the way to Budge Morrissey."

"I'll never show you the way—not even if I knew it, I wouldn't," said Shorty. "All I'll do is put a knife in you when—"

"You know," said Joe Good, "that talk may be a waste of time. I won't waste words on you. I don't have to. You've tried to hunt me like a beast. So I'll treat you the way you would have treated me."

"Whatcha mean?" demanded Shorty, his jaw set. "You can't get me to blow on nobody. I talk after I seen a lawyer."

"This is the first lawyer you'll see," said the boy, and he made the black snake hiss before the face of Shorty.

The other ducked and winced as though a bullet had flashed past his eyes. He raised a hand to protect his face from that worse-than-a-knife cut.

"What do I get," he said, "if I show you the trail to the big black?"

39

Even the sight of the whip seemed hardly enough explanation of the sudden surrender of the other. The boy made that magic lash leap back into his hand, and Shorty regarded the disappearance of it with gloomy interest.

"Go back into the house, Betsy," said Joe Good.

She went at once, only pausing at the top of the veranda to look back with horror and scorn and rage toward Shorty.

Joe Good said: "If you take me where I'll find Budge, I'll turn you loose; if you take me there and tell me the rest that you know."

Shorty considered with an odd lack of emotion, rather as one who deliberately adds one to one and finally reaches a conclusion. Then he said: "You said that you'll turn me loose. How do I know that you'll do that?"

"Perhaps you don't," agreed the other. "You'll have to take that on trust."

"Trust ain't enough for me," said Shorty.

"You can have the whip in exchange," said Joe Good.

The stocky fellow ran the tip of his tongue across his lips.

"I'll take you where Budge is, but I ain't gunna talk," he declared.

Joe Good smiled upon him without mirth.

"You have a wrong idea, Shorty," said he. "You think that I'll treat you better than I'd treat a balky mule. But you're wrong."

"I'll yell and get help," said Shorty.

"If you yell, you'll get the flogging to start with and afterward you'll go to jail for assault with attempt to kill, conspiracy, and several other things. I have a witness of how you tackled me with a knife and a gun. Sometimes they lynch people in Fort Willow. Did you think of that, too?"

Cautiously the staring eyes of the other went on adding unit to unit, arriving at a conclusion.

"Maybe I better open my trap and do a little yapping," he said.

"Go ahead," said the boy. "How do you happen to be here, anyway?"

"It was like this," answered Shorty. "I knew— everybody that floats into town knows—that a lot of the big boys would come across with a flock of hard cash if you were scratched off the list. So I got a bunch of the boys together that I picked out of the tramp jungle the other side of town in the creek bottom. Then I started in and hiked 'em up here. My idea was that I'd start digging in the cellar, because I'd heard that the house was gunna be moved. Sooner or later you'd come down and take a look at the work, and when you come down, I'd tap you alongside of the head. That's all. Somebody would've paid big for the job!"

"Such as who?"

"Such as Alton, that lives in the big house over yonder."

He pointed.

But the boy did not follow the gesture. The loaded handle of the black snake slid down a foot or so from the tips of his fingers. He said: "You've lied to me, Shorty."

"Me?" exclaimed Shorty with an air of injured innocence.

"You've lied to me, Shorty," repeated Joe Good. "You don't realize, perhaps, that you're not the first hired murderer who's been sent on my trail. And now I'm going to get the truth out of you or smash every bone in your body. I'd enjoy smashing 'em, for that matter!"

And he raised the butt of the black snake as he spoke.

"Hey, wait a minute!" gasped Shorty.

His insouciance dropped away from him. For a moment his fingers worked as though he were inclined to dash in at Joe Good in spite of the gun and the whip. But he had tasted the latter too recently to forget the torments that lay in it.

Now he shook his head and answered: "I'll tell you the real truth."

"I hope you do, for your own sake," said the boy.

"It was this way," muttered Shorty. "A fellow by name of Wally Chase, that you might know comes—"

"I know him pretty well," said Joe Good.

"Wally, he comes and meets up with me. I'd known him before. And he asks me am I busy, which I ain't. And he wants to know if I got any friends around, and I say that four gents have come into town along with me, and all with their pockets empty and nothing to do. I ask Wally if there's any job framed where we can cut in and take a hand. He says that there's nothing framed, but if I meet him the next evening—that was last night—he'll maybe have something.

"So I drop around last night and see him, and he tells me how to plant this. He says that there's a couple of grands in it. He gives me a thousand bucks to begin with. I pass out fifty each to the other boys and break a hundred buying some guns and things for the crowd. Then I come out here, and you know what happened."

"Did Wally tell you that the money came from him?"

"No. He said that Hugh Alton was paying, and that he'll keep on paying, maybe, a long time after the job was finished, if we used our brains any. Blackmail, I guess, was what he meant."

"You didn't see Alton yourself?"

"No."

"How far away is Budge Morrissey?"

"Twenty minutes' walking."

"Where is he?"

"Down there on the creek, where the wreck of the old mill is."

"There's nothing to the ruins of the old mill," said the boy, visualizing the place hastily. "There's nothing to it at all. Just a few rotten timbers."

"There are cellar rooms under it, though," said Shorty.

"Are there? I thought that they'd be filled up with the wreckage when the mill burned down."

"Partly they were, and partly they've been cleared out."

"Budge is kept down there, is he?"

"Yes."

"Tied up?"

"No, not tied. The fool thinks that Jones is his friend and is keeping him out of danger. He's glad enough to stay there."

"How many people are with them?"

"Just the two of 'em. Just Jones and Budge Morrissey. Wally Chase might be there. He's got a grudge agin' Morrissey, and would like to put a knife in him. Alton went down there once, I think, to talk to Chase."

"We might as well start now, then," said Joe Good.

"Don't you do it," answered the other. "Don't you go and do it now. That Jones is always on the lookout, and if he seen you and me together, he'd shoot us dead in a jiffy. He can shoot, too. He's as slick as you ever seen with a gun. If he sees us together, he knows that I ain't on their side any longer. No, let's wait till evening. Then we can get close up and maybe take 'em by surprise."

Joe Good agreed promptly.

He spent the rest of that day in the small front room of the house, with the Professor sitting before the prisoner, marking every attempt of the latter to stand up.

Finally Shorty gave up his hope of escaping, and stretching himself on the floor, he went to sleep. Joe Good followed the example by dozing on a couch. In the cool of the evening they wakened and set forth.

Betsy, her eyes shining like the eyes of a cat, stood at the front door and watched them as they went out.

She said in a trembling voice: "I know my man's in mighty trouble, Mr. Joseph. But if he's burning, don't you go and throw yourself into no fire to save him!"

The husky, shaken sound of that voice was never out of Joe's ears as he walked with Shorty across the fields, keeping the other one step before him all the way. For he knew by the slowness with which the other was walking that Shorty was ready to take any measure, no matter how desperate, to escape from the plight in which he found himself.

At the heels of the master went Professor, that wise little mongrel.

They went toward the wreck of the old mill, but not directly. Instead, Shorty led the way to a point a hundred yards up the stream, where there was a more easily shelving slope to the bank, down which they could pass to the edge of the stream.

Shorty explained in a snarling guttural: "It ain't easy to find the entrance. I been there before, but I gotta use my eyes and ears both to find the way again. Walk soft. If they hear a whisper, we're likely to be both dead!"

He himself went forward with the most stealthy care. And Joe Good stepped behind him cautiously, keeping his grip on the hard handle of the black snake. With that weapon he had cut his way through some strange difficulties. But it seemed that this might be a problem harder than all the others, harder even than the battle with the great Martin.

They had only a dim light to guide them, chiefly the reflection from the quieter places on the edges of the creek. This, as a rule, flowed with a powerful current and with the rushing sound which water makes down an open flume; but along indentations of the shore line the stream in some places curled slowly in backwaters, and from the face of these the dull gold and the smoking reds of the sunset were reflected.

Even this color and light were dying fast, however; the shrubbery was blurred; and, half by feeling, they kept to the narrow, sloping trail and worked forward.

They came to a point where they left the bushes and walked on the very verge of the stream, with the banks lifting high above them.

The foundation of the old mill could not be far away now, and Shorty was moving inch by inch forward, bent almost double, when gunfire burst out at them from a nest of brush and rocks only a few steps ahead.

Joe Good flung himself backward into the shrubbery which he had just left like a man diving into black water. Still, as he lay there, panting, every nerve jumping, the bullets continued to crash and whistle about him; but he saw Shorty stagger, lean to the side, and pitch into the water. The strong current caught him at once and started him down the stream, his body whirling slowly around and around. He lay on his back, with his arms stretched out above his head, and Joe Good knew that Shorty was dead.

40

The gun fire had lasted only three or four chattering seconds. It cut down some of the branches of the shrubbery and scattered it over him. It knocked a handful of sand and gravel into his face. But that was the only harm done him.

Then, as the firing ended, he waited with every nerve on the alert to hear a sound of the slayer of Shorty advancing or retreating.

But there was no sound.

Finally, working his way on hands and knees, he himself advanced through the thick of the evening and came to that point from which the shooting had been done. Cautiously he moved through it, but the gunman was gone!

His hand fell on an empty cartridge; he saw the place where the other had reclined at ease, with the rocks perfectly in place to act both as a shield and as a rest for revolver or shotgun. But there was no sign of the destroyer.

What should he do now?

If he went forward, he could take it for granted that the narrow path would be closely watched. If he turned to the side and tried to force his way through the brush the noise he made would betray him.

At last, reluctantly, he turned back.

It seemed to him the hardest thing that he had ever done, the leaving of this trail at the side of the water, for now that he had come so close to the hiding place of Budge, affairs might take a bad turn indeed for the giant.

But he saw nothing else that he could attempt, and finally he came to the top of the creek bank and stood for a moment looking over the tops of the trees toward that distant hill where the lights of Alton's house were now shining.

He scowled.

He had done much against the rancher. The time had been when every eye turned toward those lights with respect and admiration, because they marked the house of the best-known and the most successful man on that range. All of that respect had now been torn away. If Hugh Alton advocated a cause, it was sure to be lost merely by his advocacy. Scorn and hatred followed him through the streets of the little town. And in two more days he would have to appear in court to defend his life from the charge of murder.

Hang he must!

Again, and never more vividly than on this night as he stood on the bank of Willow Creek, the boy saw the picture of his hunted father, the refuge he had taken among the rocks, and that circle of Altons who had gathered around him, and, with their rifles, at a safe distance, had shot the older man down.

To hang Hugh Alton it needed only that Joe should appear before the court of trial and give his testimony. Was it not his sacred duty, therefore, to preserve himself carefully so that he might be ready at the appointed time?

He felt the force of the argument, but on the other hand, big Budge Morrissey was in the hands of his enemies, and he could not rest until he had made an effort to free him.

He might go to Fort Willow and tell the sheriff and come out with a dozen armed men to explore the recesses of the cellars of the old mill.

But that would probably take too long. The noise of the approach of such a body of men would send the warning before. They might find Budge, indeed, but probably with his great throat cut from ear to ear.

Besides, since he had been seen with Shorty on the path to the mill, even at this very moment the men who were hidden in the place might be making preparations for instant flight; they might be disposing of Morrissey forever at this very moment!

Nervous rage burned in the mind of the boy as he thought of these things. He looked away from the lighted front of the Alton house in the distance, and down at the black face of the water. Dimly, against the polish of it, he saw a canoe turned upside down on the bank.

A new thought, a new hope, came to him.

He was down the bank in an instant and had the canoe right side up at the verge of the stream.

There was a paddle under the seat; he took that in his hand. If there were no way by land to the entrance of the mill, there might be a water road to the place!

He lay in the bottom of the canoe, only his head above the rim of its shoreward side, and his right shoulder and arm trailing the paddle over the farther side. In that way he could control the canoe, though he could not maneuver it cleverly, of course.

But he dared not expose his body too boldly, even in the dim illumination of the night. The men of the mill shot too straight!

The current now took him, shot him along at sudden speed, the canoe bouncing and galloping in the central current, and when he turned it into the shallows by the shore it still was moving at a good clip. There had been rains in the mountains recently, and the water level was high, the force of it great.

They slid down around the last bend, and now they approached the high, cut-away bank where the mill had been built. A raw and almost naked bank of earth it appeared to be now, and he felt suddenly that Shorty must have lied to him. There was nothing of the mill left on top of the bank except two or three gibbetlike timbers. And how could there be cellars remaining beneath the top level?

Yet Shorty seemed to have paid with his life to vouch for the truth of everything that he had declared. Now the canoe slid closer, gliding rapidly over what had once been the beginning of the mill race. The bank sped past him and was gone, with nothing whatever noted or seen, except at the last instant he saw on the water the rosy gleam of a light.

He stared at the shore to make out the source of it, but the shore was totally innocent of anything like a lantern or an exposed fire.

The canoe dropped speedily down the stream. At length he ventured to rise to his knees, seize on the paddle, and shoot the little craft across the jerking, dancing waters in the center of the stream.

Up the farther shore he worked the boat, slowly, for there was always a considerable pull of the current against him. He sat in the prow and dug deep and hard with the paddle, in this manner making headway.

When he came opposite the site of the mill, he studied the far shore inch by inch with straining eyes. But not a spark of light could he see!

Was it some lantern which had flashed from the shore for an instant as the bearer of it had passed between rocks or shrubs? Was it the embers of a fire which had suddenly been covered with a few shovels full of sand?

But lanterns do not flash like the light he had seen on the face of the water. There was a strong impression in his mind that the light had been a concentrated glow of radiance. It was not moving; only the water had been stirring.

The problem might be a small one, but it seemed to him more and more significant.

He paddled well up the shore, crossed again to the mill side of the stream, and again descended along the water line.

As he drew past the bank with the grotesquely suggestive, gibbetlike outline of the timbers rising above it, he heard a voice booming dim and far, a voice that seemed to rise up out of the water on which the canoe was riding.

Every vibration of it struck heavily on the ear of Joe Good, for it was the voice of his servant, Budge Morrissey. That bull's roar of a voice could have been heard from the bowels of a mountain; and now, though dim and uncertain, he made out the words of the giant saying: "I'm going to leave. I've been here too long. I'm going to leave right now. Stand away from me, Jones, or—"

The voice went from speech into a deep, short cry.

It spoke no more; and the canoe slid rapidly past the bank, until, once more, Joe Good saw the red gleam of light shining out on the water.

He was on his knees at once; and, thrusting deep and hard with the paddle, he came back to the spot where he had seen the light just before.

He was working hard now, and recklessly exposing himself to any chance observer from the shore. But the voice of Budge Morrissey and the sudden termination of his speech had called up in him a fury of excitement and almost of despair.

For it seemed to him that he could see the shadowy looming of a blow that must have struck the giant down.

Here was the light again.

He studied it with amazement as he saw that it still shone, though there was no sign of any fire or lantern burning on the bank.

Then, more startled than ever, he made out the source of the radiance—it was in the water itself!

He could hardly convince himself of this, but staring again, harder than before, he thrust in the paddle straight at the light. The reflection disappeared; it did not float on the surface above the blade of the paddle!

No, down there in the water, two or three feet down, beneath the level of the surface, there was the source of this light.

He could not believe his eyes. It seemed very unlikely indeed that there was a window of thick glass opening upon the water, and that a fire or lantern burned behind it.

The Professor, as though realizing that something strange was in the air, stood up with his forepaws on the rim of the boat and whined softly as he studied that red image in the current of the stream.

Whatever the source of that light, he, Joe Good, must find it, he knew.

He drove the canoe onto the bank, and there he pulled off boots and coat, patted the head of the dog in farewell, and dived down under the black surface toward the mysterious light beneath.

41

It was neither a long dive nor a hard one. Presently his fingers were on a ledge of broken masonry; he pulled himself under it and came up through brightly lighted water to the surface.

In a glance, as his head came free, he could understand the cause of the phenomenon of that appearance of light shining up through the water itself.

It was simply that a portion of the outer, river wall of one of the cellar rooms of the old mill had fallen out. That room had two levels; the floor of the upper level was still dry, and therefore a light shining in it struck down through the shallow water that covered the lower section of the chamber, and the illumination naturally slanted off through the river outside.

He made that observation at the very moment when he heard voices close by, and was warned that danger was ready to rub elbows with him. He recognized those voices. Almost his oldest enemy, Wally Chase, was one of the speakers.

Half in water and half out, he began to crawl forward, the depth shoaling away with every step, until he came to a row of sandbags three or four feet in height which walled the inner and higher part of the room away from the water. On top of those bags stood not a lantern, but an oil lamp with a particularly powerful circular wick burning. That was the cause of the excess of the light that had been shining down into the water.

Two men on the farther side of the wall of sacks were playing cards. In a moment Joe Good had reached a place from which he could look through a narrow aperture between two of the uppermost sacks, and he gained a clear view of what took place beyond.

There, seated on a pair of boxes, with a larger one between them in lieu of a table, were Wally Chase himself and another old familiar, Doc; that same burly ruffian whom he had flogged into better manners on the evening when Martin and the rest of the gang drove him by fire into the mouths of their guns, as it were.

A white scar across the upper cheek of Doc looked like a knife cut, but young Joe Good knew that the lash of the black snake had made it.

They were playing seven-up, carelessly, for stakes too small to keep their interest on the game. And they talked, naturally, of the evening's occurrences.

"You might've followed him up," Wally was saying. "If you dropped him in the brush, the way that you say you did, you might have a good chance of walking straight in after him and polishing him off."

Doc lifted his handsome but brutal face and sneered.

"You'd've done that, I guess?" said he.

"I would have tried to do it. I been after him long enough," said Wally Chase. "I'd gladly walk a thousand miles and swim a hundred to get such a chance at him."

"How did I know but what he might've been faking?" asked Doc.

"You said that you put a slug into him, right through his body."

"I think I did, but I ain't sure. Look at here—would you follow a wounded mountain lion into the brush in the dark?"

"Oh, he ain't a mountain lion," said Wally Chase.

"I'd rather take my chances with a mountain lion," said Doc. "I took my chances with Joe Good once, and that was enough."

He glowered at Chase.

"You took your chances with him once, too, and all you got was a broken wrist and a licking!"

Wally Chase held up his right hand and worked the fingers. The wrist was almost double the proper size.

He said: "I got a broken wrist, but it's healed up now, and I can work about as good as I ever did. You keep that idea in your head, will you?"

"I'll keep it in mind," agreed Doc. "But it don't make any difference to me, Chase. You can't talk down to me."

"Who's tryin' to talk down to you?" demanded Chase.

"You, saying that you would've followed him into the brush."

Chase stirred in his place, and his lean, dark, evil face grew blacker still.

At last he said: "You done pretty good, anyway. You bumped off Shorty when the sneak was trying to give us away. You done enough for one day, I guess. But it would've been lucky for you if you'd polished off the kid, too. It would've made you talked about, I guess."

Said Doc: "If I don't get him today I'll get him later on. And if I don't get him, somebody else from the mountains is gunna get him framed some time or other. We won't forget what he done. We been run out of our homes because of him. That's a fine, free country, I call it. They take and run you out of your own homes, they do, and yet they go around and talk about the law. I don't want that sort of law!"

"Well," said Wally Chase, "did a lot of you get run out of the mountains?"

"Twenty or thirty men, counting 'em all. The minute that Martin was dead, then the gents that wouldn't've dared to peep if he'd been alive, they got together and they took us by surprise. They done things that it makes my blood boil when I think about it! There was Garnet comes down on me and Bill and old Dunker, where we was living—comes down on us in the middle of the night in the lean-to that we'd put up. He comes down and some punchers with him, loaded down with guns, and gives us the run!"

"Did you own the land you was livin' on?" asked Wally Chase.

"Sure we did. Anyways, we'd been on that land for eight-nine years."

"Who owned it before?"

"I don't give a curse who owned it before. Garnet, maybe."

"Ever buy it from him?"

"What if we didn't?" asked Doc angrily. "After you live on a claim eight-nine years, you got a right to it. Ain't that the law?"

"I dunno the law," said Wally Chase. "But if there was twenty or thirty of you, why didn't you get together and blow the heads off of those ranchers?"

"We didn't get no proper chance," complained Doc. "I was down and out. I was sick. Old Bill was used up, too; his face had been pretty near beaten off his head when Joe Good socked him with the butt of the black snake. And there was Charley Martin dead; and nobody else seemed to have no ideas. There wasn't no leadership, is what there wasn't nothing of."

Wally Chase shrugged his lean shoulders. There was no decency, kindness, or gentleness in him, even for his rascally peers.

He said: "Joe Good threw such a scare into the lot of you, and he put such a hot idea into all the ranchers, that you didn't have no chance to fight. I know what happened."

"Well," exclaimed Doc, "you got your run from Joe Good yourself. You should talk!"

"I'm gunna murder him for what he done to me," said the other solemnly. "I don't care how I get him. Front or back. I'm gunna kill that infernal upstart."

He spoke with such a quiet fervor even Doc was impressed.

"That's why I'm glad to have you with me on this job," he said. "What's that steady dripping sound I hear?"

"Where?" asked Wally Chase.

"On the other side of the sacks."

"Oh, that ain't anything. You take a rotten old trap like this and the water is always sure to be soaking and dripping around in it one way or another. We're all gunna get rheumatism and pneumonia if we stay much longer down in this dog kennel!"

"Maybe we will," said Doc. "But we're getting paid pretty good for it. I don't think I ever heard that dripping sound before."

"I don't hear it now," said Wally.

In fact, Joe Good, when he heard the first remark, had stooped down closer to the water and pressed himself more tightly against the sacks, so that there could be no possible dripping of the water from him into the cellar water.

"No, it's quit," said Doc. "But I'm gunna have a look."

"Don't be a fool," said Wally. "Don't stop the game. I'm gunna shoot the moon a coupla times and even things up."

Young Doc already had pushed back the box he was

sitting on, preparatory to rising, but now, reluctantly, he settled down in place again, but still throwing a sour and fixed look at the wall of sacks, as though his instinct told him that there was danger on the farther side of it.

However, he now shrugged his shoulders and gloomily turned his attention to the cards.

"How could anything get in here?" asked Wally Chase. "Joe Good ain't a water rat."

"I dunno," said Doc. "But he's done some funny things."

"He's done some funny things," said Wally Chase in partial agreement, "but he's had a lot of luck, too."

"He can see in the dark," said Doc, and lowered his voice a little. "Is that luck, eh?"

"Who told you that he could see in the dark?" demanded Wally.

"Nobody told me. Nobody had to tell me. I watched the windows where he was inside, fighting with Martin. There wasn't no light in that room. I can swear that there wasn't. Martin emptied one gun and part of another, and only put a couple of nicks in the kid. And the kid, he fired just one shot, and that one was enough. It was through Martin's heart!"

He spoke with awe and shook his head as he finished.

"I seen the place where the bullet sank into Martin's breast right over the heart. I seen it with my own eyes," he continued. "You can't go and tell me. I know that this here Good can see in the dark like a cat!"

"If you wanta believe that," said Chase, "go ahead, only—"

"Hush up!" said Doc. "I hear that—"

"You got the fidgets, and your nerves is all gone," declared Chase.

"Fidgets, have I?" exclaimed Doc. "Well, you listen yourself. Don't you hear something sneaking down the hall?"

They struck attitudes of keen attention; and even Joe Good could hear the approaching step!

42

He saw guns slide into the practiced hands of the two. They did not lift the weapons shoulder-high, but at a level little above the hip; they held them easily, covering the door. Plainly the boy could make out the narrow thumb of Wally Chase hooked over the hammer of the revolver, ready to let it drop and send the bullet home.

There had been a time when the repute of Wally was very great indeed as a slayer of men; and Joe Good had an idea at this moment that the same reputation would be made to grow again upon the same soil, even though men knew that on a day Wally had been flogged with a black snake.

Who was the person walking toward that door? Was it a friend of Joe, some rash and courageous man who had come to investigate his wanderings?

The knob of the door turned, the door was opened, and there at the entrance appeared the fine, broad shoulders of Hugh Alton and that worn, haggard face which had once been so handsome, so much younger than the years behind it.

He blinked at the broad glare of the lamp and then came in as the two put up their guns.

"You might've rapped on the door, governor, and sung out," said Wally Chase. "You was in an inch or two of getting yourself tagged with a coupla chunks of lead, walking right in that way."

"I think that I'd be glad to have the bullets strike," said Alton, "here between the eyes, where my brain is going mad. What have you been up to now? Tell me what you've done? I thought, Chase, that you'd arranged—I thought that—"

"You thought that five men would've been busy at the killing of Joe Good before now, eh?" said Wally Chase.

"I know the story of how they came to the house," said Alton. "I know that you got big Morrissey out of the way. I hope to heaven that you've still got him safely here. But what made you trust the killing of Joe Good to such clumsy fools? Such a gang of half-wits?"

"What makes you think that they're half-wits?" asked Wally Chase.

"He stood to them all with his black snake—a curse on it!—and thrashed them all, and made four of them run, and he caught and held the leader of the lot and made him confess!" exclaimed Alton.

Then, running out of breath with rage and grief and excitement, he began to walk up and down, beating one hand against his forehead.

Said Wally Chase slowly: "What did he confess?"

"He confessed that you'd hired him and that he'd hired the others. He said that you'd hired them with my money. My money! I was ruined before, but now I'm the most despised and hated man on the range. They came over to call on me just now, half a dozen of my worthy neighbors, men who would rather have put guns to their own heads than show me discourtesy a few months ago. But they've changed. Young Joe Good has changed them, changed everything, ruined me. They told me that they'd been at his house, that the mulatto woman had told them everything; that her husband had been spirited away; that five men had come to attack Joe Good, and they had been driven away, the leader had confessed, and had gone off with Good.

"They were very hot about it. They swore that if anything happened to the boy they'd see me swing for it—by lynch law, if the regular forms were not strong enough to handle me. I never saw men so furious. You would have thought that the worthless young idler was the son of each of 'em. One of those men came from your district, young man."

He turned to Doc. "He was Garnet. He's come down to help Joe Good in case the boy needs help. But the point is now: where is Joe Good? Where did he go with the brainless rascal who talked so much to him about you, Chase, and about me?"

"The brainless gent," said Wally Chase with his former deliberation, "was shot dead a few minutes back by Doc, here. We seen him coming along the creek trail in front of Joe Good, and that made it pretty clear that he was gunna double-cross us if he could. But he can't double-cross us now. He's dead, and the creek has got him. And Joe Good dived back into the brush. Maybe he's bleeding to death there right now!"

"Great heavens," said Alton, "why isn't something done to make sure of him? If you can finish him off—"

"You'll pay a lot of money," nodded Wally Chase. "I know that. Looks like pretty near everybody knows that. And it's gunna be bad for you if his dead body's found, no matter where. They'll lynch you, Alton!"

The other blanched a little, but then he shook his head.

"I have to take my chance. Better that chance than the court trial, the disgrace, the prison."

He threw up his hands, started to speak, and then controlled himself.

"Have you beaten the bush to find him?" he demanded.

"We ain't beaten the bush to find him," said Wally Chase, "because we ain't the kind of men that hunt wounded mountain lions in the dark in brushwood. Are you the kind that'll do that?"

Hugh Alton suddenly caught in his breath.

"Then all you know is that he may be dead, he may be wounded, he may simply be alive and unhurt, roaming about this place, laying his plans to ruin us all!"

"Any one of them things might be true," said Wally Chase.

"Then for God's sake, man, do something about it!"

"We're doing something about it," said Wally Chase. "We're waiting for daylight to come."

"Is that all?"

"That's all. We've got nothing to do till morning except wait for the daylight and kill the big black in the meantime."

"Kill him—Morrissey, you mean?" asked Hugh Alton.

"Yeah."

"More murder, more murder!" groaned the rancher. "When a man takes blood on his hands he must bathe in it deeper and deeper, until— This wretched Morrissey, is there nothing else to do with him?"

"Nothing. We're takin' it good and easy and looking on every side of the job," answered Wally calmly. "But we can't spare men to watch him day and night, and we can't just tie him and leave him. Y'understand? The ropes are hardly made that are strong enough to tie him and keep him."

"He's a gorilla," said Doc.

"Have you tried to do anything with him?" asked the rancher. "Have you tried to win him over to your side of the business?"

"We tried, but he loves his boss better than he loves himself."

"It's a filthy business," said Alton. "But if he has to be put out of the way, why not do it and have the thing done?"

"It ain't up to us," said Wally Chase. "That other black wants the job. He likes it. That Jones, he's a hard case, and he hates Morrissey like he hates poison. He wants to have the killing of him, and he's gunna have it, I guess. I don't hanker after the job, and neither does Doc. What Jones is doin' to Morrissey right now I wouldn't want to guess at!"

"Torturing him?" said Alton, suddenly perfectly calm.

"Yeah. Most likely that. I dunno what ways. He's got a brain, though, that fellow Vince Jones."

Alton took out a folded handkerchief from the breast pocket of his coat, and with it wiped first his face and then his hands carefully.

"That's right," sneered Wally Chase, "you keep your own hands good and clean, Alton. We'll do all the dirty work for you."

"You're paid to do it," said Alton crisply. "You've been paid before, and you'll be paid again. You know that. We're not through with one another, Chase. But I want no more sneering or abusive language."

"Well, that's all right," agreed Chase. "You've paid your coin, and you've paid it on the nail. You've paid a lot, and I know that you'll pay a lot more. But what are your next ideas, Alton? We've done something. We've got Joe Good on the run, it seems like to me. We've squeezed Morrissey away from him, for one thing, and that was what kept him safe at home up till now."

Alton raised a forefinger as in solemn warning.

"You've done a great deal, Chase," said he. "I don't deny that. But everything amounts to nothing until you've stopped the heartbeat of young Joe Good. Until you've put him out of the way, your work hasn't even commenced. If you wound him, it's worse than nothing. Because once he's wounded, his infernal friends will take charge of him by force, if they have to, and that will mean that they will keep him carefully guarded until the day of the trial. The day of my death, I may as well say, for I've made up my mind that I'll never face the jury and the evidence which Good can place before it. But something must be done to him. Chase, you're a fellow of brains. And in this work you're inspired, because I know you hate the rascal as thoroughly as I hate him!"

"Very well. I'll tell you what we've got to do," said Wally Chase. "We've got to sit down and plan a little more carefully the next stroke. If he's free and unhurt, we'll have to work up our scheme to get at him tomorrow. Sit down here, then."

"This is a rabbit's hole," said the rancher impatiently. "There are a couple of other rooms in this cellar. Why can't we go into one of 'em?"

"Morrissey's in one," said Wally Chase, "and there's a lot of stinking slime on the floor of the other. But if you want a change of scene, we might as well go along. I don't care where I sit to try to talk the scalp off the head of Joe Good. Come along, Doc, I'll carry the lamp."

A hand gathered up the lamp; shadow swayed over the place where Joe Good was crouched. And the three crossed the floor to the door. As it opened, a deep, far-away groan entered the room to meet them.

"Listen to that," said Wally Chase, chuckling. "There's that bright feller, Jones, at work on Morrissey. Morrissey is gunna pray for death a long time before it comes and shakes hands with him! Come on, Doc. Makes you grin, does it, to hear Morrissey grunt? You'd be doing more

than grunt if Jones was usin' his talents up on your car-
cass, son!"

Their footsteps moved on, and the door, on grating
hinges, was drawn shut.

Then Joe Good rose and prepared to act.

43

He climbed the wall of sacks; and, standing inside of them, he did a few gymnastics and setting-up exercises to supple his cramped and half-frozen body.

When his blood was flowing freely he uncoiled the supple black snake from around his right arm and drew it several times through his left hand, pressing on it hard enough to remove the water from the oily, slick surface of the leather. He freshened his grip on it and made the long lash leap out several times in the dark.

A gentle hissing sound cut the air; that was all.

Then he went to the door.

The opening of it was a matter of a second for the others, who could afford to overlook noises. But it was only after a full five minutes of careful work that he opened it wide enough to allow his body to squeeze through into the corridor beyond.

A draft blew down that hall and struck his wet clothes, chilling his body; but he continued forward, groping through utterly blind darkness until once more a heavy groan struck him to the heart.

He knew the iron strength and the Herculean courage of Budge Morrissey. He dared not imagine what torments were being used to extract these groans from him.

That sound led him to the left, and he found the entrance to another very narrow corridor, down which he began to steal, when a door opened somewhere behind him and down the first hallway went a swinging light.

"I must've dropped it on the floor," said the voice of Doc. "I'll be right back."

He and his lantern passed the little alleyway in which Joe Good was crouched and that flash of light enabled

227

the boy to see the heavy door just beside him and mark the projecting handle of the wooden latch pin.

Presently a running step came back along the first hall, and he heard Doc exclaiming: "The door's open! Somebody's opened the door to the river room! It was closed after us, and now it's open!"

"The mischief you say!" muttered Wally Chase.

"Tush," said Alton, "there's a draft in that hall. If you didn't latch the door, the wind would work it open a little."

"I tell you, I closed that door good and solid behind us!" declared Doc. "There's somebody here in the cellar. There's been somebody in that room since we was all there!"

"Rot!" said Alton. "These underground conferences are enough to make all our nerves jump a little. But everything's all right. I'm sure of that. Who could have come in, and how? Walk from the middle of the earth?"

"That's it," said Wally Chase. "Use your brain, Doc, and not so dog-gone much imagination. There ain't anything wrong. There can't be anything wrong."

"All right, you gents can have it your own way, but that Joe Good can do funny things," said Doc gloomily, "I seen how he shot Martin in the dark. He can do some funny things, and I know it."

Nevertheless he did not persist in his idea, and now the light disappeared and the door closed, groaning, behind it.

Very much would young Joe Good have wished to overhear the results of that conference which meant life or death to him, perhaps, before many hours passed.

But another groan, not of rusted hinges, but from a human throat half closed by agony, now reached him from behind the door in front of which he crouched.

His hand, in the darkness, found the wooden latch pin, and softly, little by little, he raised it, listening with his own heart in his teeth, in dread of making the slightest sound.

The door finally began to give way. As it opened, a crack of dim light penetrated, then widened, and beyond that opening crevice he saw the interior of the room.

A big wooden pillar stood in the center of the room, upholding the roof, which probably had begun to sag long before. Against this pillar the mighty body of Budge Morrissey was lashed, foot and hand as well.

He was illumined by the dull gleam from a smoked lantern chimney, and the same light showed Vincent St. Ives Jones standing before the captive at work.

Blithely was Jones laboring, as a demon might have worked with canny craft in an inferno.

There was a smile that showed the gold fillings in his front teeth. And his eyes were wrinkled and glimmering with content.

He made no sound, but calmly went on with his task. One might have thought that he was drawing a picture of torment rather than actually enacting it.

This present device was a double thong running around the head of the giant Morrissey, and in a curve of the thong a piece of wood had been run through, which Jones had turned several times, and which he was about to turn again.

Already the cords seemed to have sunk halfway into the head of the monster. The eyes of the great Morrissey protruded from his head. And his face seemed to have been covered with glistening oil, such was the sweat of his agony.

"This here," said Jones in the softest of voices, "is just to make up for the little things that you done when I first knew you. When I didn't know you good enough to hate you, Budge. I've told you about a couple of the things. And here's another one that may interest you:

"Likely you won't remember one Sunday when you came swelling down the street all dressed up with a yaller coat and a green-and-white vest on you. You had a cane in your fist and a diamond in your necktie, and a wing collar on. You wouldn't recollect, maybe, how you went by me and my girl, that was standing on a street corner. And when you passed she turned around and she looked at you, and what I seen in her face, it made me plumb crazy, and I busted out and had a wrangle with her. I didn't see that lady home, Budge. She seen herself home, and I didn't never see her no more at all.

"Now I'm gunna pay you back for that, Budge. But you listen to me. I ain't a bad guy. I ain't the kind that would be mean. All you gotta do is to beg me to kill you and I'll kill you good and quick. But I wouldn't go and take your life off of you, Budge, without you asked me to do it. You ain't tired of it yet? Oh, no, brother, you ain't tired of it yet, but maybe I'm gunna make you tired before I'm through. We'll just give this here another twist or two, and you keep thinkin' about how fine you looked that day in the yaller coat with the bright bone buttons on it all polished up fit to kill."

He twisted the thong; the vast lips of Morrissey trembled open, and the groan came shuddering forth.

Then the boy struck.

He wanted to kill, but he could not kill from behind.

Instead, he selected a place just below the ear of big Vince Jones, and there he tapped with the loaded butt of the black snake.

The knees of Jones sagged forward; not rapidly, but slowly.

He turned his head, and with blank, senseless eyes, looked over his shoulder at the form of Joe Good, who stood ready to strike again.

He stretched out his hand and caught at the body of the man lashed against the pillar, but still he continued to sag. Presently he reached the floor and sank in a massive, shapeless heap upon it.

A pocketknife was in the hand of the boy the next instant.

He cut the ropes that held Morrissey's legs first of all. Then he slashed the device on his head, setting it free. Finally he cut the bonds upon his hands and arms.

Morrissey made one long stride from the pillar and sank helpless over the body of Jones!

It was a dénouement which poor Joe Good had not dreamed of. He had reached the heart of the enemy's camp; he had set free his friend from the more immediate danger, and now he had a helpless hulk on his hands!

Was he dead? Had the terrible pressure of the cords reached to some vital nerve at the back of the neck, perhaps?

No, the heart still beat, but the body was utterly inert. If there had not been enough pressure to kill, there had been enough to take away consciousness.

When would he revive?

There was no sign of returning vitality or consciousness. He might remain this way for a long time!

But Jones was already stirring, beginning to sit up,

muttering slowly to himself, and raising a hand to the spot where the loaded black snake had struck him.

A big man was Jones, and with one grip of his hand he could paralyze easily all of the power that was in a slight fellow like Joe Good.

Moreover, he was armed.

That gun belt the boy unbuckled, took out one of the revolvers, and dropped the cold muzzle of the gun against the back of the man's neck.

"Jones," he said softly.

"Jones," said the stunned man. "Where you gone and kept yourself, Vince Jones?"

Then, with a gasp of breath, he seemed to recover himself.

"Jones," repeated Joe Good still more softly. "Steady; don't stir; don't make a sound. Look at me."

The head of Jones rolled slowly far back.

At last he looked up by that dim lantern light into the face of the white man.

His jaw sagged. Horrible fear distended his eyes beyond any belief.

"Joe Good—the whip!" he breathed.

"Don't speak again, Jones," said the boy, "or I'll kill you now. I want to kill you, except that you can still be useful. And this is how: Stand up!"

Silently the frightened Jones rose, rolling his eyes, cornered as a beast is cornered.

"Now," said the boy, "you pick up Morrissey and carry him. No matter what he weighs, no matter if you break your back. But you carry him out of this place; and make no noise, because if your precious friends hear a sound you'll die."

44

They turned out through the corridor, Jones walking first, bent and crushed under the vast, loose bulk of Morrissey, but spurred to an immense exertion by the jabbing of the revolver into his side.

Vince Jones pushed open a door. Outside there was the fresh air of the open night, the stars, and the soft, swift flow of the creek waters. Hardly a step away was the canoe from which the boy had landed not so long before.

Jones had lowered his burden and stood propping him. There was some returning life in the hulk of Morrissey, for he was able to sustain some of his own weight on his legs. But his bleeding head rolled loosely over on one shoulder, and the eyes were like the eyes of a dead fish. Even by the starlight Joe Good could see this, and he could have groaned at the sight.

Clothe this giant with his real power and he would be able to charge into the mill cellar and bring out Alton, Doc, and Wally Chase by the napes of their necks in one bundle. There, in a stroke, would be the end of all troubles, with Alton himself lodged in jail on a palpable charge.

Instead of being a magnificent helper, Budge Morrissey was not only a loose bulk, an incubus of the worst sort, and there seemed no promise that he would soon recover. Perhaps his life was seriously endangered; medical aid must be found.

Glancing down the creek toward the light of Fort Willow, Joe Good realized what he must do. He must get Morrissey into the canoe, then drive with the current until he was able to land in the town near the bridge. The sound of his voice would soon bring help to that point, and he could have Morrissey quickly in the hands of a doctor.

That was perfectly clear, but he had other problems.

With the assistance of Jones, he quickly had the helpless Morrissey stretched in the bottom of the canoe, with the Professor curled up on the knees of the giant. But now it became clear that when he, Joe Good, entered the frail little craft, it would already be overloaded. There was no space or buoyancy to support the big body of Vince Jones.

What was he to do with the brute?

He lifted his revolver a little higher.

"Jones," he said, "there's no room to carry you in that boat, and I'm not going to turn you loose."

Vince Jones lost both strength and courage. He did not actually pray for a life which, he knew, was now forfeit. But he turned sick with dreadful fear and slid weakly to the ground on his knees, with his head falling back against the slope of the bank.

"Oh, my Lord! Oh, Lord, Lord!" gasped Vince Jones.

Disgust rather than pity made the boy step back. "Jones," he said, "I'm going to let you go. I can't give you what you ought to have. But take my word for it, Alton and the rest in there are gone geese. They're not going to last long. You, Jones, clear out and keep away. Because when Morrissey gets on his feet again he's apt to spend the rest of his life hunting you down, and when he gets you—"

He stepped into the canoe as he said this and squatted, with one thrust of the paddle driving the little boat well out into the current.

The force of the water dragged them along with wonderful speed, the shore by the mill, the gibbetlike outline of the ruin above it, all disappearing in a moment.

Perhaps it was the sweep of the cold, pure night air against his face that roused Budge Morrissey. But when life returned to him it came with a rush. He broke out with a violent oath, then stirred and drew up his legs.

"Steady, Budge!" exclaimed Joe Good, heartily wishing now that he had waited a little longer on the bank until the giant might recover his strength and mind. "Steady, or you'll upset the canoe."

But Budge was still not more than half conscious, and he sat up suddenly.

With desperate strokes of the paddle the boy managed to keep the canoe from turning over, but so great were those efforts that he quite lost control of the head of the canoe. It turned broadside to in the stream, and in a moment crashed like an eggshell against a projecting rock.

The boy, with one hand, gripped the rock; with the other he fastened on the coat of the big man; and the current snatched the canoe from under them and shot it down into the darkness of the stream.

Not even for a moment could Joe Good have supported the weight of the giant; but now the shock of cold water was enough to restore Morrissey fully to his wits. It was he who bounded first to the top of the rock and then drew up his master after him.

Joe Good found that they were on a little island perhaps twenty feet long and half as wide, and the creek on either side flowed shallow and broad, but with terrific speed, as the bed of the creek here sloped down at an increasing angle.

"Where might we be, Mr. Joseph?" asked Budge Morrissey. "Where might you've had to go to take care of this worthless fellah? Oh, Lord, Lord, I been nothing but a burden to you, sir! And now there's a band of fire around my head. And I deserve it. I deserve all that Jones done to me. It's enough to teach me and make me remember what a worthless fellah I am, that can't give you nothing but trouble."

"Be quiet, Budge," said the master gently. "You've served me; and in the pinches there's no master and servant, but we both work together. Try that current, Budge. It's too heavy for me to walk through it, but maybe you're strong enough and weigh enough to wade through it."

The giant accordingly stepped into the stream, but with the first pace he was knee-deep, with the second he was to his hips, and as the current caught him he was barely able to fling himself backward and catch the outstretched hand of the boy.

He clambered back and shook himself like a dog.

"It's pretty strong," he said. "The water's shooting along here so that I don't think nobody could wade it."

"We might strike out and try to swim it," said the boy.

"It's not more than thirty feet to the shore just here, and with a good jump and some hard swimming—"

"No, no, Mr. Joseph," said Budge Morrissey. "Look down there! And listen, too!"

Joe Good obeyed, and he saw through the dark of the night the faint gleam of foam here and there, and then he was aware of the roaring of broken water, a low and steady note.

"Those are teeth that would eat you, Mr. Joseph," said Morrissey with conviction.

"They would," agreed the boy. "This is bad business, Budge. It's too far for us to jump. If we had a rope we could throw the noose over a stump and get ashore that way, perhaps. But we haven't a rope. Day is going to come on here, Budge, and we're stranded not more than a hundred yards, I should say, from the mill. If any of those rascals are left there, they'll find us held ready for them. Two rifle bullets will finish us, Budge."

Morrissey muttered something unintelligible. Then he said: "I don't know how, but we're going to get to land some way. The Lord hasn't let you do the things you've done to finish you off in a cheap little way like this."

He began to pace up and down, and presently stumbled and almost fell, his feet entangled in the long, tough withes of the vines that almost covered the little island.

He straightened again, swearing under his breath, but presently he said: "Look here, Mr. Joseph, if these runners are strong enough to trip me up they're surely strong enough to braid into a thirty-foot rope!"

"They are—they are!" exclaimed Joe Good. "But we need a knife to cut the withes. They're as tough as leather!"

"We don't need any knife. I've got the hands that can break 'em!" said Morrissey.

And straightway they began to manufacture their rope.

It was surprisingly easy to make it. Morrissey tore up vines, roots and all, stripped away the runners, and tested them one by one with the pull of his arms. Those that snapped were discarded into the stream; of the others they began the weaving of a rope that was rather thick and heavy and clumsy, but which, nevertheless, seemed strong enough to endure the weight of a man pulling on it.

But they worked with great care. For two hours they

continued that weaving, and when they had completed it
to the noose, they went up and down the little island,
carefully scrutinizing the shore for a rock or a tree stump
over which they could cast the noose and so anchor the
line.

But, unfortunately, at this point there were chiefly wil-
lows that thrust out long branches, trailing down to the
water. There was no rock, no stump, that they could
make use of.

It was Morrissey who thought of the next strange ex-
pedient.

"Mr. Joseph," said he, "the Professor knows every sign
you make to him, don't he?"

"Pretty well," said the boy.

"He'll go out and back and to this side and that if you
wave to him?"

"Yes, he'll do that."

"Then suppose I tie an end of this line around his
shoulders and throw him to the shore—couldn't you
make him walk around one of those tree trunks until the
line was fast? It's green stuff; it would stick without having a knot tied on it."

"It sounds possible," said Joe Good. "There's nothing
better to try."

It was done at once. Not around the neck of the little
dog, but over his shoulders and under his forelegs the
line was worked. Then Morrissey picked him up and
swayed him back and forth with increasing speed until, at
length, he flung the little, wriggling body far away into
the air.

There was plenty of force in that cast to get the dog to
the shore, but the rough, green rope caught against the
leg of the big man, and the Professor, falling a yard short
of the bank, was swept rapidly downstream in the current.

45

Never is the fighting instinct so strong in large creatures as in small. The big man fights with the value of his weight; the little man fights with the fury of the very flame of life. The big dog fights with the complacence of a bully; the bull terrier fights from the hunger to kill.

The little Professor, as he felt the deadly power of the stream take hold of him, looked back through the gloom of the starry night, saw the shadow of his master, and then struck out valiantly. The branch of a willow swept close over his head; he reached up and seized it in his teeth; the force of the current, dragging at his body, pulled the branch down. He scrambled for it with active feet, worked along it, and dropped down again on the dry shore, from which he turned, having shaken the water out of his hair, and looked back toward Joe Good for approval.

He saw, clearly enough, the wave of the arm that sent him to the right, and toward the right he trotted, past the trunk of a stanchly rooted willow, paused, and saw the beckoning hand that waved him in, then to the left, then to the right again, in toward the shore, and so three times he was sent around the trunk of the tree.

The signals now ended, and the Professor sat down to ponder, perhaps, upon the eccentricities of mankind.

Then he sprang to his feet and ran toward the water a step before the rope of green withes stopped him, for his own beloved master was in the force of that current, pulling himself hand over hand toward the shore.

Suddenly the rope slipped around the willow trunk. The body of the little dog was crushed against the tree. But a moment later young Joe Good scrambled on the shore and was patting the head of the dog. The past was forgotten!

Now Joe Good himself held the end of the rope, and big Morrissey waded into the water as far as he could, leaped off from a rock, and hauled himself in hand over hand. The withes, under that strain, parted at last, but not until Morrissey was so close in toward the shore that he could reach at the willow branches.

By then the giant hauled himself in and sprang upon the shore, laughing.

"Now what, Mr. Joseph?" said he.

"There," said the boy, waving toward the lights of the town, now much fewer and farther between, since the night had grown older. "We go to Fort Willow, because we may need help!"

And they struck across the fields, found a trail, and ran along it until they were on a street of the town.

To the house of Sheriff Dick Purvis they went—Purvis, who had crossed swords with the boy once on behalf of Rancher Hugh Alton.

But the mind of Purvis had changed since then. There was no more honest man in the world, and all that he desired was a good opportunity to wipe the blot from his escutcheon.

He heard the banging on his front door and rose from bed, growling, to answer it.

He flung the door wide, exclaiming: "Well, what drunk is trying to shoot up the town tonight?"

"Purvis?" snapped the voice of Joe Good.

The sheriff held higher the lamp which he had brought to the door in his hand, and he saw the slender figure of Joe Good, bedraggled with water, stained with mud, shoeless.

"Great Scott; it's you, eh?" said he with mingled emotions.

And the boy answered: "Get your horse, Dick. We're going to call on Hugh Alton, you and I. I have a new charge that will put him in jail till the trial commences."

"What charge?" asked the sheriff, and he looked past the boy toward the immense shoulders of Morrissey and the head of the big man, rimmed with a circle of red that passed above the ears and across the forehead.

"Charge of conspiring to murder me," said the boy, "and of abducting my friend, Morrissey, here."

Morrissey stretched his lips in a meaningless smile. But it would be something to tell Betsy that the boss had referred to him as "friend."

The dry, hard voice of the sheriff said: "You've got your proofs?"

"I've got Morrissey for one proof. Look at his head. He's been tortured by Alton's hired men. Is that proof enough?"

The sheriff stared.

Then he said: "I'll have a horse saddled in two minutes. Come along; you'll need horses, too. I dunno that I got anything that will carry Morrissey far, but Alton's place isn't a long way off."

They went out to the stable behind the sheriff's house, and there they found horses in plenty. A rough, roach-backed roan was given to Morrissey; Joe Good got a more slender bay gelding, and the sheriff himself took his best stayer, a washed-out chestnut whose courage offset the faults of his color.

Then, together they rode out through the black of the night, and from the town cantered across the hills. The air was still. Two or three great clouds bloomed sullenly across the faces of the stars as they reached the entrance of the Alton place, and the gravel of the driveway made crisping sounds beneath the iron-shod hoofs of the horses.

They dismounted, tethered the animals at the hitching rack, and the sheriff in person beat with the knocker on the front door of the house.

Thrice he beat before a sound came to answer them; and a Chinese servant opened the door a crack.

His slant eyes turned round as he saw the sheriff.

"Get Mr. Alton," said the sheriff, and walked in.

The Chinaman fled, and the three, the sheriff in his usual costume, the barefooted, bedraggled Joseph Good, and the immense Morrissey stood in the big front room.

The mind of Joe Good went back to another night when he had stalked through that room, in the middle of the night, to burglarize the study of the rancher. He looked at Morrissey with a smile, and Morrissey looked back with a mere lift of the upper lip.

The eyes of Morrissey were slightly reddened. The lines of his face were drawn. Humor was not nearest the surface of his mind just then.

Footsteps came faintly down the upper hall, along the

stairs, and toward the door of the room. There appeared Hugh Alton and his son, Harry, his favorite. They were fully dressed, which explained the delay.

"Evening, Dick," said the rancher. "What brought you—"

Then he saw the strange forms of Joe Good and Morrissey, and his voice stopped.

Harry Alton, shocked by the sight of these men, had drawn back beside the door. One hand, his right hand, was inside his coat.

"Tell that fool of a boy to take his hand off his gun," said Joe Good to Alton.

The message did not need to be repeated. Harry Alton's hand appeared again from within the coat, holding no weapon.

Said Hugh Alton, mustering a high air: "This is a very odd business, Mr. Good. As I have understood our affairs, you are hardly a welcome guest in my house either by night or day."

"He's come to make a charge agin' you, Alton," said the sheriff roughly. "I dunno just what the reasons are, but I guess he's serious. He and Morrissey, they don't look like they was playing any practical joke, would you say?"

Alton looked at both and shrugged his shoulders.

"Whisky is probably behind this little prank," he said. "People don't generally come sodden into my house. What's the meaning, Purvis? Or perhaps Mr. Good himself will explain?"

Joe Good stepped forward a pace and dropped his left hand on the edge of the center table. In his right hand was the butt of the black snake that had cut a way for him through the difficulties of his life.

"Alton," he said with something like a smile in his eyes and on his lips, "you've tried to buy my murder a number of times before this and—"

"Slander and blackmail," said Alton, "will get you no further in your cause, whatever it may be!"

Young Joe Good shrugged his shoulders.

"I was in the cellar of the old mill tonight," he said. "I suppose Vince Jones told you that?"

"I don't know what you're thinking about, my boy," said Alton. "Harry, close the door to the hall."

Harry closed the door and remained outside of it! Joseph Good went on: "I was in the cellar for some time.

I was behind that wall of sandbags when you were talking things over with Doc and Wally Chase. I heard every word you said to them, Alton, if that means anything to you!"

Hugh Alton strove to speak. He had words in his mind, but he could not bring them to his lips. A cold hand was taking him by the throat.

At last he managed to say: "God forbid that I should understand anything that you—"

The boy raised a hand and pointed a forefinger like a gun.

"Were you at the wreck of the old mill tonight or not?"

"I? Yes—no—I mean to say—I—"

The rancher broke down utterly.

It was a wretched thing. Dick Purvis, accustomed as he was to handling criminals, looked away.

And Joseph Good went on: "I heard you tell them that I had to be killed before your trial begins. I heard them tell you that Doc had shot Shorty when he was guiding me to the entrance to the mill. I heard you say that the three of them had to plan the coup de grâce for today. I heard you say that I would not live to face the court on the trial day!"

Hugh Alton could not speak, and the sheriff said at last: "Alton, you'd better come in with me. I arrest you in the name of the law!"

Sickly greenish-white was the face of Alton; then his head dropped. Guilt, like a horrible crown, was on him.

And he said: "I'll go with you, Dick. I'll say good-by to my wife and meet you here in five minutes. Is that all right?"

"Certainly," said the sheriff.

And Alton left the room.

46

Joe Good said at once: "You've let him out of your sight. Do you think that you'll ever see him again?"

"See him?" exclaimed the sheriff. "Why, man, that fellow won't throw up everything he has in the world and turn himself into an outlaw. The land he owns is too doggone valuable for that. You think that he'd beat it?"

"He'll beat it, all right," said the heavy, hoarse voice of Budge Morrissey.

"Never in the world," protested the sheriff. "I know something about men. They gotta be broke before they stop hoping, and he hasn't stopped hoping. He'll go on hoping till he's wasted every cent trying to bribe the judge and the jury. The hound! Joe, I was a fool in the old days!"

And Joe Good said: "You weren't a fool for thinking that Alton was right and that I was all wrong. It was trying to find out the proofs to sink him that made something of a man out of me. But now he's sunk, I think."

"I've seen enough in the face of him to convince any judge," said the sheriff. "God knows I pity him. But what put him on your trail, Budge?"

"Budge worked for me," explained Joe Good. "And Budge looked after me better than any watch dog ever could. That was enough for the Alton gang. They had to brush Budge out of the way. And they nearly managed it. But I've an idea that we'll pay them back for everything that they've almost managed to do!"

He set his teeth as he spoke, but the face of Morrissey did not alter. He had the look of one who is prying far into the future.

"How long d'you think that we ought to wait here?" asked Joe Good.

"Oh, ten minutes, perhaps," said the sheriff. "Don't make any mistakes about it. Alton ain't going to try to break away."

"He's gone already," said Morrissey suddenly.

"Gone already?" repeated the sheriff. "That's nonsense!"

"He's gone," said Morrissey firmly. "I heard the noise of horses padding along away from this place. That's Alton, and his gang with him."

"Hold on!" said Dick Purvis. "You don't mean that!"

"Open the window," said Morrissey.

But he himself raised the sash, and then, clearly, they could hear the trampling of galloping horses already at a considerable distance.

Dick Purvis rushed from the room into the hall.

"Alton! Alton!" he thundered.

Harry Alton, very white of face, came to the head of the stairs.

"Where's your father?" asked the sheriff.

"He's in the room with my mother," said Harry Alton. "He is—"

"You lie!" said the sheriff. "And if you lie, I'll have you for conspiracy to defeat the law. Tell me the truth! Where is he?"

That threat was enough for the feeble soul of Harry Alton. He surrendered like a craven and muttered: "He went out the back door a minute ago."

"Who went with him?" shouted the infuriated sheriff.

"Wally Chase," said the coward, "and Vince Jones and another fellow they call Doc."

A stream of oaths burst from the lips of the sheriff.

"You were right, and I was wrong," he exclaimed. "The dog has run, and his pack along with him. Four of 'em— but there are three of us. Will you fellows back me up? I know you will. We'll get some horses out of the Alton corral for second-string mounts."

He was running down the front steps as he cried out these words. The other two followed hastily.

At the bottom of the steps, as he flung into the saddle, Joe Good said: "The Professor can follow the trail for us. He'll bring us up to 'em before the end of the night. Here, Professor!"

He reached down, and the dog leaped to his stirrup, to his knee, and so to the withers of the horse.

That was the burden that the boy carried to the stables.

There the sheriff quickly picked up three fresh horses from the string in the stable, while Morrissey, running about on foot outside the place, located suddenly the trail of four horses that traveled away through the trees.

His outcry brought the others.

Joe Good gave to the nose of the Professor a hat of the rancher taken from the hall rack. It was easily distinguished, because Hugh Alton always appeared in clothes, hats and boots specially made to increase his dignity.

And with that scent to follow, the little dog streaked like lightning down the trail.

They left the trees; they swooped down over the rolling hills, almost on a straight line toward the house of Good.

He therefore ventured to race at full speed ahead, and near the fence of his pasture his whistle brought Molly, the mare, swinging like a bird over the fence.

He did not change the saddle to her at once. Instead, he preferred to use the mustang of the sheriff for the first burning part of the run. Molly might well come in later on.

He swung in beside Dick Purvis and heard the other muttering: "We'll catch them. We've got to catch them. This makes or breaks me, this job. Makes or breaks, makes or breaks! Joe, if I managed to land the crooks, I know that you'd work on my side at the next election?"

"At every election," said the boy. "Don't doubt that. But what are we? Are we deputies, or sworn-in posse men, or what?"

"You're posse men," shouted the sheriff. "Listen to me, and repeat it after me. You hear, Morrissey?"

"I hear you, Mr. Sheriff," said Budge.

"Repeat after me: I, Budge Morrissey; I, Joseph Good."

And so he shouted out to them the formula of the oath, and as they galloped hard over the hills, those two voices answered. They had hardly finished that oath which made them servants of the law for that night, at least, when they came to a broad sweep of naked rocks, where the little dog lost the trail.

Joe Good called him to the horse and carried him swiftly across the obstacle.

There he put the dog down and made him cast to the right and to the left; far down near the verge of a tangle of brush he gave voice again, and the party streamed away behind the Professor, his yipping voice and his bobbing tail.

He was picked up as the way led plainly, clearly up the center of a shallow ravine.

But halfway up the ravine he was put down again; luckily, for he led them straight over the left shoulder of the little valley and into rough, broken ground beyond.

"They're laying a twisting course," said the sheriff, "but they're bound for the mountains. There's no kind of doubt of that. If only the nags can hold out, and if Morrissey's weight don't break the back of that mustang!"

But Morrissey's horse bore up surprisingly well, particularly when they reached the steeper slopes. The reason was easily apparent. It was simply that the animal did not have to bear its rider up the worst of the climbing, for when they came to a sharp pitch, there Morrissey bounded to the ground and ran like a rabbit, in spite of his great weight.

He spoke not a word, for he was saving his breath, and in his mighty breast there was burning a fire of revenge which could not be reduced to language. The labor which he gave himself was beyond credence, but he never flagged, and his horse, overburdened as it was on the flat, was never far behind.

The little Professor, quite unable to hold a sufficient pace across level spots, was picked up continually by the boy, and put down again whenever there was a doubt of the way.

So they worked through the night, through what seemed endless hours.

But neither the sheriff nor Joe Good spoke of deserting the way. The small dog still found the trail, and through the starlit darkness they moiled and toiled at the great slopes.

They used up their first string of horses, shifted to the second lot, shifted back again.

And so they rode, at last, into the sullen gray of the morning, noticeable first as the big mountains turned blacker than the sky about them, and then emerged from the darkness as thin edgings of light appeared around their summits.

Steadily and gloomily they held upon their way. Then their hearts began to rise, for now they could see the tracks before them. It was not necessary to put the exhausted dog to the ground nearly so often. He could rest on the back of Molly while their eyes picked up the sign before them.

The gray light of dawn turned to rosy gold. The mountains bloomed under it; all the world wakened; birds sang in the thickets; the hawks took the upper air, and the buzzards, circling higher toward the zenith, began their all-day watch from the towers of the sky. Far behind them they saw the lower rolling lands where Fort Willow lay, but the town itself was invisible until the sun rose and flashed on the distant windows.

They seemed to be in the balcony of a vast theater, where the gods themselves were holding the upper boxes, among clouds and winds. And the trail held before them, ever freshening.

To one who leaned from the saddle and looked closely it was apparent that the fugitives had passed that way only a short time before, since the down-beaten grass was slowly rising again; or, where the way was over sand or earth, the grains from the corners and the sides of the depressions were still falling down.

That was enough to encourage them more than bugle blowing and the cheering of crowds. They were silent now, for they were watching every covert and every nest of rocks out of which a blast of rifle fire might be poured into them at any moment.

The hunted men would shoot, and shoot to kill. They were clearly riding for their lives, and they would take the lives of others to save their own.

47

It was inevitable, perhaps, that the thing should happen finally. They had pressed on too closely, and the rocks and trees were constantly grouped in strategic positions ahead of them.

Suddenly bullets whistled about them, followed by the clanging noise of the reports, and Sheriff Dick Purvis spilled sidewise from his horse.

The firing ceased; far away they heard the rattling of hoofbeats over rocks.

But the boy and Morrissey were already dismounting at the side of the fallen man.

He had been struck by a bullet on the right shoulder, and the weight of the blow or the shock of the pain had been sufficient to make him lose his stirrups.

They cut open the shirt and saw that the bullet had not inflicted a very dangerous wound.

It had been deflected, glancing from the shoulder bone without breaking it, and ripping its way out again through the deep muscles that padded the breast.

The sheriff understood its rightful significance at once, and he exclaimed, as Morrissey and the boy made the bandage: "Don't give up the trail. They're dead beat or they never would have started shooting at that range. Follow 'em up, boys. You're only two against four, but one of you is Joe Good, and the whole world's a liar if Joe Good isn't equal to any other three men since Martin's dead. Ride on, and ride hard, and good luck to you both. It'll heal me more than a year in bed to know that you're closing in on 'em! Get 'em; get that hound of a Hugh Alton and I'll be a happy man if I have to die for it!"

They did not need much urging. They left the sheriff in the shade of a tree with a canteen filled with water, and then they took the remaining horses and pressed ahead.

Over the crown of the next hill they forced their way, and down the long, long slope beyond.

Then the horse which the giant Morrissey was riding stumbled, staggered, and stood still.

"He ain't dead, but he's close to dyin'," said Budge.

"Take another!" urged the boy.

"They're done," said Morrissey, drawing the rifle from the saddle holster and slinging it across his back. "Just lemme hang onto a stirrup, Mr. Joseph, and I'll keep up some way."

Keep up he did as they rushed down the slope. Then, rounding the hill at the foot of it, they saw a stretch of flat-floored valley before them, with the narrow mouth of a ravine opening to the left. There, in full view, hardly two hundred yards away, were the four fugitives.

Big Budge Morrissey, with a groan of relief, dropped to one knee, raised his rifle, and prepared to fire.

But they were seen.

All four riders, in answer to a wild yell from Hugh Alton, swerved their horses to the left and dashed for the mouth of the ravine.

Twice and again Morrissey fired, the rifle, to the ear of the boy, sounding strangely faint and small in the thin mountain air. It was just beside him, and yet it rang out as though a hundred yards away.

Those three bullets brought no response from the four; they did not attempt to return the fire; neither did any of them fall from the saddle.

But the boy was shouting: "Budge, Budge! I think we have 'em! That's a box canyon, and if we can follow 'em to the wall right there. Come on!"

One hand on the stirrup, his body straining forward, his long legs flying over the ground, Budge Morrissey raced at the side of his mounted master, and they reached the mouth of the ravine in time to see the other riders sweeping around the next turn.

"Now, now! Run for it!" cried the boy. "They'll see that they're fenced in. Drop away, Budge, and let me go on alone."

Budge Morrissey let go his hold obediently, and Molly

flashed away like a bird. To the very curve of the valley wall rode the boy, then checked his horse and flung himself to the ground, with the Professor panting beside him.

He was but barely in time as he unsheathed the Winchester and leveled it, peering over the breastworks which a great rock offered to him.

For the four riders, streaking it at full speed around the bend of the canyon, had discovered too late that they were indeed cooped, as in a corral, the sides of which were granite walls forty or fifty feet high.

Swinging into that pocket, where the upper course of the ravine was a flat surface of rock that rose almost sheer, they had pulled up their mounts, looked for an instant on the blank face of disaster, and had realized that there was only one way out of the trap. That was to turn and try to charge through their pursuers.

Why had they fled in the first place, being four against two, except that the name of Joe Good was terrible in all their minds?

Now swinging the horses about, they came full tilt back toward the elbow curve of the ravine wall.

The boy, watching them come, thought he rarely had seen a sight so fine, so stirring. Riding in a good cause, a whole nation might have cheered those magnificent riders and those splendid horses. For every one was of the best breeding, worthy of carrying as rich and a more honest man than Hugh Alton.

Joe Good fired straight before them, pumping in the shots rapidly.

He was wild and high with the first one. It went above the heads of the line. His second struck the ground, throwing up a spray of fine sand and gravel into the nostrils of Doc's horse.

His third split the difference and fanned the very air before the face of Vince Jones.

That was enough for Jones.

His exploits had generally been performed, exciting though they were, when the backs of his enemies were turned toward him. A stealthy footfall and a dark night had generally helped him to his ends.

Now, with a howl as though the bullet had smashed through his ugly face, he pulled up his horse and fled, though there was no sanctuary toward which he could ride.

That defection scattered the charge. Men who ride together cannot help being ruled by the weakest spirit in the crowd, and under the erratic rifle firing of the boy, they fanned out. As they scattered, each man turned his horse, Alton the last of all, and rushed it back.

It was the end. For now Budge Morrissey was at the side of his employer. And if the rifle of Joe Good was a very chancy weapon, that which the great hands of the giant wielded was a different matter, for Budge Morrissey had learned to shoot in the school where a miss is rewarded with death. And his rifle was hugged now against his thickly muscled shoulder.

Yet he did not shoot at once. Crouched there on one knee, behind the same rock which was a fortress to the boy, he looked out on the quarry and saw that it was all in their hands.

They, hidden from the bullets of the four riders, could survey every inch of the granite walls and fire at leisure, bringing them down.

So Budge Morrissey began to smile in a way that was not good to see, and he waited contentedly, letting the heaviness of his panting subside a little.

There was time—there was much time. And why should not the others taste the approach of death before the actual firing began?

Wally Chase and Doc, falling flat on the ground, behind a totally insufficient hump of ground, prepared to sell their lives as dearly as possible, but Hugh Alton and Vince Jones still dreamed of safety in flight.

One of the two at one side, and one in the center of the far wall of the ravine, they began to scramble up the surface of the rock.

Budge Morrissey laughed, with a tenderly brooding sound in that sound of mirth.

"Oh, Vince Jones, Vince Jones," said he, "there ain't nothin' I'd rather see. You think you going to get out from under old Budge's gun? Try that, Vince Jones! And try that!"

Still chuckling, he fired twice, and neither bullet struck the laboring body of Vincent St. Ives Jones. But one struck the rock to the left of his face, and the other to the right of it, scattering splinters of rocks, the spray of lead piercing his face.

It was too much for the fugitive.

Unnerved by those hammer blows close to his head, he lost his hold. With a shriek, he slid down the face of the rock to the floor of the ravine, where he doubled up in a knot, and with his hands above his head, began to howl for mercy.

Wally Chase turned, half rose, and struck Jones with the butt of his gun over the head; and Vince Jones dropped with a quiver and lay still.

But Budge Morrissey paid no more heed to Vince Jones. He had a better target now, and that was none other than the chief of that quarry, the oldest and most venomous enemy of his master. There was Hugh Alton, now high on the cliff, not ten feet from the upper rim of the rock.

Valiantly he worked away, a few arm hauls from safety, a few infinities he might as well have been, with the terrible rifle of Morrissey now covering him as a target.

As the rifle of the giant settled into the hollow of his shoulder the hat fell from the head of the rancher, and the morning light flashed on the silver of his hair. Dark and glossy and young had it been in color only a few months before. Now it was the tint of age. Body and soul, Hugh Alton was far riper for the grave now, but the boy put out his hand and knocked up the barrel of Morrissey's gun.

"Let him go!" said Joe Good.

48

Budge looked in utter bewilderment at his employer. "Mr. Joseph!" he cried. "You know what you're saying and doing now, sir? You know what it all means?"

"I know what it all means," said young Joe Good. "It means that he'll get away and keep on running like a beaten cur the rest of his life. It means that his family will have to smuggle him money to live on. It means that he'll shrink away in some far-away hole and corner of the earth, and there, with a different name, he'll sit and watch faces and pray that nobody will remember him. That's what it means, Budge. And why should we kill him now, it he'd rather live like that? He'll do no more harm in the world. You can be sure of that. There'll be no power or spirit left in him for that. So let him go. He's done enough wrong to need killing. But you and I are not the judges, Budge. Let him go, and God forgive him! I'm almost sorry for him, Budge!"

The white-haired man, reaching the upper lip of the rock, flung himself forward and rolled literally over and over like a frightened dog into the shelter of some bushes.

These closed over him, and he was lost to view.

"And them others?" said Budge Morrissey. "You want 'em to live?"

"Jones is your own business," said the boy. "But the only man I ever killed was Charley Martin—and I wish that I could forget that night. You'd better let Jones go. He deserves killing, I know. But you'll sleep better if you let the law work for you!"

Morrissey heaved a sigh that was almost a groan.

"Mr. Joseph," he said at last, "I hate to say it, sir, but dog-gone if what you're sayin' now don't remind me of the way that Betsy talks. Vince Jones? That hound? Well, maybe you're right. It ain't a bullet through the head that'll pay him back for what he done to me. It's waitin' in prison. It's waitin' there for the years that don't never go by, but that stick, like the way that a snail sticks in its own slime. That's what I'll wish for him! There's Wally Chase gittin' ready to give himself up. There's Doc, standing 'longside of 'im, too!"

In fact, Wally Chase, plainly seeing that the game was up, threw his rifle far from him, unbuckled his gun belt, and stood up with his hands high above his head.

Doc imitated his example, and Jones came cowering behind the two men, as though hoping that their bodies might shield him for a moment, at least, from the inevitable impact of the bullets.

Slowly the trio came on.

One of the horses began to follow at the heels of Wally Chase. It seemed a touching thing to young Joe Good when he saw the honest horse following that scoundrel.

When they were not far from the rock that covered Morrissey and the two waiting rifles, Wally Chase said: "Joe, you've got us, all right. Whatcha gunna do with us?"

And Joe Good answered: "Wally, you've been after my scalp for a long time. And I want to ask you a question. If you were where I am, with a rifle at your shoulder, and I were standing where you are now, what would you do?"

Wally Chase did not answer for a moment.

Then he suddenly straightened his body, his arms fell and were crossed upon his breast. The old manliness which he had possessed when he was known as a slayer and a tyrant over other fighting men came over his face and his bearing.

And he shouted: "If I was you, and you was here, I'd put a pair of bullets right through the center of your cursed face!"

The answer rather stunned Joe Good. He had more than half expected wheedling lies. This sudden statement of the truth almost disarmed him.

"Wally," he said, "you've been a bad one, a black bad one. But I'm not going to take your advice. I'm going to let the law have the handling of you and Doc."

Young Doc let his head drop far back; he seemed to

look up to the sky and give thanks for this mercy; but he said nothing.

And the lion's roar of Morrissey now filled the canyon with booming echoes as he shouted: "Stand out there, Vince Jones!"

Jones, finding that the two white men had stepped away from before him, looked ahead, saw the gleaming rifle barrel leveled at him, and bent double, with his arms wound around his head.

"Budge, don't shoot!" he screamed.

"Look at him," said Budge Morrissey. "He called himself a man and a fighter. But he's no fighter. He's all yellow, inside and out. I'm not shooting you, Jones, because you're not worth the price of a slug of lead and the powder behind it!"

So spoke Budge Morrissey; and so four lives, on that bright morning, ran the gauntlet and came through the shadow of death to life, or what, perhaps, could better be called a living death.

They took the three of them down to Fort Willow. In the interval Jones had confessed the facts concerning the lawyer's part in the plot to kill. And in the end, Wisner paid a just penalty. As they rode into the town, the wounded sheriff rode with the captors, making a grim and glorious spectacle; and, not unnaturally, proud of the blood that stained the rude bandage around his arm and breast. Budge Morrissey, also, huge, tattered, with the frightful bloody mark of the thong clearly visible on his forehead, seemed to many of those who looked at the strange procession the very symbol of frontier law thoroughly enforced.

But young Joe Good slipped away, and by back alleys got to his home.

Betsy was not there.

The uproar in the town, like a Fourth of July celebration, had called her in haste to the middle of things, seeking news of Budge Morrissey. News she found, too; news that entrenched Budge far deeper among the lovers of the law than he ever had been entrenched among those who despised it.

But Joe Good was glad that Betsy was gone.

He found hot water ready, and he poured some into the old, battered, tin bathtub and stripped off his clothes and bathed. Then, wearily, he dragged on fresh clothes, for he knew that before long he would have visitors on his hands.

After that he went with the Professor to the rear veranda, and sitting there, went soundly to sleep.

He wakened later with sand under his eyelids and a mist before his eyes. A chill gripped him; nauseous sickness followed, and then a fresh wave of sleep. Very dimly he recognized certain forms near him—Garnet, Kate Garnet, Betsy, and the great Morrissey.

"Hello, Kate," he said. "I didn't know you were here." She stood close beside him.

"Get him to bed, Budge," said she. "It's nothing serious, and you don't need to roll your eyes. He's just plain fagged out, and there's a touch of malaria."

The boy opened his eyes with difficulty.

"It's good to see you, Kate," said he. "The trail's over, now. And it's good to see you. How long can you stay?"

Her voice was brisk, intensely practical.

"I intend to stay indefinitely, Joe," she said. "I'm planning to help Budge and Betsy for the rest of my days, Black-snake Joe!"